THE KISS & THE KILLER

Faery Bargains Book 2

MELISSA MARR

THE KISS & THE KILLER

QUALITY CONTROL:

This work has been professionally edited and proofread. However, if you encounter any typos or formatting issues, please contact assist@melissa-marr.com so it can be corrected.

CHAPTER ONE

No one had ever accused New Orleanians of being subtle. Carnival season still launched with Twelfth Night, despite the *draugr* who were going to be noshing on the tourists. Much like drunken excess was inevitable, deaths and injuries of careless tourists were expected. The best we could do was be careful and warn the tourists who weren't prepared for the biters.

I watched out the window of my accidental fiancé's car as we zipped through the city. Sometimes seeing the world this way made me wish for a life without walled cities and restrictions. I wanted to not worry about biters—but that was impossible with my genetic soup. It was a well-guarded secret most of the time, but I was half-*draugr*. Any blood tests to move into safer cities would expose me. Admittedly, I suspected that I would always love New Orleans better than anywhere else. The trouble was simply that knowing I couldn't move to any other city rankled. Most cities—and all airlines and train stations—had blood tests, and those cities that didn't have that still had temp checks at the gate of the city.

I'd always been able to pass the temp checks, just a simple

brief energy pull to make me warmer, but a few months ago, I was injected with venom. It was intended to be a murder, but I was half-*draugr* so it just . . . woke that up more. Could I still get through the temp check? Had I lost that, too?

I was like a cat with a closed door. I disliked rules and limits.

I wanted to have the choice to move before ultimately admitting I was already where I belonged. This was home, and I wanted nowhere else long term. It would just be nice to have a choice.

Right now, I was enjoying the ferocity of the decorations that were draped from balconies. No mild colors or modest sizes. New Orleans was larger than life in most things, and this was no exception.

"Are you unwell, Geneviève?" Eli prompted. He was smart enough to realize that I was only this silent when I was feeling moodier than usual. A more rational man would avoid poking the proverbial bear. Luckily for me, Eli was not as rational as people thought the fae were.

"I need a holiday away from here," I admitted.

Maybe this summer. Maybe in the fall. Right now, I couldn't leave the city even for a holiday. Carnival was deadly these days, so I patrolled to mitigate the stupidity of tourists. That wasn't my *job*, but since I was one of the only people in the city fast enough and strong enough to stop a hungry biter, it was my avocation. Such speed was atypical for the living. The only other person strong enough *and* alive was driving the car. Eli. My fiancé. My partner. My friend. If I stared at his hair, I could see a universe I wanted desperately to touch.

"Geneviève?"

"Mmm..?" I watched him the way I suspect prey watches a predator. I was vulnerable—and not just my heart. Eli could overpower me. He could pin me. It was a new and absurdly thrilling reality.

But it wasn't the *only* reason he had my knickers in a knot.

His features were sharp, more cut glass than museum statue. His mouth was full and luscious, and the energy woven into his very fiber had called to me since the moment we'd first met. His magic called to my own like we were made to be together. His skin held the kind of energy that felt like electricity.

"You're staring at me, bonbon."

I sighed. "You're supposed to pretend not to notice when I stare."

"Is that a witch tradition I am unfamiliar with?" he teased. "The fae do try to follow traditions." He glanced at me with the half-smile that made me want to pounce on him and asked, "Is there something you need, Geneviève?"

I was saved from replying that far-too-loaded question when I felt my phone buzz. NEW ORLEANS POLICE DEPARTMENT.

I declined the call but reached out and turned down the car radio.

"NOPD," I said.

"Ought you answer?"

"Maybe," I allowed.

He didn't remark that I'd already turned down the radio. We both knew they'd likely call again, and eventually, I'd answer. Satisfying my curiosity was irresistible to me sooner or later.

Eli cut off the music. He strongly believed in everything being the best possible quality, so the car stereo had been blasting some medieval sounding band that refused to play in my hometown on account of not wanting to get eaten by draugr. They weren't meant to be played quietly.

Honestly, I was trying to justify a trip to see them live. Maybe that was going to be my holiday plan? Of course, that meant going on a trip with Eli—and *that* held levels of commitment I was not prepared for yet. Maybe ever. Couple trips weren't my thing.

And any sort of holiday meant abandoning my post, which wasn't a thing I could do easily. Maybe it was guilt, but I felt an obligation to New Orleans. She was mine, and I protected her people. These days, people either moved to walled cities with no-fanger rules or learned to coexist. I coexisted with a generous side order of magic and swords—and the police tolerated it because, well, they thought I was "just a witch."

I liked it that way.

My relationship with the police was that I called to report "mysteriously beheaded" draugr, and they stressed that I was not a sanctioned officer and should not behead anything. But no one asked too many questions.

They rarely—if ever—called me.

It rang again; I declined again.

"Have you decapitated anyone interesting of late, Buttercream?" Eli asked, looking at me longer than was strictly safe while driving. "Threatened any influential tourists?"

"Not that I know of." I met Eli's curious gaze—although he ought to be watching the road. He was the sort of driver who would terrify a calmer person, but fae reflexes likely meant he could stare at me and still drive better than most people.

He looked away and his little blue convertible moved with a near-silent engine as we raced through the city.

When the phone rang again, I saw "Gary Broussard" on my ID. I might not answer for NOPD, but Gary was my friend.

"What's it take to get you to answer your phone, Gen?" he grumbled.

"Are you okay?" I asked in lieu of politer greetings. Gary was a sort of father-stand-in for me, sparking more of a paternal affection in me than anyone else ever had. "Are you in the hospital? Should I—"

"No." He laughed. "Bulletproof, kid. I'm bulletproof thanks to you."

"Why the call, then? I don't think I broke any major laws today . . ." I hedged.

"Got a job for you."

"A *what*?"

"J-o-b, kid. That thing where you do something, and get paid for it." Gary sounded like he was trying not to laugh.

"I'm not really NOPD material, Gary, and raising witnesses is iffy business. People aren't reliable even when they're alive. Plus, I work best on my own. It's safer and—"

"Freelance. Take a breath, Crowe."

"So raising the dead? For . . . you? Or the department?" I glanced out the window, watched the increasing darkness. No foot traffic remained on the side streets in the Central Business District once dark fell.

"No raising. Freelance *killing* dead things for the department," Gary clarified. "Temporary position. NOPD got a grant for it, specifically to hire you."

I paused. We'd always sort of agreed to officially pretend the NOPD didn't know that killing was part of what I *did*, although I had left enough bodies to pick up that it was hard to deny. I was about as subtle as a sharp sword.

I guess we were finally officially admitting that I hunted the creatures that tried to eat their neighbors. "I'm not sure I'm the person for—"

"Biters are cutting into tourism. We need an exterminator, Gen. Just come down and hear them out," Gary said. "Plus, the grant's only good if we hire you."

That set off alarms, and I tensed enough that Eli noticed.

"I'll stop in this week. I'll call you." I disconnected and stared at the phone for a moment.

Who wanted me on the street? Who wanted the NOPD to

know what I could do? Did someone know what I really was? Magic sparked in blues and purples along my skin, a side effect of my temper that had accompanied my recent brush with mortality.

Eli stopped the car, ignoring the honking car behind us.

"Job offer," I said, gesturing toward the road. "Drive, please?"

He gave me a raised brow, but said nothing as he looked back at the road and sped off. Eli wasn't a talker when he could convey his meaning with a look—or an action. He accelerated, cutting through the city, traveling at a speed that was only safe due to fae reflexes. Every spin of the wheel or drift around a curve was inviting me to comment, to object, to say something.

I fought back a laugh.

If anyone else had the wheel of his little blue convertible, I'd be doing more than objecting. I'd climb into the driver's lap and stomp the brake pedal whether they liked it or not. Instead, I was pretending not to notice how close to cars he zagged or how fast he zigged into intersections.

He glanced at me, and I just grinned.

I liked *making* him ask questions, and right now, I cherished the distraction of his provocative driving. Eli had the kind of charm and looks that meant he was used to everything falling into his lap—except me. We had the chemistry, and at first I thought that was all we had. Then he became one of my best friends, so I refused to get naked with him despite sparks. An accidental engagement complicated my resolve, and lately, I realized I'd been wrong. We *fit* in every way.

Of course, that didn't mean I was going to fall over myself to charm him or make things too easy. We'd *both* be bored if I did that. So I waited as he steered his fae-modified car around several slower cars, clearly trying to provoke me.

When I stayed silent even as he all but grazed a sign turning a corner, he laughed and asked, "I give, Geneviève. Would you care to elucidate?"

I bit my lip. *Elucidate?* Eli could make the most mundane things sound sexy. It was one of his less-irritating traits, although it was hell on my self-control.

"NOPD wants to hire me freelance for the season," I explained, forcing my mind away from thoughts of Eli's voice or body or charm. "To 'exterminate' the troublesome biters."

"And you plan to . . .?" Eli prompted.

"Grab the spot by the black SUV." I motioned to a parking spot that was more challenging than usual. Carnival season had only just started, and we already had more tourists than I liked. Once upon a time, New Orleans was always tourist central, but then came the biters.

Having walking parasites eating the tourists changed things —until the city found ways to adapt.

Eli slipped his little convertible into a spot that only he could manage. The car was the epitome of elegance, silent unless Eli was in the mood to make it growl, so cutting off the engine was unnoticeable.

"Bonbon?" He turned toward me and prompted, "What will you tell the New Orleans Police Department?"

"I'd be out there anyhow. If they have some sort of grant to pay me, maybe I should con—"

"A *grant?* From whom?" Eli frowned, obviously as uncomfortable as I was at that detail.

"Why me? Who wanted me involved? Why? Was it to help or harm me?" I nodded. "Their budget is shit, but . . . the grant is *specifically* to hire me."

"That is concerning," he murmured.

"Precisely. I need to know who funded it," I said. "Even if I refuse, I want *that* answer. To get that, I must meet them."

Silently, Eli got out and came around to my door. I'd given

up resisting his insistence on opening the door. He extended a
hand once he'd opened the door.

Instead of pursuing the issues of who was funding the grant
or that I ought to take a few weeks off, Eli pronounced, "I will
not expect compensation."

Despite myself, I laughed. "For?"

And my partner looked me in the eyes and pulled me in for
a kiss that was more territorial than usual. I melted into him,
wrapping around him like it was the best idea in the world to
forget that there were monsters, murders, and midnight
revelers out there.

When he released me, he stepped back and said, "You're the
affianced of the heir to *Elphame*, Geneviève, and there are traditions that—"

"Short version," I interrupted.

"Where you go, I go. Where you are hired, I shall be.
Where you behead, slaughter, or defend, I shall be. As long as I
am able, this is how things shall be." He lifted my hand to his
lips. "You are my warrior bride, Geneviève Crowe, and—"

"We've discussed this. I'm not a *bride*." I pulled my hand
away, trying not to swoon at the thought that he would be at my
side for the innumerable years to come if we ended up married.
"The engagement is just a temporary state and—"

"*Hush*, Geneviève." He gestured toward the cemetery with
the same grace that he used when he escorted me before his
uncle, the king of *Elphame*. "Shall we hunt?"

"Yes to hunting, no to—"

"Be aware of the traditions, Geneviève Crowe. If you end
our courtship, my time in your world ends as well." His voice
held genuine fear this time. A carefully worded faery bargain or
two had bought Eli a reprieve from the faery king's edict on his
heir's matrimony.

I didn't want that reprieve to end. Neither did he. And if I wasn't careful, it would. So instead of marriage, we were currently planning on the world's longest engagement. Committed enough to keep him in my life, but not committed enough to trap him in a marriage with a half-dead witch. To succeed meant keeping up the ruse that our engagement would lead to marriage.

Because, unfortunately, what most sane people thought of as "tradition" was a *law* to the fae, and I was blundering around trying to thwart centuries of traditions-but-really-laws without ending up married or losing the man I was falling irreparably in love with.

"I need to kill something," I muttered.

"Yes, dear," he murmured softly, as he offered me his arm to lead me to the cemetery wall we were about to scale.

CHAPTER TWO

As far as nights out went, scaling brick walls and creeping around rows of mausoleums might not rate. This wasn't a *date*, though. Christophe Hebert had been on a list of "possible victims of injections" that my current research assistant, Ally, had created. I checked the graves on that list with the hope that the dead were resting quietly where they'd been planted. The last three had been, so I was hoping tonight was lucky number four.

"Ally says Hebert's mother was a significant SAFARI donor," I told Eli as I scaled the wall landed next to him on the ground inside the cemetery walls.

My elegant fiancé muttered a curse word in his people's language that my tongue still struggled to pronounce.

"She would know," he added as we walked past darkened graves.

Ally—Alice Chaddock to most people—was a widow who had hired us to check on her suddenly deceased husband. The late Alvin Chaddock was easily twice her age, but the young widow had been genuinely in love. Sometime between injecting me with *draugr* venom and murdering the "mastermind" behind all the deaths, Ally had become my friend and employee.

I didn't pay her well enough to justify calling her my employee, to be honest, especially considering what she did for me, but she was one of the wealthiest women in the city so she didn't ask for much of a salary. My meager checks weren't even a drop in her ocean of money.

But Eli wasn't willing to let *anyone* forget that Ally had been a member of SAFARI, the Society Against Fae and Reanimated Individuals. They were a hate group opposed to increasingly tolerant attitudes towards *draugr* and, for reasons not-quite-clear, they lumped the fae in with the biters.

"Not all of the dead SAFARI members have been raised," I pointed out, but I still drew my single-handed sword.

"Hebert had enough of Alice's little stars to make note of her." Eli moved far enough away that he wouldn't obstruct me if we were startled. My sword wasn't the sort of metal the fae could handle easily, so I was more cautious around him anyhow.

"Not all children are like their parents," I snapped. I was feeling sensitive about that detail of late. My baggage from my own Daddy Issues—and no, not *that* kind. I simply hated the man.

"Enough SAFARI members woke that you know there is a link between them and the injections." Eli paused at a sound.

"True." I scanned for movement. Technically, the cemetery was closed, but this was New Orleans, and the Carnival season was underway. It was more likely that there was someone in the area than not. The question was just whether they were dead or alive.

"Is Madam Hebert still alive?" he asked.

"Very. She owns an estate at the border of the ghost zone, but she's living outside the city, somewhere over in Houston." I tried and failed to keep the disdain out of my voice.

I had no issue with Houston. It was a fine city, in fact, but people who abandoned New Orleans and still meddled in our affairs were high on my shit list. To abandon the city *and* funnel money back here for a racist organization was a level of asinine I couldn't understand.

"Good riddance," Eli said, drawing a small silver dagger.

The Society Against Fae and Reanimated Individuals was tangled up in an attempt on my life in the fall, among other heinous things. Racists, not surprisingly, weren't too keen on the continued life of those of us who were different, and while I wasn't officially on their hate list, some of the SAFARI folks lumped bisexual, Jewish, necromancing witches in with *draugr* and fae. That hostility had made murdering me seem like a lovely idea.

"Was Christophe a member or just his mother?" Eli asked, as we made our way deeper into the rows of mausoleums. They were often beautiful, but they did make hunting a bit challenging.

"Just her." I stared at the shadows, feeling the comforting whispers of the dead resting in the earth. Since my brush with my own mortality, my tie to the dead had grown stronger than I liked. It used to be that I had to bleed to hear them.

Now, the collective whispers of the grave rose up like breezes through dry corn husks. I had to actively refuse to answer, and we hadn't yet seen what would happen if I bled more than a droplet or two on grave dirt. Before my near-death event, my magic was already off. Now, I was apprehensive of testing that change. So far, my *draugr* speed had come in handy on that front at least.

"Is it worse?" Eli asked. "The voices."

I didn't think it was worse or better to hear the dead more easily, simply different. I wasn't sure I wanted to explain that to a faery, though. His people's understanding of death was so different from human death. The fae ancestry, memories of the family, were accessible to those who were in their lineage. Their bodies, however, dissolved in such a way that their dead were not able to be resurrected the way humans were. No fae-*draugr* mixes. No fae bodies to call from the grave. The dead were simply absorbed into nature, and their memories were carried forward in their descendants.

Humans, however, could be brought back as draugr or via necromancy. And all the dead were my domain. Not that I controlled them, but thanks to the magic of my mother and the *draugr* DNA by the deadbeat who fathered me, I could feel the presence of anything dead. It was useful for killing some and resurrecting others. Yeah, I killed the kind of creatures that had fathered me. Daddy issues weren't just for debutantes.

"Bonbon?" Eli prompted.

"Stronger," I clarified. "My magic is stronger."

By the time we reached Christophe Hebert's grave, we had ascertained that no one else was sliding out of their graves nearby. We'd learned the awkward way that checking for surprise biters first was essential.

The dirt over Christophe's resting spot was not disrupted tonight, but it had been recently. Someone had patted it back into place, and even added a few stolen flowers in the mound of mud.

"That's not suspicious at all." I scanned the area before crouching down.

Eli moved so he could watch a larger swath of the darkened rows of graves. We were looking in opposite directions. He took our partnership even more seriously than our romance, and *that* was saying something.

"Anything?" I asked.

"No. All clear." He held his dagger out.

I pricked my wrist on the sharpened tip. A simple droplet

worked better than a slice, plus I hated hand injuries. A cut in my palm made my hilt bloody, and that could hamper my grip in a fight.

My blood dropped onto the ground.

One drip . . . two . . . *there.*

I felt like I was sinking into the soil. Spectral hands reaching down for a body that was meant to be there.

"Christophe Hebert," I beckoned.

I held my arm up to keep more blood from falling. Eli slapped an adhesive patch over the cut. It's not all blood and magic in my business, despite what people want to believe. Sometimes it was blood, magic, and cartoon bandages.

"Christophe Hebert, wake for me," I ordered. I sometimes used prettier words, French or Latin or the occasional Gaelic, for clients, but magic wasn't rooted in pretty pronunciation. It was in will, genetics, and sometimes emotions.

And blood.

That part was true. My blood had power for the dead.

No one answered my summons, though. Christophe Hebert was not in this grave—which almost certainly meant that he was walking around my tourist-filled city looking for a bite to eat. If we were lucky, he had caught the draugr queen's attention and she'd already handled it. But Beatrice was dealing with her own issues lately, so I had a strong suspicion that this particular biter was going to be mine to handle.

"If he was injected, what are your minions able to. . ." Eli started, his voice sliding into that cautious tone that meant he was aware he'd broached an awkward topic.

I held up a hand. "I'm not collecting minions, Eli."

"Would you be able to bond him as you have your *associates* so we can gather answers?"

I sighed. It wasn't as if I hadn't considered it. I had the awkward ability to revive *draugr* so he or she was a sentient being upon waking, but who wanted the responsibility of minions? I didn't call them that, but they wouldn't object. Tres, who was dead but still running his businesses as if he had never passed, wouldn't object to anything I called him.

I shuddered.

"Just because I *can* fix the newly dead, doesn't mean I want to. Plus, I don't know if I even can rouse them once they are already transitioned to *draugr*. Christophe's grave is empty, but he is already walking."

"Swords ready, then?"

Unfortunately, I didn't quite know how to answer. I had no desire to create my own little army of biters, and the average *draugr* was a slathering, biting monster the first century, but we'd discovered that I could shorten that period of "toddler" years so that a newly-risen biter was perfectly coherent. I just didn't like the side effects.

"Stay alert," I said. "If Hebert is attacking, we take his head. If not, I'll . . . try to talk to him."

Eli didn't question me. There were times when he was in control of our actions, but this was my job, my calling, my fucked-up genetic soup, so in this, I was the decision-making body.

"To behead or not behead," Eli pronounced in a remarkably adept Shakespearean tone. "*That* is the question."

"To behead if necessary," I agreed. I wasn't immune to *draugr* venom, and I had no idea what it would do to Eli if he were to be exposed. Fae biology wasn't a class in any curriculum in New Orleans—or anywhere in the world as far as I knew.

We were both biological oddities.

"Lead on," Eli said with a sweep of his arm.

By the time we'd searched the entire cemetery, we'd found no biters, no foolhardy kids tempting fate, only one pair of tourists with their cheap "protection" chokers—as if biters only gnawed on throats. Some genius sold them with a remarkably compelling marketing campaign. "I've never been bitten" testimonials scrolled through their ads. No one mentioned that the Bite Chokers weren't field-tested around actual biters.

"Are you stupid?" I asked.

"Are you a . . . *fanger?*" the man asked.

"No," Eli answered, saving me from the half-lie. I was, in truth, sporting fangs these days. After an attempt on my life a few months ago, I was newly fanged.

I lifted a sword and pointed the tip at them. "If I wanted to bite you, that junk wouldn't stop me."

"No one wearing this has *ever* been bitten," the woman started.

"Probably because no one has worn it around a biter." I looked around at the shadowed graves. If there was a dead thing here, these two would be bleeding already.

Dumb asses. Too much booze made tourists wander off like snacks-on-delivery. And as much as I wanted to dismiss it as simple Darwinism in action, I couldn't. I had an overactive need to save people.

I motioned for them to stand. "Come on."

"Where are you taking us?" The man moved his feet like he was going to stand and fight, and as much as I respected the instinct to save yourself, it would serve him better if he'd had that self-preservation urge before coming to a cemetery at night.

Before I could say anything else, a *draugr* arrived as if summoned by their foolishness.

The dead lady was standing in the periphery of my vision. She *flowed* with the speed of a century-or-more corpse. Dressed in a cream linen suit coat that was cut for a woman and a pair of trousers that matched, the *draugr* looked like a well-dressed woman who'd merely forgotten to wear a blouse under her suit jacket. Her hair was all but shaved, and she wore no jewelry that I could see. If not for the pervading feel of death that flooded me, I might think her human from this distance.

But my magic was grave magic. She was human once, but from the feel of her, it had been at *least* a century.

Sword up just in case, I called, "On my left."

Eli moved toward the nice, human tourists and raised a lethal blade that looked like it had been cut from moonlight. The man had an uncanny ability to hide weapons that I wanted to study in detail.

The human woman gasped as she saw that short sword. "Oh my goodness, oh my—"

"Hush," the man said, pulling her close.

Then, the *draugr* was beside us, *flowing* with the serpentine motion that typically only came with age and experience. She was one place and then the next, faster than vision can track. It probably looked like magic to the tourists, even though it was simple—albeit remarkable—speed.

"My lady has a question for you, Ms. Crowe," the *draugr* said, bowing her head to me briefly before she glanced at the humans who were currently protected by Eli, and then back at me. From this close, the *draugr's* serpent-like slitted eyes were impossible to mistake for human.

She flashed a grin at me and put a hand to her chest. "Oh, no, a flimsy clasp and a cheap piece of metal. Whatever shall I do?"

Eli raised his sword as she took a step toward the tourists. "Nothing."

Before she could *flow*, I moved up to her back, lifting my dagger. I stopped my cut just at the kiss of her throat.

"Don't," I whispered, behind her, sharpened blade at the right side of her throat.

The *draugr* reached up with her left hand and shoved my arm away. She *flowed* so we were face-to-face and punched me.

I stumbled, feeling foolish that I'd underestimated her. Maybe the "lady" she referred to wasn't Beatrice. I'd gotten so accustomed to all things *draugr* being my dead great-times-great-grandmother's domain that I'd assumed. Possibly incorrectly.

"Ouch." I grasped my sword, but before I could retaliate, I felt the echoing voices of the waking dead under the earth. "Donkey dongs!"

In my stumble, my hand sliced along a grave, and my now-bloodied hand slammed down on to the soil. It wasn't a large cut, but it was my blood on grave dirt. Blood filled with grave magic was like wakey-wakey juice for the dead.

I looked at Eli. "Get them out. Now."

I urged the waking dead, "Stay where you are. Please."

We come.

Mother.

We are yours.

Who struck you?

We protect.

"Protect," I echoed.

Protect!

Their voices rose, twining together like so many threads. I hadn't ever been fond of raising the dead *en masse*, but the combination of my rage and fear had tainted my blood this time. I'd summoned them, and in my exhaustion, I'd given them purpose by repeating that word.

"Witch," the *draugr* said, making the sign-of-the-cross over herself.

For some reason, seeing a fanger make a religious gesture struck me silent, but then Eli yelled, "Geneviève!"

The woman shrieked.

I looked over to where he was hurrying the human couple out of the maze of graves. The earth looked like it was bubbling from the number of bodies surging to the surface. Hands, knees, heads. Bodies were surfacing, as the dead came to my defense in various degrees of alertness.

"Protect," one after another whispered.

I could see the animated corpses, clad in magically-restored clothes from eras past. Fifty or so reanimated dead folk stumbled, crawled, and stomped toward me. At least I didn't hear thundering inside the mausoleums. So far, my grave magic hadn't broken through the stone tombs.

"Call them off," the *draugr* ordered, watching as the dead eyed her as the threat. If they caught her, she couldn't *flow* to safety. With enough hands and force, they'd pull her apart, tearing her limb from limb. It was a horrifying possibility.

"I don't know how to stop them," I admitted in horror. "They see you as a threat to me. Until they remove the threat, they're here. Run."

"And you call *us* monsters, Crowe?" The *draugr* fled, *flowing* out of the cemetery with a far more impressive speed than her arrival.

And I was left watching the expectant dead look at me with a mix of awe and hunger I wasn't sure how to stop.

CHAPTER THREE

ONCE THE *DRAUGR* WAS GONE, I HELD MY ARMS ALOFT AND declared, "I am safe. You have protected me."

The corpses watched as if other threats were at the edge of their soil-tainted vision. Mouths gaped open as thoughts both of my safety and awareness of their location crowded newly-repaired synapses.

I clambered on top of a nearby stone, angling between the vast wings of an angel. I looked like the misshapen Andrew Jackson equestrian statue that used to stand in Jackson Square.

"I am protected," I yelled, trying to project over the crowd of walking muttering corpses.

But they kept shoving closer and closer, a mass of writhing bodies.

My bloodied hand tightened on the stone angel's wings, and the other lifted my sword high. I wasn't interested in slashing my way through my accidental corpse army, but I wasn't keen on being trampled either.

"You cannot doubt your authority," whispered a voice, a male voice that was not Eli.

I looked around.

"Geneviève, focus! They were summoned by your blood. Your magic. They are yours to command. Be commanding!"

"Listen!" I called out to the corpses all pushing to reach me.

When they paused, at once like a hive mind, I exhaled. One woman looked remarkable alert, as if she'd merely been resting. Another, a teen, crossed his arms belligerently as if resisting my command to listen. A few older men took their hats into their hands respectfully.

"I am safe." I gestured at my body. "Unharmed."

They still stared. A few frowned.

"Good. Thank them for their aid," the voice urged.

"Thank you," I echoed. "You have protected me, and I am grateful for your aid."

The dead folk started to smile and nod, a few congratulated the others, so that the air was filled with the rasp of whispered and scratches of long unused voices mixing with more recent dead who sounded nearly human.

"You should rest now," I urged, shoving my magic clumsily into the words. It was what I did with one corpse, so in theory, it would work here.

A few corpses, younger ones from the look of them, started to wander away.

"I'm safe," I said.

And the crowd of fifty or so people dwindled in groups of two or three.

"I'm safe," I repeated every so often. "You can rest again. You protected me."

As they cleared out, I saw one older man sit down and stare. He had a walking stick, ebony handle almost as dark as the night, in one hand. His suit was vintage 1800s, and his ring and watch were elegant. He was in his late-40s-50s, but not *old*.

"You can *rest*," I said again, putting another push in the word.

He smiled. "No. I'm not going back."

"What? I'm fine and you—"

"Girly, you don't have the knowledge of a goose." He shook his head. "What kind of hexen are you that you cannot put the rabble back?"

"Excuse me?"

"You need a hearing horn, too? Awkward things. I have a recipe to fix that." He pushed to his feet and brushed dirt off his sleeves. "My luck to be summoned by a daft hexen."

"Go," I ordered, making a shooing gesture. "Rest now. Your work is done and—"

He stomped toward me, and I realized that in his time he must have been intimidating. "You're a bungler if protecting you takes that many bodies," the dead man grumbled. "You clearly *need* me, so my work is far from done."

"I do not need you. Now, *rest*," I demanded, shoving magic into the word.

He laughed, a rich chortle, and pointed his cane at me. "Ah, so you're not a *weak* hexen, then. Good. I can teach you, Geneviève Crowe."

Now, I've never been the world's best trouble-avoider or problem-solver, but I usually have a plan even if it's "stab someone." In that moment, however, I was clueless. What exactly did one do with a dead man who refused to go back to the grave?

I paused. *Could* I simply leave him there? Was that an option? Option B might just be shoving him in a mausoleum— or maybe I should see if I could kill him as I did with a *draugr.* He was far more sentient than most *draugr,* though. They were slavering biting messes more often than not.

"You cannot refuse to go back to your grave," I started, figuring logic might be worth a try before I started slashing limbs at random.

"Ignatius Blackwood," he said, thoroughly confusing me. It wasn't like I needed his name to put him back. Typically. Maybe he was helping. . .?

I opened my mouth to start to try to send him back by power of name.

Then, he nodded toward the shadows.

"Master Blackwood." Beatrice's voice arrived before she did. "How unexpected to see you."

Blackwood smiled, moonlight catching a fake tooth of some sort of metal. "It *is* you! Beatrice."

She curtsied, and then glanced at me. "Had you wanted a Hexen Master, I'd have sent someone. You didn't need to call Blackwood out of his retirement."

The dead man chortled. "Being dead is . . ." He paused, titled his head. "Well, I have no idea, but no matter. I'm sure this is better." He looked at Beatrice, then. "Aren't your sort to be skulking, Bea? Instead, you are out here shinning around."

"Bea?" I echoed. "*Shinning around?*"

The rather austere *draugr* pressed her lips together. "He means to say I move quickly. He's out of his era. Significantly." Then she turned to glare at him. "Perhaps," she said sternly to the dead guy, "you ought to go back to the grave, Ignatius David Blackwood. Crawl into your grave. *Now.*"

The weight and magic in her voice was enough that I wanted to obey, and I wasn't even dead.

"Ah," he said in a laugh of a voice. "*You* didn't pull me out of the grave, Bea, and I don't think this one can put me back until I fulfill the mandate."

Beatrice sighed, shoulder slumping slightly. "Now Iggy. . . "

"Bea . . ." Ignatius matched her cajoling tone and stared at her, increasingly cheerful. "Are you still the queen of the dead here?"

She nodded once.

"No longer crouched in the shadows either?" he prompted. Beatrice nodded once more.

"And the hexen?" He inclined his head toward me.

Beatrice's eyes tightened, but all she said was, "Geneviève Crowe is under my protection."

I'd been watching them, mildly fascinated, until that moment. I tensed at my great-times-great-grandmother's evasion. Why wasn't she admitting our connection? She'd been very public in her regard of me, so her careful wording was telling. Who was Ignatius that she felt the need to lie? Or was she just in a mood? I had only known her a short while, despite our shared ancestry, so I wasn't able to read her.

"Oh, this is going to be a wake snakes experience, Miss Crowe. I can tell that already," the dead man said.

"Wake snakes?"

"Fun," Beatrice said flatly.

"*Do not bind him to you,*" Beatrice whispered into my mind. "*Whatever you do. Come see me without him when you can.*"

I made no overt motion to indicate I'd heard—but when I met her gaze, she smiled.

I asked, gesturing at one of the nearby above-ground tombs. "If you open a mausoleum, I can shove Dead Iggy Pops here into it. What do you say?"

Beatrice *flowed* over to the nearest tomb with a door. "That's not the worst plan you've had, Geneviève."

"Now, see here, Beatrice!" He jabbed his cane into the dirt, and my skin prickled with the zing of magic the dead man was pulling to him. "You know damn well that if the hexen had no need of me I'd be moldering again."

I looked at Beatrice, who dipped her chin in a slight nod of assent. And it wasn't as if I trusted most *draugr*—but she was also the only other *draugr*-witch in the world. Admittedly, I was genetically both witch and *draugr*, whereas Beatrice was a witch who had become a *draugr* when she'd died. Still, in some matters, I trusted her. This felt like one of those times.

"Fine. Iggy can sleep in the corner at my place," I grumbled.

"My name, Miss Crowe, is 'Ignatius' or 'Master Blackwood' if you prefer." He straightened, hand tightening on his cane.

I waved away his words. "I don't cook. I don't like interruptions, and as soon as he *can* go, he *does* go. . . or"—I pointed at the mausoleum—"we execute Plan B. Clear?"

I waited long enough for a nod of assent from Beatrice—and then I *flowed* as quickly as I could to the gates. If Iggy was so sure I needed him, he could find me his damn self.

CHAPTER FOUR

WHATEVER HAD BROUGHT BEATRICE OR HER LACKEY TO THE cemetery remained a mystery that I would not be solving tonight. She hadn't wanted to speak in front of Iggy, and I wasn't sure I could shake him to go to her estate. Only one way to check if I could dodge the dead guy, though: I'd put it to the test.

After I *flowed* away, I hopped into Eli's car and ordered, "Drive. Fast."

And Eli, Goddess and G-d bless him, didn't ask questions.

In as long as it took to turn on the engine and slip into gear, he had the car flinging through the city at a speed that defied words. My temper was simmering, and the lingering taint of magic—the lashback—that rode me after I'd summoned the dead wanted only two things: fight or fuck. Unfortunately, one would result in me becoming the queen of *Elphame*, so that left fighting as my only viable option.

"Too much energy," I admitted.

Eli knew me in that way that didn't require excess words, so in short order we were walking into my apartment building. My apartment spanned the ground floor of the building; no one else wanted to live in a ground floor unit where the dead could look into—or crawl into—the windows easily. I'd divided it into living space, work-out space, and one unit I'd kept as intact apartment—like a glorified guest room or mother-in-law suite.

The security door slammed closed behind us.

"Sharps?" Eli asked as I led us into my apartment. The open space just inside the door looked like a martial arts studio, but with the occasional shoe or coffee mug scattered between weapons and workout machines.

I tossed him a brass sword. "Blunts."

I didn't draw steel swords with Eli because of the whole fae-allergy thing. The stuff was toxic to him, but his uncle, the King of *Elphame*, had recently sent a collection of fae-made brass swords for us. They were obscenely expensive, but not as much as the silver coated brass swords Eli often had. Those could pass for ornamental steel if he needed to hide what he was.

"Come get me, cupcake," Eli taunted, circling and trying to draw me out with feints.

For reasons I couldn't—*wouldn't*—explain I always needed him to make the first strike. When he finally lunged at me, I let out a sigh of relief. Foreplay was well and good, but I needed actual combat.

Soon the clatter, slide, and slam of metal-on-metal filled the space and cleared my mind. The slither of swords was the symphony that punctuated my life, and I was grateful that Eli was a part of it. He made me feel . . . girly. No one alive had ever been able to best me in a fight, so practice was drills and actual fights against the dead.

Until Eli.

He had me pinned against one of the fight dummies, sword to my throat, and grinning in a way that told me that my better half hadn't been holding back at all tonight. The more at ease he was with me, the more I saw the parts of him he typically hid from those in this world. Fae prince, sword fighter, and shrewd deal-maker was a far-cry from the laissez-faire bar owner he pretended to be.

"Feeling any better after attacking me, bonbon?"

"You won," I pointed out.

Eli laughed. "I did. Are you going to pretend to be a sore loser?"

"Noooo . . . I just thought the winner might want a victory prize." I leaned forward, grateful that the sword against my throat was blunt, and pressed my lips to his briefly. "Anything you want, fiancé of mine?"

"Are you inviting me into a faery bargain, Geneviève Crowe?" His voice drew things from me that I couldn't help but like.

"Maybe," I admitted. "What do you have in mind, Eli of Stonecroft?" I was taunting the one creature who could best me with a word, who had claimed me when I thought I was opposed to such things.

So maybe I liked to play with fire. It wasn't the top of the list of daft things I'd done.

He gave me that increasingly familiar look that was as much love as it was lust, and I was increasingly doubtful of the wisdom of taunting him. "Be careful, Crème Brûlée. Faery bargains don't typically go your way."

"But don't they?" I asked, admitting a question I'd been pondering recently. I thought about the bargains we'd made. The first made him my fiancé, but it allowed him to save my life. The second allowed us to stay engaged without rushing toward an actual marriage. And the bargains—as with every deal with the fae— were binding. No one, not even the king, could force us to move toward an actual wedding.

"A wish." He stared at me. "One wish. One magically bound wish in my reserves for when I need it."

"A wish?"

"Or refuse me, bonbon," he taunted.

"What do you offer in exchange?" I wanted things that weren't the purview of bargains, but I had no doubt he had a plan. My beloved *always* had a plan.

"I'm yours though all of Carnival season. Any way. Anything you need," he offered. "My sword. My kisses . . ."

"Don't I have that already?" I was suddenly unsure. He'd been my partner, my lover in all ways that we were allowed.

"Ah, bonbon, you did. Yet, you started to make a bargain, and I am beholden to offer that *which you most desired* when we began negotiating." He gave me a small sad smile.

The weight of that alarmed me. He knew what I wanted, so that was how he picked what he offered?

"You can read my . . ."

"Desire. If a bargain is begun, the fae making the bargain knows what you most desperately want." Eli gave me a look that made me want to squirm. "We know your heart's desire in that instant."

"Oh." I lifted my chin, refusing to be embarrassed that each bargain was drawn from my own desires.

"There is still much to learn of my people, and I could not tell you that truth unless we were wed or mid-bargain. So, Geneviève Crowe, I ask again, do you accept this bargain? Grant me a magically binding wish in exchange for my sword and my body at your *use* for as long as you want me?"

"Eli . . ."

"It's a simple question." He stared at me with so much lust and love in his expression that this felt anything but simple.

"And if I say no?"

"You're on your own. No more aid at your work or in your pleasure." He sighed. "I would have preferred that you'd had other desires, but I am as bound to the laws as any fae is. *Those* were your desires. Pleasure and partnership."

"That's not fair. We . . . you . . . we're *engaged*." I hated myself for the whining in my voice, but I'd quickly become addicted to my fiancé.

He stepped back, gave me a serious look, and admitted, "I cannot say that the loss would be easy on me. In *any* way. I want you in my bed, and I want to stand at your side against all threats. But faery bargains supersede everything, Geneviève. You invited the bargain, and now we must address this. Think carefully. You tend to lose our bargains. All humans do—and that often includes those with magic."

I caught my hand in Eli's hair and held him to me, sword still against my throat hard enough to bruise. "What have I *lost* so far, Eli?"

"You are caught in my snare," he hedged.

"Oh, woe, forced to spend my time with a handsome, talented, clever—"

"Why, Geneviève, you sound as if you might fancy me. You'll give a man ideas with such flattery." His tone was light, but that was how he managed to keep me from running. Well, that and the reality that if I ran for real, the king would summon Eli to *Elphame* and the man I loved would be out of my life for good.

"You know, I . . . I mean, you know how I feel." My hand without the sword tightened in his hair, and his free hand curled around my hip. "I've said it several times."

"Said what?" His words felt like physical things against my lips.

"That I love you, Eli."

He kissed me again, and I felt like everything might be possible, like fairy tales might be true, and happily ever after might be mine. While I might not want to get married, I was terribly, irrevocably in love with Eli.

What harm was one wish?

I was just about to agree when I felt the unmistakable presence of someone dead. I pulled back from our kiss and instead of saying "yes," I said, "Eli! Sword!"

I gripped my sword hilt again, ready to warn Eli that we were not alone, when a voice said, "You keep company with the *fae*?"

Iggy materialized beside me, body appearing after his voice

Eli snatched a sharp brass sword from a nearby wall rack. He raised it in one hand and shoved another sword at me. That one was steel, undoubtedly burning his hand.

"Geneviève." Eli moved to give me room to swing steel, but he was still half-blocking me as if he'd rather sacrifice himself to whatever intruder had come into my home. His chivalry made me feel all swoon-inclined. Most people stepped *behind* me.

I pointed my sword at Iggy. "Mind yourself."

"He is fae, Miss Crowe. They are deadly and—"

"Only one of you was invited here," I interrupted the corpse. "And it was, most definitely, not you, grave-breath."

Iggy straightened his suit jacket in the way of pompous men the world over. "As you will. Yet, I must fulfill the mandate, Hexen. You are not safe with one of the fae. They'll beguile you and—"

"Eli, this is Iggy." I touched Eli's wrist to draw his attention to me. "He's dead and won't go away."

Eli gave me a glance that promised more questions later.

I nodded in response, and then looked at the dead man. "Iggy, this is Eli of Stonecroft, heir of the fae throne, prince of *Elphame*, and my fiancé."

"Master Blackwood," Iggy corrected. "You, sir, may call me

Blackwood or Ignatius." Then he turned his attention to me. "You are beguiled already."

I sighed. "No."

Eli looked at me. "Oh?"

"I mean, yes, but not through some fae woo-woo. I like—"

"Ahem," Eli said.

"Woo woo. . .?" Iggy said at the same time.

I walked over to the fridge and popped a few grapes in my mouth. I needed a little something to take the edge off my stress. I wasn't going to get blitzed on fruit, but a few grapes were the witch-*draugr* version of a shot of tequila.

"Look. I have to find a dead guy. Not you, Iggy. A different dead guy. One who's killing people." I popped a few more grapes. "Deal with the police. Find out what Lady Beatrice needs. And figure out what the fuck to do about you."

"Vulgarity is not necessary in ladies," Iggy said primly.

"Aaaargh!" I grabbed an apple and bit a chunk off. Tonight was starting to feel like I needed more than a nip of intoxication.

I glanced at Eli. "I'm going to crash soon. Lashback. Stay?"

Oblivious to everything but his Master Hexen objectives, Iggy said, "I respect your attempt to escape. It shows cleverness. However, you cannot evade me, Miss Crowe. In the entire world over, you are the one spot of warmth for me. I can always find you simply by following the heat trail you leave in your path."

"I see." I hadn't, of course, but I wasn't going to admit ignorance just then. "So like a hunting dog?"

"No. Like a reanimated being drawn to the energy of the magic you used." He gave me an almost kindly smile. "You roused me, Hexen."

"Right but—"

"Your wards," Iggy continued as if I hadn't tried to reply,

"were quite adequately done. I've made note of areas we could improve, but they're passable."

To Eli, I whispered loudly, "Iggy thinks he's my coach or something."

"Ignatius," came the reply from the dead man.

"Where did he . . . when . . . *why?*" Eli asked in a surprisingly calm voice.

"Grave, earlier tonight, no fucking clue." I ticked my answers off on my hand. "He refuses to get back in his box."

"I see," Eli said. He sounded flustered, but I was starting to think part of my appeal was the drama I seemed unable to avoid. "Do you have a plan?"

I shrugged. The corporeal dead do not simply appear. That was a law—and yet here he was. I wasn't in the right frame of mind to come up with a workable plan.

"Sleep on it?" I suggested.

Iggy wasn't going away, and I wasn't sure what to do. The magic cost of tonight's activity was pushing at the walls I'd erected. Those walls would crash, crumble to pieces, and I needed a way to direct that energy.

So I walked toward the far end of the room where my guest apartment was. It was impersonal, looking like a floor model or fancy hotel, but it had a door—and boundaries were important in any roommate situation.

I jerked open the door and pointed.

"This will be where you stay, Iggy." I held his gaze. "We can discuss what it is you want to teach me, but this"—I waved the sword around the apartment—"is my home. You want to be out here in my space, you knock or text or something."

"Text? What is—"

"Tomorrow. We'll cover texting tomorrow," I said with a reluctant smile. "Otherwise, you go read a book or something. Tonight, I'm going out. You are staying here."

"I should assist you, as a teach—"

"No. I give my word that I'll return, but I need a recharge. Without you around." I glanced back at Eli, who was watching the whole thing in curiosity.

"Perhaps the fae is the one who is beguiled," Iggy murmured.

I flipped Iggy off. "We'll have boundaries, or I swear to Pete, I'll lock you in a box and salt it enough to mummify you. I'm going out. I'll be back; this is my *home*."

"Tomorrow." Iggy held my gaze with an assertion I was not expecting. "Or I will find you."

"You will not follow tonight, though."

Iggy nodded once. "My word."

And I don't know if I was on to something with the threats or Ignatius was just courteous, but he went into the guest apartment without another word.

CHAPTER FIVE

"WOULD HE BE ABLE TO FOLLOW US INTO YOUR HOUSE?" I asked. Waking up in Eli's arms wasn't something I wanted to let myself get used to, but I already found myself sleeping in his guest room more and more. I pretended it was convenience—central location or some such excuse—but tonight, I *needed* that security. I needed the fae sanctuary Eli had created.

"No. Nothing can enter my home without consent." Eli grabbed a pair of swords and gestured to the door.

The trouble with Eli was that he understood what I needed before I did most days—but he rarely pushed me, so when he did, I tended to be pliable. I think that was the secret that allowed him to get closer when no one else had. Well, that and a judicious use of faery bargains, a clever mind, and a body that . . . okay, fine. There were a lot of reasons he was The One.

I glanced at him as he led me to his car. "Shouldn't you be angry?"

He shrugged. "Perhaps."

I waited as he opened my door.

"You are never boring, cupcake." He watched me get settled.

At least he was still referring to me in dessert terms. That was a fae thing, the intense love of desserts, rich and decadent treats, and it would irritate me to no end if any other person did so. Eli, though, had this tone in his voice that promised sinful hours, and I had to resist a shiver lately. We hadn't crossed *all* the lines because we were engaged, and the fae were tradition-based people. But I knew all too well what that tone promised.

"Were you planning on yelling?" I asked when he got in the car.

"So civilized, Geneviève. Asking me. Waiting for my outbursts." Eli didn't look at me. "How is it that you can be so rational and infuriating in cycles?"

I sighed. "I should've mentioned Iggy."

"True." He slipped the car into traffic, driving cautiously as if he had to control everything in order to control his temper.

"I'm sorry . . .?" My voice rose at the end, sounding more like a question than an apology.

"You are not. You are sorry I'm displeased, but not at all sorry you withheld information that would've taken a second to—"

"I was embarrassed," I interrupted. "You have everything together and I just accidentally raised a wing of a cemetery, and oh, by the way, I have fangs now. And did I mention I'm also *accidentally engaged to a faery prince*—"

"A handsome faery prince," Eli interjected in a laughing voice.

"Fine." I slouched in my chair. "A gorgeous faery prince."

"Gorgeous, is it?"

"Yes."

Eli laughed. "Pouting, Geneviève?" He reached over and took my hand in his. "You can trust me. You can talk to me about feeling overwhelmed or angry or scared or raising corpses who refuse to obey."

"I *know*. I'm just not used to sharing things before I have a clue," I admitted.

"Or at all." He squeezed my hand as he said it, taking some of the sting out.

We drove in silence as he took us to his home, a building in the Garden District that felt increasingly like my home, too. I wouldn't say we were living together, but more and more I found myself here at night. Several nights each week, I slept alone at my place, but just as many nights found me here.

The house wasn't ostentatious like a lot of the Garden District homes. It had no balcony or gallery, no porch or Ionic columns. But even as plain as it was, there was a feeling of age to it. Eli's home looked like it could have been one of the first in the city. A stone fence surrounded the house and yard, and a wooden gate opened at our approach. That gate was undoubtedly expensive, as everything wooden rotted in this humidity—unless it was magic.

The benefits of being fae were sometimes subtle.

Still silent, we entered the house, and I felt peace fill me. The foyer floor was marble so polished it could be glass, and the wood under the bannister was dotted with buds and blooms. It was as if Eli had transported part of *Elphame* to this world. We walked to the second-floor landing of Eli's home, opening the door—wood inlaid with silver and brass—as Eli murmured words in his language that I didn't understand but could replicate if ever I needed.

Just inside the door I slipped my shoes off, and Eli did the same. He put the swords on a rack that he had added there for this very reason.

"Geneviève. . ."

I met his gaze.

"I can feel the energy pulsing from you," he said.

"Lashback," I whispered. "Raise that many dead and . . ." I

shrugged. "The fight helped, but the thought of losing you has me unsettled."

Eli removed his shirt, holding my gaze. "I am here. There is nature, flowing water. Let go."

I shook my head.

He shed his trousers, and I couldn't look away. I told myself that it wasn't sexual. The fae were an almost obsessively clean people. He was in the cemetery. He'd handed me my steel sword. The foyer was where the outside world, violence or death or anger, was left.

I could tell myself that I felt such peace here because of those things.

I had.

It was a lie, though. I felt this way because the naked man in front of me was here; he was my peace. My haven.

I stripped in silence.

He walked away, passing the main room and going to one of the most beautiful rooms I'd seen anywhere. Inside was a marble rainfall shower behind a wall of plants. Beyond it was a stone tub, with a small waterfall that splashed into it. It was the sort of decadence that made me remember that he wasn't merely the fae bartender he pretended to be most of the time—much as seeing him with a weapon made me remember that. He was a prince. A warrior. He had no need to be ostentatious as he had no insecurity there.

It took all of my resolve not to kneel before him in worship when he was this free, just as it took all of that resolve not to bend him to my will when I saw him with a sword in hand.

"What thoughts are in your mind, bonbon?" Eli stood so that the water of the shower was cascading over him, and I could forget that we were inside as he stood naked with stones under his feet and plants shielding just enough of him to make me need to move closer.

I moved so the water from his body splashed me.

"I catch a few stray words as intensely as you are thinking. Tell me, Miss Crowe. What are these thoughts that you are resisting?"

"Rules," I whispered. Our mental communication thing was spotty, but since I'd been injected, it was harder to keep him out. "Thinking of the rules . . ."

Eli shook his head. "That's not what you were thinking. Something about swords in hand . . ."

My gaze fell to his hand, watching it reach out toward me. "No swords here," I said, trying for lightness. The pressure from the lashback in my body made me feel like I was shaking, but I couldn't tell if that was real.

"Shall I take something else in hand, Geneviève?"

I stepped closer and nodded. "Me."

He pulled me into his embrace under the water. "Let go," he whispered. "I have you."

And I did; I let my restraints fall. All of the residual magic trapped in my skin after my accidental necromancy flooded him. He swayed with me, letting me fall into him and his back brushed the plants around us.

I whimpered as my body made contact with him from thigh to chest. It wasn't sexual in a way that could result in faery matrimony, but it felt good in a way that sensual and magical all at once. My eyes fluttered against the pleasure of his fae energy crashing into my grave magic.

Perfection.

Life.

. . .

Obviously, the plants in the room appreciated the surge. The wall erupted into a veritable jungle as the grave magic let go of me. I slid to the stone pebbled floor and looked up at Eli, who was as aroused as I was. The trouble with my grave magic was that it was life affirming —and what could be more life affirming than sex?

"Geneviève?"

I took him into my mouth. *That* act wasn't forbidden to us, although Eli had made a point to avoid it.

I paused and asked, "Rules?"

Eli's hand reached down and caught my hair. His voice was as delicious as any dessert as he said, "None for me. I am yours, bonbon."

Our entwining magic crashed again, and all the tension I'd had rose. I found that pinnacle where there is only sensation.

"Geneviève. Love . . ." As Eli groaned my name, I fell tumbling into bliss, and in that moment of mutual release, I admitted that every act was a miracle with him.

How the fae thought *this* wasn't sex was a mystery! Thank the Goddess and G-d that these things we did weren't sex *enough* to result in our having an actual wedding.

Afterwards, Eli carried me to the guest room. I didn't have the energy to stand. The lashback was equal to the energy used, and I had created an accidental jungle in his bathroom.

"Are you still anchoring in this world?"

I nodded.

"Any urges I ought to know?"

I mustered a grin. "Pretty satisfied, *bonbon*."

He laughed softly. "I meant nourishment, but I shall accept that compliment despite you doing the heavy lifting, as it were."

"Just need to recharge." I snuggled closer. "Freezing."

Eli was polite enough not to admit that I failed to tell him just how much magic I'd summoned earlier tonight. I only felt as cold as the proverbial grave because of depletion. I snatched the shirt he had on the side of the bed. I rarely opted to sleep in a shirt, but when I grabbed it, Eli simply pulled it over my head since my arms were too weak to lift the fabric.

"Geneviève?" He crawled into the bed beside me, and I practically crawled on top on him seeking warmth.

"Mmm?" I managed. I couldn't pry my eyes open. Magic and lashback had left me near comatose.

"Later," he whispered when I couldn't rouse myself to reply.

I fell asleep in Eli's arms, in his guest room, which was one of the many adjustments we'd made to cope with one or the other of our issues. For him, I avoided certain words, iron, and of course, tried my damnedest to accept the six hundred or so rules that the fae lived by. For me, we slept in a guest room, avoided traditional intercourse, and tried to cope with the rules that my biology required. We compromised.

But sometimes, I still woke in a panic. Tonight was one of those nights. A few hours later, I slipped out of bed.

Eli, half-asleep, caught my hand before I was out of reach.

When I looked at him, he met my gaze with sleep-heavy eyes. "You're safe, Geneviève. If you want to leave me someday, I'll release you."

I stayed, concentrating on the logic of his words, the logic of Eli. The fae don't lie. Eli was one of the most trustworthy people I'd met in my life. He'd risked his life, happiness, and even his ancestors' memories for me.

He released my hand, and I walked to the window.

"We can figure it all out," he reminded me, voice soft in the darkened room. "It's all happened so quickly but—"

"Has it?" I turned to look at him. "We've been friends for a few years."

"And if someone hadn't tried to kill you, we'd still be slowly building to where we are," Eli pointed out. "I didn't choose to rush this. I know you."

"How long were you planning to wait?"

"How long were you?" he parried. "You talked yourself out of my bed more than a few times before you ended up here . . ."

"I'm in the *guest* bed," I pointed out, stressing the fact that it was a guest bed.

Eli laughed. "Of course, my cherry pie. *My* guest bed."

In a move intended to remind him I trusted him, I *flowed* back to the bed. In less than a blink, I was back on the bed, crouched over Eli.

He looked up at me. "My bed. Guest room or not, it's *my* bed in *my* home. You rest in *my* arms."

"I know." I brushed my lips over him before adding, "Trust me. I know exactly where I am."

"I wanted forever before you realized it," he said. "I waited."

"And here we are . . ." I no longer wanted to do anything quickly. I wanted every last second to last. "You look like cat who's caught the canary, Eli."

He chuckled. "Odd . . . I feel rather like I'm the canary when you pin me down."

We both knew he could throw me off him, could return to *Elphame*, could leave me. That was the part that I couldn't stand some nights. He spoke as if I was the one with the power, but he held my everything in his hands. If he left, if he got tired of my chaos or mistakes, he could simply leave—and I could not follow.

"Are you caught then?" my voice was embarrassingly vulnerable.

"As caught as you are, love." His hands traced up my sides, under the loose shirt I had worn to sleep, caressing but cautious even now.

I lowered myself over him. All that was between us was a sheet, and that was only over his lower half. It felt somehow like too much and not enough.

I was what was politely called "sex-positive"—and impolitely called words that had led to my fists in more than a few faces—but the most adventurous nights of sex had never felt as important as the smallest touches with Eli.

His thumbs on my nipples made my thoughts evaporate and my hips grind down.

"*Geneviève...*"

"There's a sheet between us," I whispered, bending down to kiss him and pressing myself closer to his obvious arousal.

What was meant to be a simple kiss became a clash of tongue and teeth that had entire body buzzing with the strange magic that had been between us these last weeks. When he pulled back, I admitted, "I always feel drunk on you."

"Geneviève," he tried again. He swallowed and asked, "Rules . . .?"

I sat up, took his wrists in my hands, and then I angled my hips. Pushing his arms above his head, I pressed myself down and rubbed against his body. With sheet between us, we weren't breaking the rule.

"I want *you*, Eli," I confessed.

"Bonbon . . ." He groaned as he pressed his hips up in time to my movements. "*Rules?*"

"No intercourse," I said, as I always had to say since I'd discovered the unpleasant truth of fae engagements: True love and sex created an unbreakable marriage bond with the fae.

I was pretty damn sure that what we felt was love. Saying it was as good as admitting I loved him—and that I knew he loved me. Maybe that was why he had started forcing me to say it every time we'd touched intimately. He was aware that my refusal was an admission.

"No intercourse," Eli repeated in a low voice. "And you want my pleasure. Anything else?"

Any negotiation with a faery was dangerous, but I couldn't care in that moment.

"That's all, love," I said, enjoying the way he reacted to *that* word.

I bent to kiss him again, and I wasn't sure whether it was his need or mine that had me wishing there was a way around this no-intercourse issue. The fae were literal enough that I figured we could safely do everything *but* that. And I was increasingly insistent on finding that exact line and skating along it.

"May I kiss you, finally?" he asked.

I blinked at him.

"You crossed *that* line earlier." He breathed the words against my throat. "Would you deny me the same?"

I let out a sound that was more noise than word as I realized what he'd meant. "Kiss me" was a polite euphemism. "Please. *Please.*"

"Begging so soon?" Eli chuckled.

In the next moment, Eli had reclaimed the control I'd held. I was flipped over mid-kiss, and in short order I was topless, legs spread, and Eli had slid down my body. There was something incredibly exciting in knowing that he could probably hold me down if he wanted—and that he wouldn't do so if I said the word.

I wasn't saying anything, though. My thighs were parted for his attentions, and I had no words left.

"No intercourse, peach," he whispered, "because you'd be *mine* forever."

At first, I managed not to answer. I had no words with Eli's mouth on my body. He held me tightly enough that my thighs would have fingerprints.

Then, just when I was about to crash into bliss, he paused. Staring up my trembling body, he asked, "No intercourse, my delicious peach, because . . ."

I slid my hand between my legs, and he chuckled and batted it away.

"Eli. . . *please*."

A few casual strokes of his devilish tongue, and he prompted, "No intercourse because. . . you dislike me?"

"No."

"Ah. You fear I'd disappoint?"

"No."

"Because you love me, but aren't ready for marriage?"

I looked down at the beautiful man who continued to torment me just enough to keep me hanging on a precipice. "Yes. . ."

"I do love you, Geneviève," he swore.

And then he stopped teasing.

CHAPTER SIX

BY MORNING, I WAS IN FAR CHEERIER MOOD THAN I HAD thought possible at this unholy hour of the day. I didn't even remark on the designer jeans or new undergarments in "my" drawer that obviously cost more money than reasonable people spent on clothes.

"No shirt?" I glanced over my shoulder at the naked faery watching me from the bed. The sheets weren't covering anything, and I let myself look my fill. Witches weren't particularly hung-up on modesty, and fortunately, neither were the fae.

"You can borrow any one of my shirts." Eli's voice was mild, but it felt like a test of some sort. "Or bring a few to put in my closet."

I grinned. "But pretty things magically appear here, why would I do that?"

"Because I am fae, bonbon." He stalked toward me. "I like the scent of you on my sheets. Wear my shirt, or you could hang some of your things next to my clothes."

I shrugged like it was no big deal. "Sure. I like the dark blue one of yours."

Eli left to his closet and returned with six blue shirts—and I tried not to admit that I liked the smell of his clothes, too, although I know he saw me sniff one of the shirts.

"I wore that one briefly yesterday," he said.

"I'm terrible at being courted." I pulled on a sleeveless shell he'd brought, too, and then put his shirt on over it like it was a jacket. "Maybe you should—"

"You're exactly the one I *want* to court, Geneviève," he said with a quick kiss, nothing more than a brush of lips but it somehow still made me feel like some foolish maiden about to swoon. Then he added, "So, *no*, you aren't terrible."

The buzzing of my phone told me that my designated driver was outside. Eli glared at the phone.

"Do what you need," I said. "Ally will take me home and then we'll handle the Christophe Hebert problem."

"You could stay here," Eli suggested. "Sleep more."

"I need to deal with Iggy, and you need to go over to the bar."

"I need to hire a manager." Eli sighed, but the reality of the matter was more complicated.

The fae need a "normal" amount of sleep—and sunlight. I was the opposite. For most of my life, I'd needed little sleep, maybe four hours a day unless I was injured. I had a peculiar metabolism that meant that I could do a low-grade activity while my body recharged. Watch a show? Take a bath? Things that required no activity on my part recharged muscle and organs. After the attempt on my life, that changed. I could sleep longer, but if I wanted to stay awake, there was a cure.

That cure was waiting downstairs in a cup.

"This afternoon," Eli said. "I'll be at your side to locate Madame Hebert in Houston, but there is a faery bargain left unanswered. If you do not accept the bargain by tomorrow, you are on your own, Geneviève. I cannot offer you aid or pleasure. Think about that, about how you tremble at my touch, about who else could provide the strength or pleasure you need . . ."

"Eli . . ."

"The decision is yours." He kissed me thoroughly and once I was breathless, he added, "I would be bereft to lose what we have, and I cannot express how it would pain me to see you go unprotected into danger."

"Not playing fair."

"Fae never do, Geneviève." He kissed me again, nipping my lip and demanding entrance.

Once I managed to pull away, he caught my hand and added, "I am yours, Geneviève Crowe. Accept me as I am or free us."

Then he left me there, speechless and confused.

I left the house without the ability to speak coherently. I knew I was right that our bargains so far had benefitted me as much as him, but how could I grant anyone an open-ended wish? That sounded far more dangerous.

A tiny reasonable voice reminded me that this was Eli, that I wasn't randomly granting a stranger power over me. This was the man I loved. . . and yet a lifetime of self-preservation made me unable to simply say "yes."

Outside, I slid into the passenger seat of Ally's car.

She handed me a travel cup with a cheery, "Blood orange juice!"

"Juice?" I gaped at her. "Allie, we talked about this. Fruit makes me drunk, and I don't have time to be dr—"

"Blood, silly, not blood oranges," Ally whispered. "It just"— she looked around although the car window was up and she was whispering—"seemed like a dangerous thing to say. What if. . . one of those SAFARI people heard and—"

"Got it." I took a big gulp of vodka and blood. "Thank you, Allie."

"Oh! We need a code word." She shifted into gear and pulled onto the street. "Like carrot juice? Beet smoothie? Oh, what about lava juice? You know, because lava is red."

I'm fairly sure I replied, but sometimes Ally required a special degree of attention that I had trouble with during the daylight. I paused in my thoughts and looked at the window. "You had the windows tinted darker."

"I hate your headaches, Boss." Ally didn't add that it was because she had a strange maternal need to nurture me since I'd resurrected her stepson, Tres, but it was there. Whether it was gratitude or guilt for attempting to kill me or magic, Ally was devoted to my health and well-being with the fervor of a new mother.

"Where to?"

I gave her the address of Christophe Hebert's mother's home and settled back in her luxurious sedan. Whereas Eli went for a flashy convertible, Ally drove her late husband's cars. All of them. Today was a Lexus with its distinctive front grill, leather interior, and climate controls that were surprisingly useful in New Orleans' omnipresent humidity.

I was just going to pop by Madame Hebert's house, ask a few questions, and then I'd go home to deal with Iggy. That was the plan. I didn't need Eli's back-up for this. I'd take him with me to Houston—assuming I could still enter the city—but this was just swinging by an empty house. *Draugr* were even more sensitive to sunlight than I was, and I could feel them nearby, so I wouldn't be exposing Ally to danger.

It was perfectly safe.

And sure, I still had a dead guy in my apartment, a police request to attend, and an engagement to navigate, but I felt confident that I could handle it. Maybe it was the orgasms last night or talking to Eli. Maybe it was arrogance. Who knew? All

I could say for sure was that I had an optimism today that I hadn't felt standing in the graveyard last night.

"Sing for us, Allie," I said, and not *just* because I wanted to distract her. Alice Chaddock had such a beautiful voice that it would make even angels weep, and although I was far from angelic, I was fairly sure that it was a holy experience to listen to her sing.

She started to sing some gospel song about "going to the river," and it felt like exactly what I needed.

I couldn't tell if it was the sex or the blood that had me so cheerful, but either way I was positively optimistic when Ally parked the sedan outside the Hebert family estate. Admittedly, Madame Hebert wasn't local these days, but they'd kept the family estate on the edge of the city. It was close enough to the ghost zone that I had no idea what awaited me, but I knew that *draugr* were asleep during the midday hours.

"Well, this looks just peachy," Ally drawled.

The wrought iron gate in front of the estate was looking rough. Several fat padlocks and thick chains held it shut. Vines twined up it as if they had been there for years, and some of the fleur-de-lis at the tops of the fence spikes were cracked off. The weeds had consumed the front lawn, but the flagstone walkway was clear. Someone had been here recently.

"I think you'd better stay outside." I got out of the car, foolishly thinking she had the sense to obey me on this.

Ally got out and slammed her door. When I glanced over at her, she scowled. "Do I look like I want your fiancé to put a boot up my butt?"

I paused, looking away from the ruined estate in front of me. "Eli is not going to kick you, Ally." She opened her mouth, but I held up a hand. "And your roots are showing again . . ."

"Damn it!" Alice Chaddock took several steps toward me. "I relax around you, Boss. Then I get all . . . hillybilly-sounding."

I grinned. "You're fine. Still the socialite. Still the widow Chaddock."

She relaxed slightly. "Still, maybe we ought to get help. Eli—"

"Is busy, and anything in there is asleep," I pointed out. That was the benefit of coming during the day.

"I still think you need protection! Back-up or whatever." Ally crossed her arms like a petulant child.

But before I could argue, I felt the dead. Here. Behind me.

"And who is this pretty bit of frock?" Iggy said as he stepped to my side.

Ally was done pouting and aiming a massive gun at the corpse in the next moment. "Should I shoot him?"

A part of me wanted to let Ally shoot Iggy. Another part wanted to know why the socialite wife, one of the wealthiest people in the city, had such ease with guns—or where she hid a .45 in a designer pantsuit. Someday, she was going to answer those questions.

For now, I said, "No."

"Just once?" she whispered.

I stepped in front of her. As much as I was bound to her, I still remembered that she was a hair-trigger sort of woman.

"Iggy, I thought I was fairly clear on the no interruption thing

Iggy walked around me and bowed to Ally. "I apologize for startling you."

"And for calling me a pretty bit of frock," she added.

"Ah . . ."

"*Say* it," Ally ordered, raising her gun to his face.

Iggy laughed. "Things certainly have changed since my death, haven't they? I apologize for calling you a pretty bit of frock, my dear lady, but you are quite beautiful."

She poked her gun into his chest, and Iggy vanished—only to reappear beside her. "Lovely piece."

"I'm not a *piece*," Ally hissed.

"I meant the revolver." Iggy shook his head. "Now, tell me what my hexen needs protected from . . ."

CHAPTER SEVEN

ALLY WALKED OVER TO HER TRUNK AND PULLED OUT BOLT cutters and an axe. "Boss?"

"Where . . .?" I was used to cute shoes and mugs with silly sayings, but an *axe*?

"Always prepared," Ally chirped. "It's like the assistant's code or something, right?" She paused. "Do I get a merit badge for this?"

"A merit badge?" I blinked at her. It took me a minute to realize she was teasing me. I took the bolt cutters, snapped the chains, and handed them back. "You *will* wait here, Alice Chaddock."

She sighed like she was deflating. "Can I shoot the dead guy at least?"

"No," Iggy and I answered in unison.

Then Iggy looked at me and said, "I will be your extra eyes, Hexen. I am impervious to the tempers of humans." He glanced at Ally. "And their revolvers."

Ally crossed her arms and jutted out her lower lip. Honestly that pout worked on me more than I ever wanted to let on. Ally was becoming some weird cross between annoying little sister and child in my mind. No one else understood my fondness for her, and I couldn't truly say I did either. She'd tried to kill me. That was definite hold-a-grudge territory, but the mere thought of her in danger made my temper prickle.

"Stay," I repeated. "Or else."

Now, "or else" was a lame sort of mom-threat, but it worked. Ally's eyes widened, and she got back into the sedan.

I studied the fence. It wasn't electrified from the looks of it, no wires attached, so I could simply go over. I glanced at Iggy. "Can you go through it?"

He looked affronted at the thought. "I am dead, Hexen, not a ghost."

"You materialized in my home. That's ghost stuff."

"Magic, girl. Not ghost traits. And afterward, I had to repair my magical depletion." Iggy glared at me in a way that made me feel like I'd failed a pop quiz.

I started snapping bolts and chains. *Trespassing. Destruction of property. Breaking and entering.* I skirted more than a few laws in my job, but today—with a pending appointment with the NOPD—I was acutely aware of it.

Iggy walked behind me, looking like an elegant reveler dressed for another era. Honestly, a small part of me wanted to be sure he was *actually* dead because he looked as lifelike as anyone in the city. He stepped around the thorny branches of a rose bush grown wild, pushing hip-high weeds aside with his walking stick.

"Serpents," Iggy said, pointing at the rattling tail of an impressively sized rattlesnake. "Mind where you step."

He moved in front of me then and started whacking at the grass. Startling the venomous creatures wasn't my preferred tactic, but I made note that even when one struck his leg, Iggy was fine. If anything, the snake looked injured. It fell limp and shuddered. Apparently, whatever manner of dead Ignatius was, he wasn't good to bite.

"I have spelled boots, Iggy," I mentioned as I took the lead again. "This is nowhere near my first encounter with fanged things."

Iggy chuckled and followed me to the front door. Despite the ruinous state of the yard, the porch was intact. It looked like it had been carefully kept up. No sagging planks here—and that was a challenge in the humidity of the bayou.

"Monkey nuts." I glared at the door. There, beside the front knob was a security panel. The house was wired with an alarm, and while I could argue that my B&E was justified, I hated having to deal with police officers more than absolutely necessary.

"Monkey . . ." Iggy scowled at me. "What kind of thing is *that* to say?"

"I'm trying to cuss less often." I spared him a glance. "I need to go in and see why the house is locked up. I'm hoping to find clues on SAFARI and the late Mr. Hebert—"

"SAFARI is still around?" Iggy grimaced. "As bad as the KKK, they are. 'Course back in my day, most folks didn't know about the *draugr* or the fae so—"

"Can we catch up on history lessons later? Maybe when we aren't breaking and entering? Unless you have a solution to get me inside . . ." I said.

My dead helper was unable to function like a proper ghost. Just my luck! A proper ghost could go inside and have a look-see . . .

"Solution proffered." Iggy murmured unfamiliar words and a zing of energy built at my side. The dead man put his hand over the box, and in the next instant, it began sizzling and smoking.

"No!" I clutched his hand, getting a jolt through my arm as thanks.

Whatever chance we had of stealth was gone now that the alarm was shorted out. That, undoubtedly, sent an alert wherever it was routed. Police? A security company?

"Fuck a duck!" I slammed into the door. Whatever time we still had, I was going to use it. "Office. Office. Where's the twice cursed office?"

Iggy went another direction as I prowled the house, hoping to find an office with information. The house was supposed to be empty, un-used, but it was dust free and none of the furniture was under sheets. Someone had been here recently.

"Crowe!" Iggy called from wherever he was within the house. "You need to see this."

"I need to find answers!" I yelled back, hoping that the security system didn't include a video or audio recording set-up.

"Geneviève Crowe, come *here*!"

Something in Iggy's voice made me want to know what had the dead Victorian ruffled. Terrible décor? Rats in the larder? I went toward the sound of his voice and found myself not in the kitchens, but in a sitting room. It was, admittedly, terrible decor. Dusty doilies and a sort of excess that spoke of no personal sense of style. And arranged on the chairs in various macabre postures were six formally dressed, dead people who were seemingly playing cards. Three women. Two men. And one person with no clear answer. They'd all been beheaded.

"What the fuck . . ."

Iggy shot me a look.

"Some situations require cussing," I said.

"Indeed." Iggy stood beside a corpse in a ball gown. Her hair was blood-crusted, and the bodice of her gown had been soaked with it. "Dry."

"So at least a day? Maybe two?" I circled the corpses, studying them. I'd seen dead bodies before, but nothing quite like this. "Why are they arranged like this?"

"Perversity," Iggy offered.

I pulled out my phone and began documenting details. A photo of the entire grisly scene. Another of the cards, seemingly nailed to their hands. Several images of identifying traits, fingerprints in blood, and anything else I could think might be useful to recall. I wasn't sure, though. I was a necromancer not an investigator.

"What is that?" Iggy asked.

"Phone." I snapped a picture of him and held it up so he could see his stunned expression. "Calls, internet, camera, music."

"Should we notify the police? An alienist? Beatrice?" Iggy stayed at my side, but he watched the doorway as if the murderers were still inside—and they very well might be. I heard no sirens yet, no voices at the door, so I figured that we had a few minutes.

I looked to the sweeping staircase. "Come on."

Upstairs were three bedrooms—one with a sitting room and walk-in closet—as well as an expansive bath, an office, and a smaller bathroom. Nothing looked touched. The only mark that anyone had been up there was a shattered window. The glass crunched underfoot as I went to look out at a towering oak that the intruder or intruders had obviously climbed to reach the window.

"What are we seeking?"

"Answers." I glanced over my shoulder at Iggy where he stood watching the hall and stairway. He made a fairly good back-up. "Someone came in. Broke this window. Was it the guests in the sitting room? Or were they invited? Why are they dressed for theatre night? And who posed them?"

I walked out of the bedroom and to the office. A heavy writing desk—which must've been a chore to tote up those stairs—had correspondence on the top. Bills. A letter to a congresswoman. Nothing damning.

A scream rose up, audible though the broken window.

"Ally!" I tore down the stairs and was outside in a heartbeat or three.

A man stood outside Ally's sedan, punching her window. He was sizzling in the sunlight—which was unusual under any circumstances. Ally had her gun aimed at him but shooting him meant shooting her window.

My sword was in hand, and his head was severed in as long as it took to notice that her window already had cracks in it. The bubbling dead man thumped to the ground as Iggy came running through the gate and onto the street.

Ally shoved the door open. "Weasel dick," she yelled as she kicked him in the side.

"Ally . . ."

She looked at me. "He was trying to kill me!"

I sighed. "You could've left."

"I would never leave you, Boss." Ally looked scandalized. Then she whispered, "I did call Prince Eli."

"Ally!" I rubbed my face. Eli was going to be pissed off. In my defense I thought I was visiting an empty house or maybe questioning a tenant.

I hit autodial for the number Gary had used. I wasn't sure if it was at the police station or a cell phone.

He answered on the second ring. "Kid? You alright?"

"Yeah. I, umm, need back-up at"—I looked at the house and rattled off the address—"stopped by to talk to the owners. Door wide open. Six corpses inside—"

"Biters?"

I paused. I wasn't sure. They had been beheaded. Who could leave so many biters like that?

To Gary, I said, "No clue. The one trying to bust into my car was though. . . I think. Hell, I don't know. He was sizzling."

"Sizzling?" Gary echoed. "Con Crew?"

The Contamination Crew collected dead *draugr* during daylight only. There wasn't always a good way to check if the *draugr* were dead. Even animated, they had no pulse. Daylight tended to make them sleep, so it was safest to gather them in the light and contain them to see if they woke at evening.

"Send a few people. None of them have heads attached."

"Even the one who sizzled?"

"He was attacking. I am a beheading sort of woman . . ."

"Course you are, Crowe." Gary sighed. "Anything else?"

"Let the Con Crew know," I said, disconnecting as Eli's car slid to a stop.

My fiancé was out of the car and stomping toward me with an expression I'd rarely seen.

"I can explain," I started.

Eli glanced at Ally. "Thank you for the disaster notification. It was appreciated, albeit later than acceptable."

She curtsied. "I couldn't stop that"—she pointed to the corpse—"but I couldn't let it go inside after the boss."

"Understood." Eli turned to me. "Why was there a *draugr* in daylight?"

"No clue." I shrugged, hoping he didn't ask what was inside.

But he didn't have to because Iggy asked, "Do you think that creature was what slaughtered the people inside?"

I winced.

"Slaughtered . . ." Eli looked from me to Iggy and back to me. If a look could sting this was it. Ice hung in his words as he prompted, "Geneviève?"

I turned to Ally. "Would you please go home? I cannot focus on what's next while worrying over you."

"Are you mad at me?" Ally asked, glancing at Eli before looking back at me.

"Not at all." I smiled, hoping I sounded convincing. I wasn't. Not really, but I was frustrated in the whole situation.

Iggy straightened his lapels again. "Well, Let us—"

"Go with Ally," I interrupted. "I need to know she's safe, and I cannot explain *you* to the police, Iggy."

I watched them get into her sedan and depart before turning to Eli. "So . . . hi."

"Geneviève." Eli's tone was frigid. His use of my actual name always meant that we had witnesses or that he was being serious.

And we had no witnesses other than the headless corpse on the sidewalk.

CHAPTER EIGHT

"I WASN'T EXPECTING TROUBLE . . ." I STARTED AFTER A LONG tense moment. I didn't take a step toward him, despite my worry that this conversation would lead to words we couldn't erase. That fear hung in my mind larger than the moment. Words said hastily were still said, and if we quarreled, the cost could be our entire relationship. The result was that I stared mutely at him.

"Geneviève?" he prompted. "Do you care to explain why Alice called me screaming?"

"She was in danger, not *me*." It was a weak excuse, but it was the best I had. I gestured toward the house. "That was just unexpected."

"The slaughter inside?" he prompted, and I made a mental note to talk to Iggy about boundaries again.

"No one could expect what is in the house." I walked away, figuring Eli would come with me or leave me there until that flicker of rage was quenched.

He followed me into the yard, and the entire place shifted. Seeing Eli in that overgrown yard when his temper was sparking would be enough to disprove any thoughts that he was only half-fae, which was the rumor he encouraged. Eli was far from human. Plants twisted, sprouting tendrils that reached toward him. Grasses wove themselves into a pathway, and the serpents in those tall grasses paused for his crossing.

The fae were one with nature in a way that was seamless. Witches could connect to nature through will and the occasional spell or blood. My peculiar jumble of witch and *draugr* genes made me sensitive to energy in odd ways. No one, no being, other than the fae could do as Eli just had.

Which meant his magic was unbound.

Which meant he was furious.

"Eli?" I whispered.

He turned, and I swear there was a forest lurking in his eyes just then. "Geneviève."

"I was not being careless."

"Oh?"

I shoved my own temper back. I would not fight. Not him. Not now. I squared my shoulders. "How many times have I done my job? How many *years* have I done so? I invited you to my side on hunts or night excursions, but I am still me and this is still *my fucking job*."

Okay. Maybe my not-fighting decision was failing a bit.

"Do you think I am unaware of that?" Eli sounded near growling, and G-d help me, I liked it. I liked him when he was soft, but I liked his darker streak just as much.

I stared, biting my lip to stop from saying something foolish.

"I know who you are," Eli continued. "I love you for who you are, Geneviève Crowe."

"Don't start the full name thing," I snapped. "I am not some fae princess that—"

"You are, though. You *are* a princess now. My princess. My

affianced. My future queen," Eli grabbed me and pulled me closer. "And I am allowed to be alarmed."

"Oh." I met his gaze. "So, you're not angry?"

Eli pressed his lips to mine. It wasn't an answer, but desire surged. I felt tears in my eyes, and when he pulled away, a moan of need slipped through my lips. It was altogether possible that my own temper was twisted into fear.

"I don't want to lose you," I admitted. "Don't give up on me."

After an oddly long moment, Eli said, "That is precisely why I was . . . *am* angry. I have sought the perfect mate, the woman who would be my equal, for decades. Here you are. And you were in peril." He made a growling sound again. "I wasn't here."

"That *will* happen."

He caught my face in his hands and held my gently. "Do you think I don't know that? I've stitched you and carried you. I've watched you get stabbed. You were nearly dead in Autumn. Last month, you were attacked. Honestly, bonbon, you are out fighting creatures who are faster and stronger than you. That is not to count the humans and—"

"I'm sorry," I interjected before he could continue to list all the dangers. "This is who I am. You know that."

He sighed, and then in an uncharacteristic move, he laced his fingers with mine. "Come. Show me what you stumbled into this time."

I leaned up and kissed his cheek. "I was careful, you know. These bodies are dead, and really, the only threat was to poor Ally. I dispatched that threat in a blink."

He squeezed my hand. It was not quite an apology, but I wasn't sure which of us ought to apologize.

· · ·

By the time we were done taking my second survey of the corpses, I realized that they were not, in fact, all human. Two likely were, but the others were *draugr.* Who left twice-dead *draugr* in a house arranged as if they were at a gruesome poker game? Or humans, for that matter?

"I feel like we're missing something," I admitted, looking again at the nailed cards. "Why are they in the Hebert house?"

Eli shook his head.

"And the one outside . . ." I looked toward the street. "It *sizzled* like acid on it."

The police arrived, and I heard the distinct voice of Gary Broussard barking orders at the rest. I stepped onto the porch as Gary and two other people in NOPD uniforms entered the yard.

Gary looked at the woven grasses and at me. "Kid?"

I shrugged. Saying my angry faery fiancé did it seemed pointless—or confessional. Either way, I motioned Gary forward. "Inside. Strong stomach required."

"No newbs here, kid." Gary met my gaze. "Official report?"

I squirmed at the implied warning there. He was forewarning me that one of the cops was a by-the-book type. I carefully explained, "I'm looking for Madame Hebert. Her son was . . . missing."

"Alive?" one of the others asked.

"No. Missing from his grave," I clarified. "I came to check on the deceased's next of kin—"

"Why not call us?" the same officer, a young woman who looked vaguely angry, asked. Her voice was all Midwestern intonations, so I figured she was new to our fair city.

"I am a necromantic witch, officer. I don't need to call you," I pointed out, voice level despite her attitude. "I'm authorized to conduct my business."

"And him?" she prompted, inclining her head toward Eli. "Half-fae, right?"

"My associate was not here. I called him when I called Gary." I answered quickly because Eli couldn't actually claim to be half-fae. The fae don't lie, and Eli revealing exactly who he was would create a shit-ton of complications for both of us. The world had such an odd fixation on royalty and on the fae, so if they learned that he was the heir to the throne of *Elphame*, we'd be under scrutiny neither of us needed.

"I was shaken," I said. "There are . . . six bodies inside. None are Madame Hebert. I was about to call you when I was accosted by the *draugr* on the street."

"Biters don't come out in daylight," the woman said. "Was it in the—"

"Look. I am well aware of what they do and don't do." I stepped closer, hand dropping to my sword hilt as my temper flared back to life. "I grew up right here, Minnesota."

"Geneviève is a witch, Trelawney." Gary met my gaze and shook his head slightly. "Gen, Officer Trelawney came out of St. Louis before this."

"Walled city, huh? Must be different there." I smiled, ignoring Gary's head shake. "Learning the ropes from books must be interesting."

I walked off, leading them to the parlor with the corpses. "Here you go. All dead. No biters that will resurrect."

"How can you be—"

"Witch, Minnesota. I'm a *witch*. I can summon the dead. Necromancy, *draugr* location, that's my job." I pivoted.

"Kid!" Gary didn't reach for me, but he followed fast enough that he was in my path. "Do you need to antagonize everyone?"

Eli muffled a laugh.

"Sometimes," I admitted with a rueful smile. "It's been a morning."

"Broussard? You're going to want to bring Geneviève in here," a tech called.

"Now what?" I wasn't sure much else could rattle me here, but the tech was a senior member of the Con Crew, too. I'd seen her around often enough to remember when she got the scars on her throat and shoulder.

Inside the room with the corpses, the tech—Suzette—gestured to the floor. Under the table was a box, wrapped in silver and blue. The lid was wrapped separately, so the bow didn't need to be undone to open the package.

"Suz?" Gary prompted.

"Geneviève Crowe." Suzette said my name oddly, as if we were strangers or . . .

She pointed at the label on the box, and then she added, "It's addressed to you."

I stepped closer. "Open it."

Inside the box were the heads of three crows, and a bright red Carnival mask. The whole mess was resting in ribbons and glitter—and crawling with maggots.

"Well . . ." I exchanged a look with Eli.

Three crows.

Me, Mama Lauren, and Beatrice?

Was this a threat against us? Was I misreading it?

"Anything you know?" Gary asked.

"Some sicko put bird heads in a box." I shrugged, not willing to show anything else here. "Someone knows I work with you all? Maybe they knew the owner's son wasn't in his grave so they expected me?"

"Looks like a threat." Gary looked at me like he wanted to say more, but then he glanced back. Minnesota was eaves-dropping.

"Must be a day that ends in 'y.'" I shrugged. "Plenty of threats. What can you do?"

Eli was silent at my side, but I saw him nod to Gary. Maybe it was man-code. Maybe it was to verify that Eli understood Gary's implications.

"I'm okay, Gary." I gave him a reassuring smile. "No worries. I'll see you at the NOPD meeting, but unless you need me here . . . I have things to do."

"Sure, kid," Gary said.

"Suzette." I nodded to her. "Stay safe."

"Kid? You are *legally* allowed to bring him"—Gary nodded to Eli—"to the meeting. Or me. Or both."

Then he turned away and began ordering the forensic techs and the Con Crew in a combination of evidence gathering and corpse awareness.

CHAPTER NINE

ELI OPENED THE PASSENGER DOOR OF HIS LITTLE convertible. "We are near enough the ghost zone that it might be simple encroaching."

"And the box?"

"Well, that changes things." Eli looked around, as if the killer was out in the open watching us like on some television program. "Although, I suspect you do have enemies in the ghost zone."

I snorted. The cities were where living folks clustered, and the immediate space outside that—the ghost zones—were where *draugr* gathered. Admittedly, there was mingling, but in a sort of perversion of city-suburb-rural, the ghost zone—formerly the suburbs—was now the most dangerous place most living folks would encounter. Sure, *draugr* still roamed the city proper, but if people went inside at dusk, they could mostly guarantee a long, relatively safe life.

"We should talk to Beatrice," I admitted out loud. "Tell her about . . . all of it."

"Already going that way, bonbon." Eli steered us onto the bridge, taking us out of the edge of the city and into the ghost zone. The Hebert house was at the border, but it was still, technically, in the city. If not, the police wouldn't have come. No one patrolled the ghost zone.

It was eerie in the way of many a ghost town. The occasional tourist or scavenger went there, since the former inhabitants left their homes without taking most of their possessions. Entering the houses meant that the risk of *draugr* encounters was high.

"Should we see your mother, too?"

I glanced at him. "I'll address that with Beatrice."

"We could warn her, bonbon. Three crow heads. Do not think I am not drawing the same conclusions you are." Eli reached over and squeezed my hand. "If the NOPD knew about Lady Beatrice . . ."

I sighed. My relationship with the *draugr* queen was new and still something I'd rather not share widely. Once upon a time, Beatrice had been a witch who had woken as a *draugr*. Before her death, she had a child. Over a fair number of generations, Beatrice had watched her descendants—until my mother. Mama Lauren knew Beatrice, knew of *draugr*, knowingly conceived a child with one, against Beatrice's wishes.

And that was me.

My mother followed her own path, a mix of Judaism and paganism. Beyond the ghost zone was the Outs, where I grew up. Nature. Wild West law—shoot first, ask if you got around to it. It was the new frontier, and my mother, Mama Lauren, was still there.

"Another day," I said. Eli had met my mother last month and part of me liked how easily they got on together. Another part, one I was not examining, was ill at ease with it. "Let's see Beatrice. I still need to follow up with Madame Hebert, locate Christophe Hebert, and meet with NOPD. I can leave Beatrice to warn my mother. I cannot spend the night there."

Instead of pressing me, Eli drove us into the Outs. No utility services. No law. It was wild nature, and even I wasn't going to travel here after dusk. And staying over in my childhood home with Eli was a sort of "welcome to the family" that I wasn't quite ready to handle. Hell, we still slept in his guest room. If I couldn't welcome him into my apartment that way, how was I to manage overnighting at my childhood home?

"I wasn't rushing you about seeing her." Eli stared straight ahead. "We are *engaged*, Geneviève. We spend between fifty and sixty percent of our nights in bed together. Your clothes carry the scent of my skin. Your mother was threatened. It is perfectly reasonable to see her."

"She would shoot anyone not welcome, and Beatrice likely has guards there already." I crossed my arms. "I cannot deal with her emotions *and* you overreacting to me doing my job today."

"Does no one worry over you? Want to ease your stress? Dream of your safety?" Eli's voice made me feel embarrassed. "Am I to love you but not worry?"

I squirmed at the topic. My friends, my assistant, Gary, my mother, they all worried if they knew too much. So, I kept a lot of secrets. It was easier. I wasn't great at letting anyone know everything. I hedged, "I tell you more than I share with anyone else, but you can't worry like this just because—"

"I worry because you are precious to me, Geneviève." Eli took my hand. "And I will not ignore that." He paused. "I've hired a part-time bar manager. I'll pay her profit share and a salary. Say 'yes' to the bargain I offered you. Let me stay your partner."

"I don't need you to—"

"Christy. I hired Christy." Eli glanced at me.

And honestly, the man was not playing fair. Christy Zehr was one of my dearest friends, and she worked the pool tables there often. She was a towering Black woman who researched freelance and hustled pool. She was smarter than ninety-eight percent of everyone I'd met, with a two percent margin of error. It was sometimes like having precog, though she swore it wasn't magic. Whatever made her tick, she was a rock in my life and these days, she was dating my childhood bestie and surrogate brother, Jesse.

"Damn you." I scowled at Eli. I couldn't object to him offering her the job. She could run a con, run a table, and possibly run the world without breaking a sweat. Typically, though, she'd vanish for stretches, and no one knew what she did then.

On the other side were Sera and Jesse, who had stores. Jesse had a book shop, and Sera a coffee shop. Small businesses could be risky, but during Carnival season, they'd all turn a profit that would carry them for months.

"It frees me up to be at your disposal." Eli adopted that do-not-panic-and-run voice. "I will still own and run the bar, but now that I am returned to my family, I have access to my funds. I have no need of work."

"Then why not sell it?" I asked even though I wasn't sure I was ready for the answer.

Eli lifted one shoulder in a half-shrug that only a man like him could pull off: elegant, careless, and utterly telling all at once. That half-shrug of his was often to avoid discussions— usually for my benefit. "My fiancé is not sure she wants to live as a queen, and I will surrender the throne to *Elphame* before giving up on my love."

My mouth gaped open.

"If I do that, I will need to have an income," Eli continued.

Nope. Not ready for that answer at *all*. I didn't bother pointing out that I would not ask such sacrifice of him. He knew that.

"Obstinant ass," I grumbled.

"Pot, kettle," he said cheerily.

I said nothing else as Eli drove us deeper into the Outs and to Beatrice's small castle. What was there to say? We didn't agree. It would crush me to lose him, but what other choice did we have? I could not pass on my genetic nightmare—or even carry a child most likely—and he *had* to have a biological child with his wife.

We had no viable answers that I could see.

So I held my silence and watched the nature outside as we made our way to the home of the dead woman who had once given birth to a girl who was my ancestor. Beatrice, all *draugr*, was human once. My ancestor was a human, Jewish witch, who had become a *draugr* powerful enough to rule this region of the world. Her genes were mine via my mother, and my *draugr* heritage was a result of the perverse tests once conducted on her when she was human. Those tests led to my father realizing that witches were the key, and so he seduced my mother with the explicit goal of my birth.

Oddly it didn't make me feel special.

When the car stopped, we were under a towering oak. I had kept my mind busy thinking to avoid the almost irresistible urge to reply to the dead buried all around us. I had to concentrate not to send out a summons to the dead when I was in the Outs, but of late it was a scream in my head I was trying to bury under thoughts, words, and memories.

Details. That was my very mature response to the pressures. I focused on details.

Beatrice's home was ostentatious even in a place still dotted with plantations. It was vaguely modernized—no drawbridge—but there was a long stone bridge between parking and the massive front doors.

As we were walking toward it, I could see that the bridge

was already down, allowing us to cross over the moat filled with resting alligators.

"Hey, Sir George," I said, waving at the largest of the gators. He was, apparently, a man who had once offended my great-times-great grandmother. I didn't know if any of the others were alligators of the born-that-way sort, but Beatrice had admitted that she turned men who angered her into scaled pets or pigs.

Sir George flicked his tail, but I couldn't decide if it was a friendly greeting or a pissed off one.

But even as I tried not to reach out with magic, I still felt absences in pockets of space. Those were either graves or *draugr*. I'd noticed several of them last time. One, a young girl, bothered me in a different way.

Others felt older, centuries older in fact.

"Bonbon?" Eli said, entwining his fingers with mine again. "Are you well?"

I nodded. The dead wanted attention, *my* attention, and I wanted to ignore them. My plate was too full to summon the child in the nearby grave who was reaching out to me. She was more ghost than bones, but I'd rather not beckon anyone.

At the door of Beatrice's palatial home, we were met by two of her guards. All of the guards, staff, and residents here were female. One Caucasian, and one Middle Eastern. Beatrice was without racial, cultural, or religious bias in those she took into her staff. Her only rule was no men.

I looked around the medieval-style castle expecting to see Beatrice's assistant, Eleanor. I had a suspicion that both the *draugr* and the house were brought here from some far away forest. I didn't ask, though. I was still finding my way with my dead ancestor.

"Granddaughter! What a lovely surprise!" Beatrice's voice arrived before she did.

When she stood in front of us, I paused. In the city, the *draugr* queen tended toward an outdated formal attire. Ballgowns, cloaks, or something equally noticeable was her default. Here, however, she was dressed in comfort. Feet bare, the regional queen of the *draugr* stood as comfortably as I would in my apartment. Loose palazzo pants and a top that seemed to be a net of threads woven into the barest of halters.

"Son of Stonecroft," Beatrice said with a moderately deep bow.

"Lady Beatrice." He dipped his head to her. "We come with news."

"I was hoping you'd come after Daphne found you," Beatrice said regally.

"Daphne?" I asked.

"At your raising of many dead," Beatrice said. "Lovely bones, that one has . . . and a beautiful penchant for displaying flesh."

"Right." I remembered the *draugr* in the jacket sans blouse. I tried to force my brain to not think of the definite lust in my great-dead-gran's voice. "She said 'her lady' wanted to speak to me. I thought you sent her."

"She likely wanted you to think that. I did not. You are not a lackey to be summoned, Daughter of Mine, but I am glad you are aware of her. She means to cause me troubles. It's rather charming, though."

Charming?

I glanced at Eli, who shrugged.

Then Beatrice tucked my arm into the fold of hers in a way that reminded me of Mama Lauren. And without another word, she led us into the castle.

CHAPTER TEN

"GRANDMOTHER?"

Beatrice smiled at me. The familiarity of calling her that wasn't truly there, but it had a positive reaction when I did so. We both knew that it was as much to remind her of my familial tie as to attempt to forge a bond. I had mixed feelings, but honestly, the temptation of knowing anyone who was both witch and *draugr* was hard to resist—and Beatrice knew it.

"Daphne?"

"Ah. Precious thing, maybe three centuries?" Beatrice stared to the side as if summoning details from her mind. "She wants my throne."

I exchanged another tense look with Eli before asking, "Are you in danger?"

Beatrice laughed like I'd told her a ludicrous joke and patted my hand where it rested on her forearm. "You're a love! If I still had girlish dreams of love, she'd be dangerous. Quite the talented seductress, Daphne is."

"But she's not going to . . . attack you?" I prompted.

"No unless I accept her application to be my consort." Beatrice's eyes practically twinkled in amusement.

I nodded as if I understood, but the inner workings of *draugr* society were even more hidden than the ways of the fae —and they were often called The Hidden People. I had no idea what it meant to "apply" to be a consort, or even how many queendoms or kingdoms there were. All I knew was that Beatrice was the local ruler, intentionally so because my mother had been living here.

"I'm not so foolish, though she is quite lovely," Beatrice explained. "Sadly, her earldom has long ties to the Inquisition and the Witch Massacres. Daphne wasn't born then, or reborn obviously, but she lives in a community that is steeped in hatred. Of witches. Of Jews. They posture as if it's in the past, but there is not a soul in their entire earldom with witch ancestry—*or* with Jewish matrilineage."

"So hot but bigoted?" I prompted.

Beatrice laughed in a way that had probably charmed emperors or started the fall of a small nation. My great-times-great grandmother was a charming, beautiful deadly creature. It amused me to call her "grandmother" as she looked no older than I was now. Centuries of knowledge and power hid behind her laughter.

"I am hoping it won't be necessary to behead her," Beatrice continued conversationally. "Business before sentiment, though. If she continues to bother you, feel free to behead her. Her holdings are minor, but I could demand an insult penalty if necessary."

"Sure . . ." I wasn't clear on if Beatrice told me these things to increase my knowledge for my use or her own, but I was certain it was never accidental.

I mused on her long game as Eli, Beatrice, and I wound deeper into the castle.

The vestiges of modernity were remarkably absent in this part of her home. The wall sconces were electric in this passage, but the floor was worn stone under ancient rugs. One room we passed had a tapestry that looked as old as Chaucer.

This was only my third trip here. The first on a visit such as this, and the second for a soiree that ended with a murder. That, incidentally, was what I'd been there for. A *draugr* called Harold had sought to overthrown Beatrice. Motivated by prejudice and misogyny, he thought he could take her power, but I was there as her secret weapon. Harold was no more. He'd gambled on a power play and was now dead by Beatrice's hand.

His head, which she'd sent as a gift, was buried in the city. I didn't have a permit for that burial, but I wasn't really a heads-on-the-wall kind of woman. The jewels she'd sent, spoils from his corpse, were converted to money that was useful, though.

We stopped at a thick wooden door that would take several humans to push open. Beatrice flicked it open with a tap, making me wonder how strong she was. She tended toward Victorian garb, but I knew her age to be pre-1700 at least. *Draugr* accumulated strength with time.

Inside the room an opulent rug filled the center, covering stone floor. A fire, raging despite the room being empty a moment prior, created enough warmth to chase away the damp January weather. It wasn't cold exactly, but the damp was pervasive.

"Sit." Beatrice motioned to a series of over-stuffed sofas, one with lions' paws for feet. "Tell me this news that has you worried."

"There was a murder in the city, at the edge of the ghost zone, and in the room with the headless corpses was a box . . . addressed to me." I took a breath, hoping my faith in this woman was not misplaced. "The heads of three dead crows. Mask. Glitter."

For a moment she said nothing, merely held up a hand.

A few seconds later, Eleanor, one of Beatrice's most trusted, appeared. "My lady?"

"Go to Lauren. Tell her there is a threat to her and either bring her here or stay there to keep her safe." Beatrice reached a hand toward the dead girl.

Eleanor took it, dropped to a knee and kissed it, and then she stood. "My life for her safety, my lady."

Then the young woman was gone. Beatrice made a "continue" gesture. She stood by the fire as we filled her in on the grisly scene at the Hebert house. When we were done, she turned to face us.

"They were all twice-dead? You are sure?"

I nodded. "Beheaded. If they weren't *draugr*, they were still killed as if they had been."

"Of course," she murmured. "The photographs?"

I held out my phone, and she simply stared at it. "I used my phone camera."

"Show me." Beatrice kept her hands far from the device, so I scrolled through them, pausing and enlarging at her request.

I couldn't read her emotions or thoughts without her projecting them, but her expression shifted to that emotionless state that was "public Beatrice" not the more human way she had started being in my presence. If there were no witnesses, that meant she was hiding something—or upset. I understood that much.

Finally, Beatrice walked away. "They were from Prague. The deceased. Not local. Not *my* subjects."

"*Prague?*"

Beatrice moved toward a small bar that I hadn't noticed at first. "They are a new tendency." She gestured with a still-empty glass. "They read too much 'classic' literature in their lives, I fear. Younger. Not even a century typically. Much is made of their rebellion. The elder factions do not approve."

Draugr were as toddlers, noshing on everyone the first decade. If these were older than that, they were obviously in possession of their mental faculties. They were aware of themselves before they were slaughtered.

"They select proteges. Apprentices or some other ridiculousness." Beatrice gave a delicate little shudder. "And they call themselves '*vampires*.' As I said, too much modern literature."

"Did you know they were here?" Eli asked.

"No." Beatrice frowned. "I do not begrudge them their childish ways. In the past when we were hidden, they were a threat. Always with the melodrama. Taking up with artistes. They were why we are exposed now."

I stared at her mutely as she carried me a glass of bloody whisky.

"It's mine," she said. "You will need the strength. I will see to Lauren's safety. She may be your mother, but I am the only elder in her family. She is my responsibility."

That certainly didn't bode well. Of course, I was starting to suspect that nothing involving my grandmother did. I sighed and sipped the blood and whisky. Both were aged enough to be powerful stuff. As I sipped, I updated her on Iggy, on the police grant, and my general sense that there was a threat that was greater than dear beheaded Harold.

"Iggy is a useful man," Beatrice began in that way that said there was much she was not saying.

I gave her a look.

"He knows where the bodies are buried." She shrugged. "Once he was an assassin, and had I been seeking a lover, I would have kept him. Iggy was not much for cages, sadly. And I was never quite sure which of us would first try to murder the other." She glanced at Eli and added, "The women in my family often have regrettable taste in men."

"Geneviève seems to be an exception." Eli's voice could freeze infernos.

"Perhaps." Beatrice offered him a glass of whisky, no blood. "No bonds are made by sharing my wealth."

It sounded formal, as did the slight dip of Eli's head and murmured, "Nor expected."

"Great. Well, Iggy cannot kill me, right?" I steered right past that little *draugr*-fae drama as quickly as I could. No amount of reading or questions had quite prepared me for the long history of formality between them.

"Do not trust the man, Daughter of Mine." Beatrice caught my free hand. "Hexen have a long history of patriarchal deceits."

I sighed. "Great. This is all just *great*. Tell me something good . . .?"

"The grant is not my doing," Beatrice assured me. With a slight smile, she looked at Eli. "Have you asked your uncle? Fergus is a dangerous creature when crossed, and I doubt that he's at ease knowing that one of my sort might hold the throne."

I thought back to my encounters with the king of *Elphame*. Would he do this as a gift of money? Would he do it to eliminate me from Eli's life? I wouldn't be surprised if he had. When I met Eli's gaze, I saw the same pensive look.

"This is a wise question," Eli allowed, suddenly sounding more fae as he re-framed the grant not as a threat, but as a boon. "My uncle the king might offer such a gift to my fiancé."

Beatrice, as diplomatic as the fae, nodded. "Sadly, it could be a dangerous thing as well." She paused, glancing at me pointedly. "Witches have enemies, as do *draugr*."

"As do the fiancés of royalty," Eli added.

"Yay," I muttered. "I guess lots of people want me dead."

Eli opened his mouth to rebut my gloomy statement, but

my grandmother was faster. "You are the only of your kind. Powerful, binding three types of beings, as well as being Jewish and a woman. You are going to be hated by some and worshipped by others."

I tossed back the rest of my drink. I could practically feel the energy humming in my skin. The mix of ancient blood and aged whisky was doing its job.

"Luckily, Geneviève, being dead will only make *you* stronger. I do not want to hasten your death, but should it come, we will face it. You have allies, dead or alive. The enemies, however, can *all* be eliminated." Beatrice lifted her glass in a bloody toast. "Let us feast on their blood and regrets. No slaughter too much for the sake my granddaughter."

My ancestor was a terrifying woman, but luckily, she was also devoted to my well-being. A tiny whisper of fear made me wonder if that stance would also be handy to justify acts she would be elsewise unable to take. She had a regard for me, of that I was fairly certain, but she was also a *draugr* who had wrested power from centuries of men—and had little patience with those who opposed her.

In truth, I suspected my mother had inherited a number of her qualities. Mama Lauren, however, was human. Alive. She was a witch who was handy with a double-barreled shotgun.

And I was neither alive nor dead, neither *draugr* nor human. I was the closest thing to what Beatrice was, and it was both terrifying and comforting in waves.

CHAPTER ELEVEN

AFTER WE LEFT BEATRICE'S CASTLE, I COULDN'T SAY THAT I had any more clarity than before on the pressing matter of the grant. If anything, she'd added to my questions. Why were the *draugr* here from Prague? Why were they at the Hebert house? Was the connection coincidental? Was Beatrice's paramour involved?

And why the dead crows? That was obviously a threat, and I was glad that my mother was under Beatrice's protection. However, the larger question was who knew that there were three Crowe women and wanted us dead? Beatrice had claimed me in quite public ways among her kind, and I had been part of the outing of a *draugr* who wanted to usurp Beatrice.

"Bonbon?" Eli prompted as we raced the sun to reach the ghost zone at least or the city at best.

"Worrying," I admitted. "I just want to go home and hide away."

"If I go faster, we run the risk of damage to the car," he reminded me.

I nodded. Being stranded in the vast emptiness of the Outs wasn't ideal. We should be fine on time. I'd made this trip dozens of times. Honestly, the drive wasn't that long, but in January, the sun set here between 5:00 and 6:00. And we'd forgotten that the gates on the bridge closed thirty minutes before the sun began to set. It was the latest attempt by the New Orleans government to limit how many *draugr* were inside city limits.

Biters gnawing on the tourists was hard to keep quiet, and the city needed tourists. So laws and gates and fences popped up. I wondered if the grant to hire me was along the same lines. I hoped so.

The alternatives were all versions of "make me a target." And that was already enough of an issue. The timing of the NOPD grant and the box of dead crows made me suspect that there was more to the target theory than anything else.

"Will we make it before the gate shuts?" I asked Eli.

Beatrice had reminded us about the law at 4:00, and the hour plus drive on the barely maintained roads had us far from certain of our return.

"Maybe?"

We were minutes from the ghost zone when a loud thump shook the car.

"*Draugr!*" I yelled, pointing at the group of three people who had *flowed* from somewhere else directly into our path. "Swerve!"

Eli cranked the wheel hard to the left, and a ripping sound from underneath had me yelling, "Weasel nuts!"

The car shuddered to a halt, engine no longer purring. Eli's car, for all its charms, was not a battering ram. It was smooth, luxurious, and beautiful. It would also have crumpled if it crashed into the three bodies. As it was, a tree branch had caught the hood when he'd swerved and all but tore the flimsy metal off.

"Are you well?" Eli asked.

"Angrier than a goose on a holiday."

Eli gave me a look that soothed a few of my ruffled feathers. "Swords, devil's food?"

"Swords."

The *draugr* watched, not approaching but waiting. Lucky for them, they had no need to wait long. I was out of the car with sword drawn in a blink.

Across from me, Eli opened the door and pulled out a heavy brass single-handed sword from the recently added sheath mounted to the driver's door.

"Iggy, now is a good time to pop by," I yelled, thought, willed. I'd taken on multiple dead jackasses at once in the past, but I had hoped to avoid stitches tonight.

As I stomped toward them, I felt for corpses, seeking pockets of vacancy that were either the truly dead or other *draugr*. A few scattered animals were all that was nearby. Beyond that was a scattering of bodies who felt like they were screaming in their rest. Murder victims, likely. They were rarely anyone's first choice to fight.

That left either Eli and me—or assorted coyotes and one puma.

"*Furred ones. I offer the chance of a meal.*" I thought the words into my magic as I nicked my forearm on my own sword and flung my bleeding arm upward, tossing my blood onto the soil.

"What was that?" one of the *draugr* yelled. "Why is she tossing blood around?"

"Calm yourself, Tommy."

"Tommy?" I echoed. "What sort of name is *Tommy* for a *draugr*?"

"Piss off," the woman said. "We're not *draugr*."

"Yeah." The third, clearly articulate, one added.

All told the three dead people looked like they were trying

to channel the 1980s, and doing the math in my head, they very well might be. Older than a decade, younger than a century, they were the sort of *draugr* that posed more trouble in the French Quarter. The woman on the left looked like she was trying to imitate a tattered shroud with her flowing blouse and . . . *harem pants*. The man in the middle had a velvet dressing coat over what looked like a waiter's uniform and combat boots. Tommy was the least outrageous, unless you thought that mohawks and jeans with bandanas tied around them were outlandish.

As odd as they were compared to today's more sedate fashions, they could still blend with the crowds in a city—more or less—whereas dead folk like Beatrice exuded an air of superiority, a sort of laissez faire attitude that mimics the nobility mingling with the peasants.

Of course, Beatrice had her meals delivered or home prepared.

As we stood there, the sky streaking reds and golds, the three dead strangers watched us.

"Are you expecting fear?" I asked, waiting for my re-animated animal aids to come to me.

The downside of animal necromancy was that they weren't conversant in the way of humans. I felt them drawing near, and I thought toward them in images.

"We're vampires!" the woman said. "You ought to be frightened."

"Yeah!" the one in the velvet coat said. He was, obviously, not quite as old—or perhaps had a flaw from his re-awakening. Either way he was clearly not the brains of the group. That left Tommy or the woman.

"What do you want?" I asked.

Eli remained silent at my side. He wasn't usually interested in conversation with the dead—or most people, in truth. He had a sword, and he'd be in the thick of the fight if it came to that.

"Parley." Tommy jutted his chin out.

"Parsley?" the other man asked.

"Parley," Tommy repeated. "To negotiate. You killed our masters, and we don't want to die that way."

I blinked at them. Who had I killed recently? The holidays had been sort of quiet. They usually were, for reasons I didn't entirely grasp. I'd killed far fewer *draugr* than normal. I pondered my recent jobs. "Harold?"

The confused dead man started, "No, man. This is *Tommy*. I'm Scott."

"I killed Harold," I said. "And Lydia, but she was human. The guy who was punching the window." I went through my mind, pondering jobs. "There was the guy at the Cormier job."

"Human, bonbon. Weasel nuts was a human," Eli reminded me. "And you didn't kill him. Detoothed, but not killed."

"Right." I frowned. "When exactly did I kill these people?"

"This week," Tommy said, sounding less sure of himself.

"I don't think I killed anyone other than that guy yesterday," I muttered, glancing at Eli.

As we were talking, the puma, four coyotes, a weasel, as well as assorted nutria started to gather.

"The fuck. . ." Tommy said.

I shrugged. "I don't like to be outnumbered. I called aid."

"Why do they obey you?" the woman asked. "Are you a vampire?"

"No," I answered truthfully. "I'm a necromancer, and they're dead."

"Cool," said Scott.

I smiled coldly. "*All* dead things obey me if I will it. That's what necromancy is."

There was a long silence, and I started to think the ambush

was not going to result in anything other than inconvenience. I felt a twinge guilty for waking the dead predators with a hope of a meal they, apparently, couldn't have.

"At the house in the city. You killed them and then called the police." Tommy watched the animals with a fear that was almost sad.

I reminded myself that they'd wrecked our car and were trying to intimidate us. They caused this. I should be nearly home now. Instead, I was standing here arguing with daft and obtuse while their stoner buddy was adding emphasis at odd intervals. I was not in the mood for this. I glanced at the necromantic puma and let it stalk a little closer. Animals might not speak but they were more obedient than revived people.

"We want parley," the woman said. "And not to be killed."

"Wait. You mean, the Hebert house?" I asked. That was the only place I'd called the police.

"I don't know the house's name is, man. The one where you nailed cards to their hands. *That* house. Unless you do that a lot, it should be a pretty freaking short list." Tommy waved his arm around. "We are here *now* to try and get mercy. We followed you from the city, but then you went to Baba Yaga's castle and—"

"Baba Yaga?" I echoed.

"The witch, man. You went to the witch." Scott paused. He looked at the animals. Suddenly, as clarity sideswiped him, he pointed at me and whispered loudly, "Dude, I think she's a witch, too!"

Scott took two steps back, as if that distance would matter.

Don't need to outrun the witch. Just the other people, I thought. I hated being the monster.

"We didn't know there was a witch and vampire war in your city. We got caught in the crosshairs, you know?" Tommy was pacing now. "We just want to have eternal life, drink a few babes, and travel. Maybe level up enough to have wolves or be bats—"

"Bats would be so cool," the woman interjected.

"Right . . ." I exchanged a look with Eli before asking the three *draugr*, "You were part of the Prague group?"

"Totally!" Scott said with a fist pump.

At my side Eli muffled a laugh. Admittedly, the trio of abnormal dead people were still *draugr* and could still *flow*. They could be a threat, but it seemed unlikely. I wasn't quite ready to drop my sword, but I wasn't feeling terribly menaced.

"Parley," I said, testing the possibilities. I wasn't sure Eli's car would get us far, and I didn't think examining it while they watched sounded wise. Honestly, I also wasn't sure what to look for in car engines.

But staying in the open until people came to the Outs wasn't likely a great idea. There was a bus that brought tourists or citizens out into nature early morning. I could stay awake, stand guard, and wait for dawn to arrive. Or I could *flow* with Eli back to my grandmother's house. None of the options were ideal. What I wanted was to go home.

I nodded toward the ghost zone. "Are you staying there? Outside the city?"

"Yeah, man. The way you killed—"

"I did not murder them." I pointed at them with my tip of my sword, and the furred predators started to stalk toward the trio of American-by-way-of-Europe *draugr*. Animals were not as graceful as humans, but I thought that was because they were so graceful in life that the slight delay as they remembered how to stalk was noticeable. My dead mammal army slowly advanced.

"Ms. Crowe?" Eli asked. "Are you feeding these again-walkers to the beasts?"

His formal tone cut through my anger. Apparently, I'd had a smidge too much of Beatrice's blood. I felt colder than usual.

"*Halt*," I think-spoke to the furred ones.

The puma looked at me in irritation and yowled, as if to tell me to stop teasing. I suppose it could've said other things, but I did not speak puma—even dead puma.

I looked back at the *draugr*. "The queen is not Baba Yaga . . . I think."

"Chaz said she was actually Marie Antionette," the woman offered.

"Sure, but Eve said that Baba Yaga was a tsarina," Tommy said. Then, catching himself before falling into what apparently an old argument, he stared at me. "Whoever she is, she's *not my queen*. I'm a vampire!"

My head was starting to hurt from not rolling my eyes.

"Okay. I did not kill your friends. Beatrice did not kill them." I motioned toward the car. "You, however, wrecked our car, and I have places I'd rather be."

"If you can help us, we'll get the car going." Tommy smirked. "I bet you can't do that."

I growled, and the animals all growled in an eerie symphony. Sometimes the connection with furred things made me a little pre-verbal, but tonight, I'd go with it.

"Scottie?" the woman said in a squeakier voice.

Scott went over and peeled off the remains of the car's hood and tossed it aside. Eli winced, staring at his car hood when it was discarded on the ground like debris. Scott poked around in the engine. I had no idea what he was doing, but he was clearly more adept at engine's than words.

"I'm sorry about your car," I said to Eli. I honestly had no idea what a car like his would cost.

"There are worse things that could happen," Eli gave one of

his half-shrugs as we watched a *draugr* mutter and tinker with a custom car.

"We needed a way to earn money," Tommy said, noticing our stare. "Scottie can work at night off the books. He was a helluva mechanic when he was alive.

"Worked racetrack pit crews," Scottie said from under the hood. "Even faster now."

"We only drink the willing," the woman said. "So, we earn our money. I dance."

Draugr strippers were a thing in a few cities who were "embracing the future." I guess there's a club for every kink somewhere.

I was starting to feel twitchy. Unlike the fae, I'm not great at patience. "We could go to Beatrice's."

Eli nodded.

Then the *draugr* straightened and pronounced, "It'll run."

One disaster averted. The thought of *flowing* to Beatrice's estate and staying there didn't make me comfortable—and it would surely spell the second-death of the *draugr* in front of me. Beatrice was temperamental at the best of times.

"Stay in the Outs," I ordered both *draugr* and animal. I told the trio of dead people, "I'll find out who killed them."

Then I looked at the animals and pictured Beatrice's castle. With the image securely held in my mind, I ordered, "Lead them here."

With a mental apology to my grandmother for the surprise I was sending to her, I added, "The queen will look after you while I find out who did it. Tell her that the blue-haired witch sent you for parley."

Then, with a last mental order—to not eat the *draugr*—to my furred allies, I walked to the car, as if sending reanimated people and creatures into the Outs was normal.

Safely inside, I reached out for Eli's hand.

"Not depleted, are you?" he asked.

I shook my head once. I wasn't sure how soundproof the car actually was, and I didn't know if I wanted that known to the *draugr* we were leaving. I sort of trusted that they were telling the truth, but my trust was limited with almost everyone. Those I trusted—like Eli, Jesse, Christy, and Sera—I trusted enough to die or kill for, but the rest of the world was greeted with a midlevel paranoia.

Honestly, it wasn't that strange to feel that way. The list of people who wanted to harm me was longer than I'd like. Some hatred was just the way of the world, but attempts on my life weren't rare these days. Maybe they never were. I was an aberration, not just a witch but the only person born with *draugr* genes.

If my existence were revealed, I'd end up in a lab.

And then I'd have to kill people. A lot of them. Scientists. Guards. I didn't like to kill humans. I strived to avoid it, in fact.

"Geneviève?"

"If SAFARI or their associates discover what I am, you'll be at risk." I stared at him. Eli was stunning all the time, but in the low light of the late afternoon, the blacker-than-black strands of his hair looked iridescent. The fae, the shining ones, were so gorgeous that in centuries past they'd been mistaken for gods or fallen angels.

The look that my fae beloved gave me brought a strange emotion to my heart.

"Geneviève, you are the accepted future queen of *Elphame*."

"Right . . ."

"We are not a warrior people without cause, but to defend our own, the swords are always kept sharp." Eli's usual calm slipped. "You are mine, Geneviève Crowe. And my people accepted that over Yule. Do you think we would sit idly by?"

Visions of hundreds are sword-swinging faeries made me

sigh. My imagination was surely not as lovely as the reality of such a sight would be, but I was still stunned at the thought.

"I love you," I whispered.

"Good." He squeezed my knee. "I love you enough to declare a war on humanity if I must. Never forget, bonbon, that —while I may be inconspicuous and relaxed by design—I can wade into fields of blood with just as much ease as you."

"No one out there will ever love me the way you do, will they?" I whispered. I was starting to get a glimmer of the depths of Eli, and the immensity of his sentiment and devotion was large enough to swallow me.

"You're very lovable, Geneviève. You may not see it, but I do. Surely others would." Eli's voice lightened. "Of course, I fully plan to seduce you so thoroughly no one else gets a chance."

"Eli . . ." I didn't feel worthy. I never really had, not of his love, not of anyone's. Seeing myself through my friends' eyes when I was facing death and seeing myself through Eli's eyes these last few months had changed me in some way. Not like it "fixed" everything! Sometimes, though, death and love were truly life changing. I'd encountered both recently.

"Trust me, Geneviève," Eli said, still sounding light-hearted even though the subject was far from light. That, too, was for my benefit. Then he continued, "My people are known for impossible bargains and feats of wonder. Surely, you don't think I am without contingency plans for my contingency plans?"

I laughed. "I'm not sure why you're so absurd, but I cannot imagine life or death without you at my side."

He chuckled. "Then my nefarious plans are working . . . if only you would say yes to that outstanding bargain."

"Fine," I muttered. "I, Geneviève Crowe, accept your terms, Eli. One wish. And in accepting it . . . I get what I already have."

"These terms are accepted, Geneviève Crowe. You are indebted to me for one wish at such time and place as I see necessary." Eli relaxed as soon as the words were spoken and a chime sounded, closer and louder than it had in prior bargains.

"So mote it be." I shivered. This bargain felt different, but I wasn't sure why.

E li and I made our way through the edge of the Outs and through the ghost zone. Seeing the ghost zone at this hour, with the *draugr* out and about like a Friday night on Greek row was surreal. They were gathering in groups, and aside from a few exclamations as Eli navigated the car through the cluttered streets, it was a painless albeit tense encounter.

I had no illusions about the trouble we could face if we broke down there, but we kept a steady, much faster than when we were in the Outs, speed. And soon, we were crossing the bridge.

The gate was closed, but Eli paid a bribe that was enough for his car to be kept safe, and we walked the rest of the way into the city where Alice was waiting in a different car.

"I was about to get into the tub," Ally started. "Do you need a drink? Are you going to Prince Eli's or—"

"Alice," Eli interrupted, much to my relief since my assistant was rapid firing more questions than I could face.

"Sorry." Ally took several deep breaths. "Why are your eyes slits? Were you fighting?"

I glanced at Eli, and he nodded once.

"We were visiting Beatrice," I said.

"Did you fight *her*?" Ally sounded awed at the thought—and rightly so. My odds of surviving a fight with one of the oldest *draugr*, who was also a witch, were slim to laughable.

"No!" I couldn't fathom that. "She had some strong drinks for me. Then, I . . . umm . . . summoned animals."

"Oooh! Could you summon Mr. Snickers?" Ally asked. "He was just the sweetest little muffin, and—"

"I do not summon dead pets." I glanced out the window at the twinkling lights of my city. I felt more alert than I had in months. I suspected that the blood from Beatrice, my body's adaptation to my new state, and my general swooniness toward Eli were all factors. I asked Eli, "Are you up for the bar? I can call the gang, grab a few drinks . . ."

Eli smiled. "A night off?"

"I think my brain needs it," I admitted. There were more questions zinging around, and I needed a bit of chatter and laughter to let the questions simmer. Tomorrow, I'd deal with the rest. In fact, I told at Alice, "Call NOPD. Leave a message that I'll take their meeting tomorrow."

"What if they can't do it on such short notice?"

"Well, that's their problem, isn't it? They're the ones trying to get me to commit to a schedule and get *them* funding." I thought about it more as I spoke, processing aloud.

I liked this idea. If they refused, I had an out. Obviously, the grant would pad my account, but it felt *off*. Off too often resulted in death threats. Add that to a box of crow heads, and it felt like getting this resolved sooner than later was becoming essential.

I continued, "If they want it to happen, they will adjust. If not, that's one problem resolved."

I wasn't terribly optimistic, but maybe being difficult would make them drop the matter altogether. I just had an increasingly bad feeling about the situation.

CHAPTER TWELVE

I TEXTED JESSE AND SERA TO MEET US AT BILL'S TAVERN. Christy was already there, so I figured we'd surprise her. It was Eli's bar, the reason we met and the place I had called home for several years. I used to think it was just the ambiance. Inside was a polished wooden bar, low bar lights, and a remarkably good liquor collection.

Recently, I'd learned that the liquor collection was custom designed for me. Eli had been wooing me far before I'd realized. To keep me there, he'd hired me to handle *draugr* problems— ones he could've managed on his own. He claimed it was about protecting his persona of laconic and charming bar owner, but he did so in the fae way that was both honest and incomplete. He might not be able to lie, but he was able to misdirect like it was an art.

The doorman nodded at us as we walked in, although he did give us a once-over in search of any injuries. The staff at the bar had all accepted our relationship, but they grumbled at how often I left blood on the floor or tables. About half the time it was someone else's blood, but I'd been stabbed recently. At the time Eli had been too worried about me to properly clean up. And I was unable to do so.

Inside, Eli motioned for a bartender, and in a matter of moments, we were walking away from the bar with a bottle of tequila and a stack of glasses.

"Gen!" Christy came out of the office. She hugged me and then looked at Eli. "No issues to report, Boss."

"Take a few hours off then." He motioned to a table.

"I texted Jesse and Sera." I poured glasses for the four of us, leaving the other two empty for now.

Ally wrinkled her nose and pushed her glass back toward me. "Nope. I'm too tired for that."

Guilt flashed through me. She was likely too tired because I was draining her energy.

"Stop it." Ally swatted my hand. "I know that look."

She pulled a bottle out of her bag.

"I don't need—"

"Not for you, chickpea." Ally grinned. "I got me a special mix of electrolytes and supplements that were recommended by a mutual friend."

I stared at her.

"B-e-a-t-r-i-c-e," Ally whispered each letter loudly. "Said it would keep me full of energy. Energy that's also stored in my blood!"

I emptied Alice's rejected glass of tequila. Honestly, what was I to say? 'Thanks for taking supplements so I can leech your blood' didn't really have the right tone. Ours was a complicated friendship, founded in murder, built on blood.

Luckily, before the awkwardness could go on too long, Jesse and Sera arrived at the table with a flurry of greetings. Eli watched all of it with the sort of fae reserve we all used to interpret as dismissal. I knew better now. He was simply not expressive around most people—and I felt a surge of joy that I was an exception to his rule.

"Is this one still treating you well?" Jesse asked with a nod toward Eli. They weren't *not* friends, but Jesse had taken up the "big brother" role in my life for years. He thought it was his duty to be suspicious of anyone looking at me with interest.

Eli looked at me and raised his brows. "Am I?"

"Yes." I felt like blushing at the topic, so I turned it away from me. "Christy? Is my obnoxious brother looking after you?"

"Hey!" Jesse objected with a laugh. "You're to be asking if she's looking after me!"

Christy leaned over to me and whispered loud enough for everyone to hear, "Poor thing is trying to keep up."

"What is this? Pick on Jesse night?" Jesse looked around at the table in faux outrage.

Eli started, "My sympathies, Christy. Do I need to find you someone more—"

"Nah. He's the one I want." Christy leaned into Jesse's embrace, and he tugged her until she landed in his lap with a victory yell from Jesse. They had taken years to finally try dating, and if they weren't tangled up in forever soon, I'd be stunned.

Sera and I exchanged a look. Instead of feeling like an "extra wheel" because our friends had found love, we both were glad. I wished I knew someone who would make Sera feel as content as my other two best friends looked, but she was in no rush.

And Ally had the glimmer in her eyes that was the hint of tears. *Again.* I was glad she wasn't drinking, to be honest. Liquor made Alice maudlin. She'd known she'd outlive her husband; Alvin Chaddock was easily twice her age. She'd thought she had more time, though, and a couple glasses of booze meant that was all she could discuss.

Just as I was about to start scrambling for anything that

made Ally avoid tears, a man strode into the bar in that hyper-focused way that said that he only had eyes for one person. Unfortunately, I was that person.

"Gen?" Sera asked, voice ringing with the questions we always had these days—was he a *draugr*? Did we need to do something?

"Iggy." I had a moment of hostility, but it wasn't his fault he was not in his grave. At least I thought it wasn't. Honestly, magic wasn't a hard science. It was somewhere between science and art, not quite as precise as things like biology but more so than literature.

"Not a *draugr*." I stood, watching the increased calm ripple over my three oldest friends. They were still adjusting to my near-death, and the memory of my body's reaction to the venom seemed to haunt them more than me.

In fairness I was unconscious for parts of it though. They witnessed everything.

"Not a *draugr*." Iggy scoffed. "Rather skilamalink to hide me if I were."

"Ignatius Blackwood," I said with a nod toward him. "Magician and general lesion."

"*Skilamalink?*" mouthed Jesse.

"Lesion?" Iggy scowled. "You are, quite possibly, the most infuriating hexen I've known. I was summoned. Rousted from my restful—"

"Stop." I rubbed my head and glanced at Eli. "Fruity something?"

"Bowl of garnish coming right up." Eli vanished, leaving me to explain to my friends why there was a dead man at our table.

"Iggy here is a witch," I began as Iggy stood arrogantly at the table.

"Hex—" he started to interrupt.

"Died in the 1800s," I continued. To him, I said, "Chair."

A flicker of surprise slid over his face as I invited him to sit. I felt guilty, realizing that he was probably as unable to leave as I was to get rid of him. He had to be lonely. Probably confused. But then, he tried to sit next to Ally, who looked about as friendly as a wet hen with a fox approaching.

"Revolveress," he greeted her.

She folded her arms and glared at him. "I'm married."

Iggy looked around. "Ah. Where is the lucky—"

"Iggy!" I took a calming breath. Ally was hard to stop once she got started on the waterworks, and I was bound and determined to have a relaxing evening. No tears. No fights.

"I have a few book questions," Jesse said, and from the intensity of his voice I was fairly sure it was not in an attempt to rescue me. Jesse's bookshop, Tomes and Tea, was half contemporary, masses friendly fiction, but he had a collector's drive that meant that the best place to find books of magic was in Jesse's store.

Technically, it was my store, too, but I ignored that detail.

The sensitive books were on display in enhanced glass boxes that were soldered to silver and steel pedestals. They couldn't be removed without the keys that were woven into his skin and mine. I bought more than a few—and I knew damn well that he sold them to me for less than they were worth. It was one of his sneaky ways of paying me.

"The *Constabulary*?" Iggy leaned closer. "Oh, that was a hard to find one even in my day!"

As they spoke Jesse slid an envelope toward me without making eye contact. I knew what it was. I used to rip them up, but that was insulting. I fronted the start-up costs for his bookstore the first year, and Jesse was still refusing to remove my name from the deed. I was also refusing to cash his checks.

Family was complicated sometimes.

And this was my family in all ways that mattered. I loved my mother, but there were no blood-siblings, cousins, aunts, or the like. We were a family of two for most of my life.

Sera and Christy were discussing bookkeeping, Jesse was scribbling notes from a dead guy on possible families who might have a copy of the *Constabulary* in an attic moldering somewhere, and Ally was singing along with whatever music Eli had queued up while he was away getting me a bowl of cherries and oranges.

They were mine. My family. My center.

My great-times-great grandmother was out there, as was my mother, but this was the family I'd chosen. And time with them re-centered me so I was ready for the next crisis.

"Bonbon?" Eli slid a cocktail glass of fruit toward me.

I popped an orange slice into my mouth as he dropped a few lime slices into my glass of tequila.

A waitress stopped by with cocktails he'd ordered, too, and I smiled as I leaned closer to Eli. Mine. That was what he was, too. Not just a friend. Not just an accidental fiancé. Not just a partner in my business.

He pulled me closer, so we were a bit more like one of those always-touching couples that used to annoy me.

"What does that look you are sending me mean?" he whispered.

"*Mine*," I admitted.

He chuckled, brushed a quick kiss over my lips, and agreed, "As you are mine."

Maybe he said it to remind me that not only *draugr* or witches have the urge to create a group, coven or nest—or maybe he was simply as relaxed as I was. Either way, I rested my head on his shoulder and smiled at my odd assemblage of family and obligations.

CHAPTER THIRTEEN

I MIGHT NOT HAVE AGREED TO PATROL FOR NOPD, BUT I still intended to do so. Eli was closing the bar with Christy, and I saw Sera and Ally to Ally's car. Ally had plenty of security—and an underground garage. So I knew that after she dropped Sera off, Ally would be fine getting home.

Jesse was gathering the last of the trash with the lingering employees. He wasn't required to do so, but he was just like me when it came to having idle time. We sucked at it.

Iggy and I were alone at the table for a few moments.

"Talk to me Iggy," I offered. "Why can't I get rid of you?"

"Because I know hexes you need to learn." He leaned back in his chair, and for a flicker of a moment I realized that he was truly relaxed here. This was a man who was fond of taverns or gentleman's social clubs in his day.

"So if I learn them, *poof.*" I snapped my fingers.

Iggy gave me a hard look. "You want me here, Hexen. If you didn't think I had knowledge, and if I didn't think I did, I'd be hustled off to my grave."

"How many spells?"

"Damfino." He lifted the cigar that had been in a pocket

somewhere and stared at it the way I stared at a pint of ice cream on a rough day. Iggy sighed and said, "I used to love a good cigar."

"Damfino?" I echoed.

Iggy grinned. "Say it slower."

"Dam . . .fi . . no. Damned if I know." I laughed the laugh of the tipsy. "If I trusted you, I might actually grow to like you."

Iggy put the cigar back in his pocket. "You've seen Bea, have you? Woman doesn't trust anyone."

"Especially assassins." I watched for reactions, but I was fairly sure I wasn't the first to ask about his avocation.

Iggy held my gaze. "You're innocent then? No blood on those calloused hands?"

"Wasn't talking about me." I shrugged.

"The world wasn't kind to hexen even then." Iggy swirled my glass of whisky. "Least I wasn't a woman, a Jew, and Irishman. Plenty of hate those days."

"Still is," I interjected.

"Fear, though, if it's deep enough makes hate pause and look for an easier victim. I was never an easy victim." Iggy lifted my glass, taking a long sniff. "Damn shame I cannot drink."

"Why would a privileged man need to—"

"Do you think I was born with this name, Hexen? That I was to the manor born?" He sounded like he was both laughing at me and challenging me. "My knuckles were bloodied, and my trousers worn when I decided to create Ignatius Blackwood."

"If I knew your real name—"

"No one does, Hexen. Not even the lovely *draugr* queen. . . and *that* one knows the map of my scars."

Even tipsy, I realized that my lack of his name might be the secret to why I couldn't force him into his grave. And I knew that he was the one telling me that truth. If I knew, I might be able to put him back, but he was banking on the temptation of knowledge to keep me from doing so.

"Going to patrol," I called. "Just looping a few blocks with Iggikins."

It wasn't quite asking if Eli minded, but I was allowing a moment for his objections. When none came, I walked over to the bar and asked, "Wait for me?"

"Haven't I been waiting long enough?" Eli murmured.

I smacked a loud kiss on him. "Soon."

Then I grabbed a sword, a go-cup of blood and coffee, and headed to the door. "Come on, Iggypoo."

"Has anyone told you that you could charm the wings off a fly, Geneviève?" Iggy groused as he stepped into the street with me.

"Nope."

"Shocking." He motioned for me to pause. "Roll out the senses. Visualize the grid."

"The grid?" I blinked at him.

"The streets, the river, the graves, the parks . . ."

As he spoke, I tried his way. It was a more orderly version of my "let my magic free" approach.

"Close your eyes," he said. "I'm at your side watching."

Typically, I'd refuse such a suggestion, but we were mere steps from Eli's place. So I let my eyes drop briefly.

"Adjust your vision. You are *hexen*. Necromancy. Magic. Chain it to your will." Iggy's voice felt like it was inside my head, like I could glimpse him out the corner of my eye. Firmly, he ordered, "Open but hold the map."

When I opened my eyes, Iggy was a shadow of a person at my side, and the city looked different. Traces of deaths were on the ground, buildings, or trees in purple splotches.

"Darker is newer," Iggy said, voice strained.

I swallowed. There was a *lot* of purple.

"Look at the map," Iggy rasped. "Hold it. *Hold* it."

The map was only about three blocks in every direction, but the details were crisper than usual. Green flecks moved on several places, and I knew without words that those were dead folk. "Only four."

"All *draugr*?"

I stared at the map that was overlaid on the street, and I saw Iggy. "You. Three of them."

"Three?" he prompted. "All *draugr*?"

"I think . . ."

"How old, Geneviève? Just like the blood traces. Look at it. *Hold* it." Iggy's hands were gripping my shoulders now, and his voice was no more than grave dirt in ash.

I strained to see the green in shades. "That one is oldest."

"Good." Iggy coughed.

And I opened my eyes to see what looked like a mummified man wearing Iggy's suit. "Fucksicles! Iggy!"

He leaned against the building, staring back at me with eyes that protruded like he was a desiccated corpse. "Go get them Hexen."

"What just—"

"Go!" Iggy coughed again, slumping more and grasping at the door. "Explain later."

"Shit shit shit. Let me get you inside before someone hurts y—"

"Dead already." He laughed, wheezing and gagging, and then pointed. "*Go*."

I opened the door and yelled, "Drag Iggy inside."

Then since no one was watching, I *flowed* toward the oldest of the dead. The younger ones were more likely to attack, but the older one would have venom.

When I stopped, stumbling a bit in my lingering bit of tipsiness, I looked around, only to find the *draugr* from the cemetery.

"Daphne, right? Dead. Trying to seduce Beatrice." I wasn't going to underestimate her this time. I watched her as I spoke.

And I had to admit that she was beautiful. She had that dressed in a man's suit thing down. Wide loose trousers and vest. Her hair was cropped short enough that I wondered if she'd been military.

"Ah, have you been to grandmother's house then?" Daphne smiled.

"Is this the part where I comment on your sharp teeth?"

She flicked an elongated fang with the tip of her tongue. "Do you suppose your grandmother would be upset if the wolf took a bite?"

"If you bite people here, I am sanctioned to behead you." I paused, hoping for some reaction. "Both by the queen and by the city."

"Wrong story, Crowe." Daphne *tsk*ed. "The big bad wolf eats the granddaughter. Gobbles her up. For now, though—"

"Look. I'm not sure what your game is but . . ." I paused as she pushed a button on her phone, sending a message. "What was that?"

"Boom." She motioned. "Fire. Some tavern or other? What was it called? Oh, I know . . ."

And I was off. Her laughter echoed behind me as I *flowed* to Bill's Tavern. The front window was shattered, and several tables were on fire.

Christy was standing at the street, gun in hand, looking like a wet avenging spirit.

Inside, Jesse had a fire extinguisher, and the sprinklers were on. Eli, however, was what caught and held my attention. My beloved was standing with his arms directing the flow of sprinklers through some sort of fae magic that was both beautiful and thoroughly foreign.

Iggy, looking slightly less cadaverous already, motioned me closer. "Earlier, I plugged my energy into yours to help direct. Go to the fae. Give him yours as I did."

"I don't know how to—"

"You do. You've pushed against him with yours. Every hexen does it when they meet magical beings. It's irresistible." The look he gave me was vaguely wicked, which was creepy as fuck while he was looking like a mummified corpse.

I walked over to Eli, who was sooty and soaking. "Eli?"

He glanced at me, and there were lakes inside his eyes.

"Hold on," I whispered as I stepped closer so we were chest-to-chest. "I'm not sure how to do this without . . ."

I lowered the cage that kept that part of me inside, the barrier I'd taught myself to erect around whatever magic writhed inside me.

"Geneviève?"

I shook my head and pressed my body even closer, erasing the slight gap between us, not entirely sure how to do this without it feeling sexual and also knowing that being quite that affectionate was very not-fae. I slid my hands under his shirt, tracing the line of his spine with my fingertips, letting the energy that lived in my skin glide from my body to his.

"All of me," I whispered against his neck. "All of me is yours."

The fires that were flickered around the bar were drawn from the surfaces where they were dancing, and in a surge of uncontrolled energy, they walked toward us.

Flames crawled over our bodies, sinking into us like a million small touches, searing me inside so that I was barely standing.

"Geneviève . . ." Eli lowered his mouth to mine as my lips parted.

And in that instant, I felt as if I could see the entire city. Every single body in the soil, every last body that walked without life, I could see each of them. I saw faces turning to look back at me.

Then, behind us, I heard Iggy's voice. "Pull back, hexen. You people, *pull them apart*."

Jesse and Christy were there, hands grabbed and shoving us apart.

"Don't hurt us," Jesse yelled.

Eli and I stood, panting, and I felt my energy snap back like it was a net being closed. I separated from the dead, closed the map, and looked around. The room was thick with steam, as if the fog rolled off the river and into the bar.

A much younger, healthier Iggy grinned like a madman "Atta, girl!"

I blinked at him. Right now, he looked maybe twenty-five years old at most. He grabbed a bottle of whisky, chugged a long drink, and lit the old cigar in his pocket. "Heartbeat! My heart is *beating*, Hexen." He took another long pull of whisky. "Tastes as good as I remembered!"

"The floor," Jesse muttered.

Flowers and moss flourished between the wooden planks, along tables, and the wooden parts of the bar now had branches. The windows were translucent stone, and a pond was burbling in a corner.

"Well, fuck me sideways." I looked back at Eli. "I just . . . offered more energy than you needed I guess?" I squirmed, embarrassed. "I'm sorry. I was too much—"

"You're never too much, bonbon." And Eli looked around and just started laughing.

CHAPTER FOURTEEN

MORNING CAME FAR TOO QUICKLY THE NEXT DAY. MY genetics had always made nighttime my preferred "day," and that was even truer since I'd been injected by *draugr* venom. It felt sometimes like my genetic *draugr* side had been jerked to the forefront with that venom. I didn't know what was going on inside me on a cellular level. I wasn't a scientist, just an aberration with a foul temper.

Draugr, even half-*draugr*, were not really morning people, and as far as gifts from my unpleasant heritage that one was acceptable. Today, though, I felt energetic, despite the sunlight I knew was glaring outside my apartment. As I woke, I realized that was probably a side effect Beatrice's blood—as were the fangs I couldn't quite convince to recede.

"Eli?" I murmured.

He was awake, dressed, and looking *fine*.

"Are you feeling okay? You definitely *look* good enough to pounce," I told him.

Eli's rumbled laugh was a salve on my mood. "You always look scrumptious," Eli murmured as he bent down to kiss me. "Sadly, now is not the time to demonstrate, bonbon."

I stuck out my tongue. "Let me grab my things."

I walked into the main living area where Alice was surreptitiously watching for me, but after much repetition, she'd learned not to speak until I addressed her.

"Welcome to the day!" Ally chirped, looking up from where she was tapping away on a laptop at my breakfast table. "Ready for a pick-me-up, sunshine?"

I flipped her off, much to her glee. I felt weirdly wired and exhausted at once.

Eli asked, "Why are you *always* here, Alice?"

"Prince Eli," she started.

"*Just* Eli," he said, as he did every damn time that she tried to use his title.

My assistant was a cheerful shit-stirrer. If there was a category of monster filled by cheerful, maddening women, Ally would be assured a throne. Unfortunately, the world was pretty basic—humans, fae, witches, and *draugr*. And since both witches and *draugr* were human or previously human, that really left it to human and fae.

Ally curtsied to Eli, who ignored her completely.

Giggling, she brought me a steaming mug of coffee and blood, which had sounded thoroughly disgusting to me until a few weeks ago. Now, I thought caffeinated-blood-of-Alice was the most delicious breakfast I could imagine.

I was pretty grossed out by the *thought* of it—though the taste was divine—which is why she keep trying to find a name for her concoction that was appealing.

"What do you think of Chicory Alice?" Ally asked as I accepted the cup. "I drank a bunch of chicory coffee throughout the day, so it would add chicory flavor to me, and then mixed Alice-Red-Juice with more chicory coffee. Did it work?"

I took a long gulp. It still tasted like bloody coffee, but I liked the taste of blood and coffee. I just didn't *like* that I liked it. I mean, lots of people put syrups and creamer and whipped cream on coffee, so adding things to coffee wasn't that weird—unless I let myself admit that what I added was people juice.

"It's really good," I told her.

She pouted. "You always say that, Boss."

And I rarely wished I could lie as much as I did when Ally pouted. She was somewhere between assistant, responsibility, and an unwelcome but inescapable relative. Of course, she'd also tried to kill me in the not-too-distant past, so I figure she will become less needy once she was convinced I won't behead her.

"You're really good to me," I told her. "And this *is* really good."

"But you said the same thing about"—she held up her hand and started ticking off names—"Caffeinated Vodka Morning, Garlic Going to Get You, Fruit Bowl Friday, and—"

"The fruit left me too drunk to stand, and I didn't like This Piggy Went to Market at *all*," I reminded her. That one was horrifying. She'd soaked her blood in a bowl of crispy bacon. I wasn't the world's best Jew, but blood and bacon? Ugh.

Ally clapped her hands. "True! No more bacon."

At first I thought her cheerful attitude was affected, but she was really just a bouncy person. And while I wasn't going to announce it, I maybe liked her a little more because it was real. I couldn't recall ever clapping in glee, and I caught myself smiling at Ally's constant joy.

"I brought a suit!"

I blinked as she darted over to one of my fight dummies. She only moved at human speed, but I swear that woman had hummingbird in her DNA somehow.

I was still sipping my energizing meal when she held out an elegant suit that obviously wasn't something she was lending me. We weren't the same size, for starters. Ally was more like a well-heeled pin-up girl, and my bust was far from generous.

"You can't keep buying me clothes," I said, harsher than I meant.

Eli shot me a warning look.

But Ally had already reverted to the person she'd been when we met—and the widow Chaddock was a mix of sobbing and angry. Her pout had turned into tears, and she glared at me through those tears.

"Alvin is dead, and I'm sad," Ally whined. "I just want to make up for being foolish, but no one else will let me. And I want you to *need* me. Tres is off being all business man because *you* sent him away. And my Alvin . . ." Whatever else she said was lost under sniffling noises.

"I do need you, Alice." I glanced at Eli in alarm. The tears we'd avoided last night seemed like they were coming one way or another.

"No, you like my blood, but you could get anyone to do that."

"Ally . . ." I opened my arms to hug her.

And she melted into me. Eli watched, silent but obviously realizing what I'd been thinking more and more. I'd had my suspicions, but the longer I knew Alice Chaddock—who had initially annoyed me to the point of wanting to stab her—the more I realized that I'd accidentally bonded her to me. Ally was my Renfield.

Eli met my gaze as I hugged Ally and pretended to bat at invisible flies.

I mouthed, "I know."

I went from being a woman responsible only for myself, protective of my three dearest friends, but untethered to being a woman with a *draugr* and a human bonded to me, a fiancé who was the heir of the fae throne, and a dead guy currently coming out of the guest suite.

Iggy and Alice were staring at one another the moment he walked into the room. She wiped her face, erasing the few tears that had escaped without smudging her perfect make-up.

Iggy, charming in the way of men who were expected to be so, walked over to a sofa and motioned to it. "Revolveress?"

"What?" Ally sounded suspicious.

"I find myself in need of knowledge."

"About?" She walked over and sat, though.

Once she'd done so, Iggy sat at the far other end. "Since the 1880s, women are prickly, wear unnatural hair color, and punch artificial men for fun." He gestured at my fight dummies. "The fae and the dead ones are exposed, and hexen have no mastery system. What else is new?"

For a moment, I felt bad for him, and maybe a little grateful. He'd defused Ally's emotions. It was a selflessness I appreciated, and I had a wave of hope that they might become friends. Iggy was dead, and he was suddenly pulled into a future that was markedly different. Ally was at a loss, tethered to me through magic and mourning the loss of her husband.

"Cities are like islands," I offered. "When the dead exposed their presence, people panicked. Telephones are tiny enough to carry around, and have no cords." I looked at my kitchen. "And we can cook food in a minute in microwaves, and cars are—"

"I noticed the cars," Iggy interrupted.

"What do you eat?" Ally asked, whipping out her phone for her grocery list.

Iggy offered a sad smile and then met my gaze. "Nothing, I'm afraid. No food or drink or cigars unless my heart is beating. Today, it is not."

"So all . . . better?" I asked awkwardly.

"Better? No. But my heart is silent." Iggy glanced away, and I felt like apologizing.

"Geneviève?" Eli glanced at my wall clock.

"Right." I took the suit Allie had brought and headed to the bathroom. I knew it would fit.

"Accessories!" she called, jumping up and grabbing a bag. "Sword holster, shoes, and a handbag with room for a pistol and first aid supplies. Designer."

She didn't bother trying to tell me brand names any more, but she couldn't resist telling me it was quality. I smiled, drained my mug, and took the bag. And I darted off to change.

After last night, I felt renewed despite my to-do list, and the Chicory Alice was already helping, boosting the energy of Beatrice's contribution. It still burned my biscuits that I failed to put Iggy in his grave, but I was starting to wonder if he might be an asset after all. I could benefit from an experienced witch's wisdom.

Maybe.

I wasn't sure what would work the same for me as for more traditional witches; I wasn't working with the same magic most witches did. Sometimes, will and words were enough, and sometimes a single drop of blood roused a full wing of a cemetery. My magic wasn't predictable, and dead things came at me when I worked any magic. Whatever else I was, I was *draugr* enough to be unpredictable. That would make me decidedly unwelcome in any of the Sanctuary Cities—or leave me dead in a few other places.

After a quick brush through my hair, I changed into the damn near perfect suit.

When I stepped into the room, I admitted, "You are a true gift, Ally. Could I get another mug of Chicory Alice?"

She preened a moment before starting, "I have a voice recorder, spare bullets, and notepad. We can take two cars or—"

"I shall accompany Ms. Crowe," Eli cut in.

I expected an objection, but Ally curtsied and dipped her head. Her increased deference to him was super-weird, but honestly, the list of super weird complications was starting to be long enough to prioritize. This one was way down the list somewhere.

"Get me everything you can on Madame Hebert," I told her as I accepted the second mug of blood, this one in a cheery cup with the words "Monkey Balls!" emblazoned on it.

Ally grinned. "It's catchy."

Eli rolled his eyes, but I smiled at her and said, "After I deal with this, I need to get that Hebert business sorted out."

I didn't have the heart to tell her about the crow heads. Ally might be a cheerful murderess, but she worried about me these days. Secrets. It was how I got by without my friends constantly being anxious.

Iggy opened his mouth, but I spoke over whatever he was going to say, "And babysit Iggy, please."

"No worries, Boss."

"That will *not* be necessary," Iggy said. "Miss Alice will be treated as the lady she so obviously is, and I will be here awaiting your next need."

"Ignatius and I will be just fine." Ally gave me a finger wave before telling him, "We could walk around the city to refamiliarize you. There are a few files at the Historical Society I need to grab." She paused. "Are you younger today?"

"No." I paused and caught his eye. "*Right?*"

Iggy nodded. "Simply feeling spry in your presence, Miss Alice." Then, to me, he added, "The revolveress will be completely safe, Hexen."

I smiled. "Thank you, Iggy. And maybe once I get this Hebert mess sorted out, you can teach me a few new tricks so you can return to your rest."

Iggy laughed. "I haven't had this much fun in my death. Of that, I am quite certain. So I am no rush to return to wherever I go in death, Hexen."

"Strays," Eli muttered looking at first Ally and then Iggy.

I ignored all of them and walked out the door.

CHAPTER FIFTEEN

I was impressed that Eli's car was outside and already repaired. I guess, sometimes, being powerful was handy. I wasn't always sure how I felt about it, but Eli was neither pretentious nor egotistical. He was simply fond of what he was fond of, and he had the resources to have it.

Walking into an NOPD office made me tense more than the restless dead or face-gnawers ever could. This one was at the edge of river, where watch officers stared out over the muddy water as if they'd be able to see under it. An awkward attack in New York where face-gnawers strolled out the Hudson last month and started chewing on people had rattled the world. Again. Dead means no need to breath, so it wasn't terribly shocking.

Somehow it was a rude awakening for New York, though.

Here at the mouth of the Mississippi, we were pretty much founded on rude awakenings. Plagues, pirates, and poverty tended to create the stories passed down for generations. The biters were just the latest on a long list of challenges—but neither hurricane nor plague had destroyed us. The *draugr* weren't going to either.

I straightened my shoulders as I walked up to the main desk, an officer I didn't know, who was tucked behind some plexiglass barrier with steel wire so we could hear to talk. Low tech? Maybe, but it worked. It had the bonus of identifying most any fae in the city, but Eli stayed back from the toxic stuff as I said, "Crowe Associates for Gary Broussard."

"You the witch?" the officer asked. He was one of those guys who looked like he'd worked out for months before coming here. The pay was one of the highest in the nation these days, but so the was the mortality rate. When I didn't reply, he added, "Broussard's witch friend?"

It felt like a pause went over the other officers or detectives or whatever the hell they were to be called properly. My hand started to drop to the short sword at my hand. I might not be able to summon the dead, but if I had to do so, I'd draw.

"I am," I muttered.

"Thank you," he said loudly.

"What?"

"If not for whatever hocus pocus you do with those rounds Gary passed out, I'd be dead instead of on the desk while I heal." He pulled his shirt collar to the side, revealing a mass of fresh scars at the juncture of his neck and shoulder. "Partner put two of those magicked up rounds in the fanger who grabbed me. I'm not dead."

I nodded mutely.

"Is Broussard ready?" Eli's voice brought me back to focus.

The officer pushed a button, activating some sort of intercom on the desk. A few moments later, the loud clank of the steel door unlocking heralded the arrival of Gary Broussard.

"Strange to see you without a corpse you're trying to explain away," he teased. At the same time, he looked pointed up and to his left. A camera in the wall was recording our conversation.

I gave a quick nod. I guess his official report didn't mention seeing me at the Hebert house. "Aw, Gary, do you miss seeing me?"

"Nah. I was telling myself you got smart and stopped hunting."

"But?" I asked.

"Saw the calendar, realized it was the holidays. Not as much fanger activity over the holiday." Gary motioned for me to walk through a doorway. "But now Carnival season is here, I bet I'll get to see you right regular . . ."

I shrugged. Sometimes, I swore Carnival season was Darwinism in action. Dumb asses arrived here by the busload, and we never needed as many buses to send them home afterward. Humans, apparently, weren't the only ones who celebrated a bit of excess before Lent.

"Imagine my surprise when we got a grant for keeping tourists alive." Gary met my eyes. "Anyone want you on the streets that I ought to know about?"

I shrugged again. The recent attempt on my life wasn't a detail I shared freely, and my ability to piss off a racist organization that had drawn in a lot of wealthy families might be a factor. Of course, I couldn't completely discount the King of *Elphame*—or a few of the rejected fae women who were irritated that their beloved prince was off the market because of me.

"Nothing comes to mind as a clear suspect," I hedged.

"So, more than a few possibilities, eh?" Gary rubbed his face as if he could wipe his worry away, but he said nothing else until we were at a conference room I wouldn't have imagined in a police office.

He shut the door. "Everything is recorded out there. A few people will be in shortly, but what I can tell you, Geneviève, is that the department will get a chunk of much needed cash *and* money to hire you. Someone wants you on the street during the season. After that crow business . . ."

"I don't know who or why," I admitted truthfully.

Gary glanced at the door. "Dead box of crow heads, kid. That's not accidental. They'll pitch civic duty, tight budget, and . . . just, if it's going to get you killed, kid, turn them down."

Then the police chief, mayor, and a few pencil-pushers came in.

"Mayor Randulf," I said politely. I didn't know the mayor, but he'd taken the helm and handled the city with what seemed like minimal corruption, so I liked him as well as any politician.

"Gen," another voice greeted from the door.

"Mr. Chaddock, I didn't realize you were . . . back," I managed to say.

Tres Chaddock, Ally's stepson and former classmate at university, stood in the doorway looking like a perfectly pressed businessman. Only Eli and I knew he was dead.

"I arrived this morning." Tres stepped into the room and reached out as if to take my hand. He stumbled as he reached for me.

I jerked away before he could touch me. Tres Chaddock had been peculiar before he died. Since then, he'd been exceedingly difficult. Maybe I had no interest in touching the man whose un-life I'd had to consider far too often. He'd been murdered and in his dying moments, Ally had "jabbed him" with a syringe of *draugr* venom.

Had I been cruel, I'd have let him stay dead, beheaded him, or obeyed the law and had him sent to a T-Cell House where the newly awakened were stored until they were in control of their senses.

But guilt and misplaced kindness had me waking him in a way that—to the best of my knowledge—was an offshoot of necromancy. So, I revived him, and now he was my burden. And like the mature adult I should be, I promptly ran, so Tres was doing his best not to aggravate me even though his entire being was keyed to my happiness. He was, bluntly, my minion.

And I didn't want him.

"I understand that my step-mother has been working with you," he said, hurt thrumming in his voice. Tres stumbled again, lurching into the table.

"Mr. Chaddock, we have a meeting now. Perhaps, you might chat with Ms. Crowe later," Eli interjected into the tension, diffusing it quickly.

I shoved a small pulse of magic at Tres, emphasizing Eli's words. Tres flinched—although no one there could tell what I'd done to Tres. It wasn't painful, just the same necromancy I used on walking corpses when I woke them. It was either that or get mauled by the dead.

"Anything Gen wants," Tres offered agreeably, watching me the way starving people might watch food. Fervently, he said, "Always at your service."

"So," Gary said loudly. "Mayor. Chief. This is Miss Crowe. She's the witch who has so generously provided the bullets that have increased our life expectancy around here."

The mayor stepped up like he wanted to shake my hand, but he hesitated. "Miss Crowe."

Eli extended his hand and shook the mayor's. "Miss Crowe is a Jewish witch, mayor. Unmarried currently, so touching men casually . . ." He shrugged in a what-can-you-do way.

Admittedly, I wasn't the sort of Jew that avoided contact with men, far from it, but I didn't offer that fact up. The beauty of the fae was that they misdirect as easily as most people blink. Eli had explained why I refused to shake Tres' hand or the mayor's hand.

Chief Caisson looked me up and down like the thought of sending me out to face the monsters worried him. "I expect Broussard explained the situation."

Eli pulled out a chair for me.

When I sat, the mayor, chief, and Gary all did. The pencil pushers followed suit. Only Eli and Tres remained standing. Eli because he didn't trust Tres, and Tres because he was grandstanding or maybe being a dick. The whole being dead thing hadn't brought out Tres' better qualities.

"Gentlemen." I stared at Tres.

There will be no dick-measuring here, Tres, I thought toward him. *Sit.*

Once Tres sat, Eli moved so he was leaning against the wall behind me, looking more like a bodyguard than anything else. I didn't bother arguing. Eli was his own man and having him watch my back wasn't a bad thing.

"If you need a bodyguard . . ." the chief started.

"What I don't need is the extra work, chief," I said with a smile. "And yet here I am. Gary is a friend, so I came to hear you out."

"We have received a donation—"

"From?" Eli asked.

"An anonymous benefactor." Chief Caisson tapped a file folder. "There are several terms here. We cannot share the benefactor's name. The funds stipulate that we can only hire you. And, of course, that we ask you to sign a 'non-liability' form holding the department or the benefactor responsible for any injury or death sustained while under contract."

"And you get a donation if I accept," I added.

The mayor and chief exchanged looks.

Chief Caisson scowled at Gary. "Did Broussard tell you that?"

I leaned back, smiling at them. "Actually, *you* just did. It was a hunch. You were awfully eager to meet me, and there's only two reasons I can see—powerful benefactor or money. Power, money, and sex, gentlemen, that is what makes our city spin, isn't it?"

They grumbled, but we all knew I was right.

"Is there a point at which I meet this donor?" I asked.

"No." The mayor scowled. "Only three people know the donor's identity. Me. Caisson. The donor."

"That doesn't strike you as odd . . .?" I looked at them, thinking a conscience might suddenly sprout. Surely, they realized something was off here! But the bottom line was that they would get funds, and that meant more to them than my well-being.

"Do you interrogate every employer?" Chief Caisson asked. "Or is it that we're the police?"

"Seriously?" I pointed at Gary. "This man is literally one of my favorite people in this city. I provide *draugr* bullets to the department. I could sell them to a lot of places for significant upcharge. I don't. I sell them at an embarrassingly low cost to *you*. Do you have a problem with me, Caisson?"

"*Chief* Caisson."

"You're not my chief, even if I accept the grant. Look, I don't know what has your panties in a bunch but—"

"I'll match whatever they're offering if you don't take the job," Tres interjected.

Suddenly, the whole room was staring at him, then arguing amongst themselves, and Eli came up behind me. He leaned down and whispered, "Tell them they have a deal."

I startled. "Why?"

"We need to lure the benefactor out." He looked over at the mayor who was pointing at Tres and then at the chief of police. Whatever was going on, they weren't all on the same page.

"Good point." I hated it, not just because it felt like a trap. I wasn't terribly impressed with the mayor or the chief of police.

"Hey!" I yelled. Once I had all eyes on me, I said, "I map my own routes, and I select my own back-up. And I don't answer questions. Take it or leave it."

The mayor gave me a patronizing smile. "Now, Miss Crowe—"

"I don't need your money," I said. "I'm accepting, and you'll get your kickback for it, but if you think that this is anything other than a set-up to get at me, you're fools."

"Why do it?" one of the pencil pushers asked.

"That's a question," Eli said calmly. "I believe Ms. Crowe has already said she doesn't answer those."

Neither the mayor nor the chief liked it, but Gary and Eli both looked pleased with my terms. That told me I wasn't being unreasonable. I didn't need approval, but I thought of my friends—and whatever category Eli was—as a metric to know if I was being as ass.

"It's that or no dice," I added when the chief looked likely to object again. "You'll lose fewer officers if they let me do my thing unaided."

Then one of the pencil pushers, a woman who looked like she ate bunnies for kicks, piped up, "The department still gets their funding if she dies. There's no protection clause in there."

NOPD needed the money, and I'd be getting paid to do what I'd be doing anyhow. There was no real issue there. The larger issue was simply who wanted me on the streets and why. I took my copy of the form, which I would only sign after legal perusal, and left.

Honestly, the whole business could've been handled over the phone. I thought sometimes the city budget could be managed better if they focused on the work of keeping the city—and NOPD—safe rather than meetings and pencil pushers whose function appeared to be note-taking and file shuffling.

But what do I know? I was a freelancer. I raised the dead, and I beheaded *draugr*. No one else in the city did either, so I wasn't really big on meetings. Most client meetings were handled by either Eli or, lately, Ally. That left me with the sword-swinging and occasional death-dodging. And *that* didn't require meetings.

Outside the police office, very much in sight of the watch, I waited for Tres. I had too many questions, not enough patience. He knew something.

"You waited for me!" Tres sounded excited, obviously not noticing the angry fae just around the corner. "I'm so—"my sword was out and tickling Tres' throat "—glad."

"Ma'am!" an officer called out.

"Personal disagreement," Tres called back breathily. "We're close friends. It's fine!"

Another officer made a disgusted noise. "Rich guys and their weird kinks."

"Is this a kink, Tres?" I asked. "Pissing me off so I consider ending your servitude?"

"Do you want it to be? If it would please you—"

"Stop." I scowled.

It bothered me more than it would've when I was single. I mean, who doesn't have at least one kink, right? But I was far from single, and even if I had been, Tres' obsessive interest in me was creepy as fuck in the best of lights. Ally, in a weird maternal move, had been micro-dosing Tres with venom before he was dead. The result was that he had been unpleasantly attentive to me since we'd met. Now that he was dead, it was like having my own personal stalker.

I lowered my sword. "Don't be gross, Tres."

He wiped the blood from his throat with a silk handkerchief because even dead, Tres was the embodiment of money and style.

Eli watched the whole thing with the air of someone utterly bored, but I saw the tightening around his eyes.

"I'll be whatever you want," Tres whispered. "I need to see you, Gen. Please."

"Stop." I poked his shoulder with the tip of my sword. "What I want is for you to be a living, breathing, not-my-problem human."

He slumped.

"Did you put up the money for the grant? Truth." I wasn't sure what was and was not within the rules of my binding, but I figured I might as well add a little magic zing to my question.

Tres' eyes fluttered as if I'd caressed him. "No. If you need money, though, I opened an account for you. Anything you need."

"Miss Crowe's needs are all met, Chaddock." Eli stood, arms folded and exuding possessiveness.

I flashed him a smile. "While my fiancé is right, I would still like your word that this grant was not your doing. So, tell me: Did you have anything to do with the grant?"

"On my life, I did not," Tres swore.

"You're dead," I pointed out.

"No!" Tres gave me that zealous smile. "Like Lazarus, I am risen. You have given me the gift of etern—"

"Right, then," I cut him off before his increasingly loud voice drew unwanted attention. "Okay, well, see you around."

I turned, fast-walking in hopes that I could simply walk away from this problem. I was a lot less than okay dealing with this particular dilemma. If I couldn't behead it, I was less at ease.

"Geneviève!" Tres ran after me and grabbed for my arm.

Unfortunately, I kept thinking of him as a human, so I wasn't out-of-reach as quickly as was necessary to evade a *draugr.* He had my wrist in his grasp, and he didn't let go. A brief temptation to stab him flickered over me, but I'd promised Ally I wouldn't stab, behead, or otherwise harm him without reason.

"Geneviève?" Eli's voice was calm, but he very obviously was not.

"It's fine, Eli. Tres was going to back up. Weren't you, Tres?" I jerked out of his grasp before things got uglier. I met Tres' gaze. "I have enough things on my plate that I can't deal with you, too."

"You have to!" Tres sounded desperate enough that I knew I was missing something.

"Why? Give me one good reason."

"I need time *with* you, near you, or I'll stop being me." Tres sounded more like a petulant child than the strong businessman he'd been when alive. "I'm trying to obey your will, stay out of sight, but . . . if I don't spend time in your presence, I'll devolve. I can feel it. When I was traveling"—he shuddered—"I felt slower. Hungry. I don't think I can leave the city again. Not safely."

I closed my eyes. I wasn't even sure I could keep a house-plant alive, and having a person need me was horrifying. It wasn't need like dating or friendship. I mean, I wasn't the best at those, but . . . this was different. Worse. I could look after him or kill him—because if he devolved, I would have to kill him. Young *draugr* were biting, irrational things.

"Behead him and be done," Eli whispered.

"I'll pay you. Hire you."

I felt guilt. Damn it. I hated guilt. "I raise the dead, Tres, or behead them."

"Well, I'm dead." Tres folded his arms. "Look. If I cannot be in your presence, behead me. I cannot go into a"—he looked around furtively before whispering—"T-Cell."

We all knew that I couldn't just behead him. It was one thing to behead those who were attacking people, or to eliminate those who attacked me, but I wasn't a senseless killer. *I couldn't be.* That was what separated me from the *draugr* part of my heritage. It was a line I drew and observed. I might be a sort-of-assassin, but not carelessly. I took on the task of killing only to protect.

And that was the line that kept me able to say I wasn't a sociopath. If I was able to kill the innocent, Tres would've been decapitated before his eyes opened. This mess was as much my fault as it was Tres'.

"Come on," I said. "Walk with me."

It was only a block to the car, but Tres looked relieved. "Thank you."

I glanced at him. "What was it like?"

Tres grimaced. "I started drooling. I almost *bit* someone in the elevator. Not a volunteer, like usual. Honestly, Geneviève, it was terrifying. I couldn't recall where I was or why. I'm missing time."

"Missing time?" Eli prompted.

"All I know for certain was that I had to get back here for this meeting." Tres frowned.

"How did you know about the meeting?" I asked.

"I have absolutely no idea," Tres mused. "It was in my schedule."

"Who put it there? Why?"

"I'm not sure, but I will be." Tres suddenly has purpose. It was if he had rebuilt himself into the businessman I'd met when I was hired regarding his father's murder.

Someone wanted me on the street, and Tres was someone here. It was likely that I should suspect him. His father was a card-carrying SAFARI member. He'd been dosed with venom, and as far as anyone knew he was alive.

Or maybe they knew he wasn't. Maybe they thought their venom-cocktail was responsible for his coherence.

"Where were you before this?"

"Houston." Tres frowned again. "Why was I in Houston, Geneviève?"

I couldn't answer at first, but when we reached the car, I offered, "Come to the apartment when Ally comes to bring me . . . supplies, or barricade yourself in your estate for the next few days. If you aren't with me, you stay there."

"Thank you. Thank you so much, mistress. I won't—"

"*Geneviève*. Not mistress." I poked him in the chest. "Don't cross me, Tres."

He caught my hand. "Geneviève. Thank you."

I pulled away after a moment. "And Tres?"

He glanced at me.

"If you harm Ally in any way"—I caught and held his gaze—"I will kill you. I don't care if it's because clarity is fading or what. She is to be kept safe at any cost."

"On my honor." He bowed.

Honestly, Tres was a little too happy affecting an old-world manner. I had to wonder why he wasn't being bonded to some other *draugr*. I made a mental note to talk to Beatrice about it again.

"Tomorrow?"

"Come by. We'll talk," I agreed.

By the time he sauntered off, Tres was walking more confidently. Eli, however, was looking at me expectantly.

"What?"

"You're still collecting strays," he said, as he opened my door.

I rolled my eyes and got into his car. Sometimes I missed driving, but I was afraid to drive his car—and anything I owned wouldn't be fae-friendly. His little blue sportscar was hypersensitive to slight turns, had whisper touch brakes, and was the result of the kind of magic and deep pockets that only a fae prince could afford.

By the time he was in the driver's seat, I'd already texted Ally for research results and let her know I saw Tres. While I waited, Eli and I headed over to his bar for a bite to eat and a few hours with no interruptions from my collection of strays.

CHAPTER SIXTEEN

ELI'S BAR WASN'T CLOSER THAN HIS PLACE OR MY PLACE, BUT I was grateful for the shared territory just then. I felt emotional after dealing with Tres—and with the police.

"Boss. Crowe." The doorman of the day greeted as we approached Bill's Tavern. "Everything good?"

"Indeed," Eli said, doing one of those weird man-speak things that I couldn't replicate even if I tried.

Today's doorman, whose name was Luc or something, gave Eli a commiserating look in response to whatever silent gesture or minor tone men used to communicate in their terse way, and I suddenly wanted to smack someone. I was not responsible—as far as I knew—for the stress that Luc had noticed.

"All good here?" Eli asked.

"A few tourists needed poured into cabs last night after you left." Luc shrugged. "No fights. No low liquor that needs your sign off as far as I heard."

"Dead?"

"Not last night," Luc glanced at me. "Seems like they heard the sheriff here was your lady."

I rolled my eyes, but the reality was that it was Beatrice not me that kept all the little dead darlings from bothering Bill's Tavern. Again-walkers were increasingly obedient to her, and I was starting to hope for a future where the face-gnawing dead were all contained.

Of course, Christophe Hebert was missing from his grave, Tres Chaddock had been one of several people injected with venom. They were made into again-walkers by human intervention—and I couldn't fathom where the humans even got the venom. Was there a giant terrarium where the dead were milked like serpents for their venom? I had questions and no idea how to investigate.

While I was pondering, Luc and Eli finished their chat and, in whatever man-code they used, they were done. Luc opened the door, and Eli tossed him the car keys. The whole thing was seamless, efficient, and infuriating. I couldn't blame it on species differences. Luc was human. It was just man-code.

Mutely, I followed Eli to his office. He unlocked the door and motioned me inside the room. It was a sort of understated posh that was a part of the persona Eli had in this world. Just a guy who ran a bar in a boozy city. Nothing to see here. Move along. Functional wooden desk, functional leather chair. If the buttons were stone and the desk had a stone inlay, it was not odd. Pretty and simple. Plants cluttered the window and the—wooden again—file cabinet. Cut glass decanter and highball glasses. The rug, woven bamboo, was plain. In all it was a minimalistic, personality-free office . . . unless you knew that Eli was not half-fae as people assumed. He was the real thing, and nature grounded him as death grounded me.

The door shut with a *snick*.

And I turned, expecting to find him ready to yell at me. Instead, he had me shoved against his desk.

"Trousers," he muttered.

My suit trousers were fastened with an iron button. I could

pretend that my assistant had no idea, but the woman had literally locked him out of my pants. That was not an accident.

"Get rid of them."

Eli watched as I tore the button off and dropped in it a pocket. Then he was pushing the cloth barriers away, cupping my bare ass in his hands.

"Mine," he whispered.

"Yes."

His kisses were enough to melt stronger reserve than mine, but Eli was fae. Rules mattered. And the closer we were to crossing the damning line, the more rules there were.

"Tell me." Eli's mouth was on my throat, scraping teeth over sensitive skin. His fingers traced the outline of where panties no longer were.

"Eli . . ."

"*Genèvieve,*" he said. "Rules?"

"No . . . that thing we . . . can't . . . do," I said between kisses. I couldn't call it fucking, but I couldn't call it sex. Sex was so much more than one act.

"No *what?*"

I swear he tore down each barrier word by word, kiss by kiss, bargain by bargain. I shuddered as he slid his fingers over my aching body.

"What can't we do?" he asked.

"Making love," I breathed as I kissed his throat. "No making love."

"Genèvieve." He lifted me onto his desk like I weighed nothing. "It's *all* making love when I touch you."

"For me, too," I confessed.

Something about that sentence tickled at my brain, and I swore I heard chimes sound around us, but then a faery—*my* faery who had more experience than seemed fair—kissed me, and my brain stopped working. His hands were magic. They always were, sliding against my slick skin, teasing until I was begging, and then filling me as I needed.

I whimpered and moaned loud enough that I suspected the entire block might hear us.

I clutched at him, undoubtedly leaving bruises. And Eli watched me as he used his hands to bring me pleasure.

"I love you, Geneviève," Eli said as I found the edge of the precipice. "I've loved you for years."

"Eli . . ."

"Tell me," he ordered.

"I love you. I fear I always will," I confessed in a rasping voice interspersed with whimpers.

"Good." He thrust his fingers deeper and faster. His thumb on my clitoris was hard and fast, and the combination tore a scream of pleasure from me.

I was trembling and, as any time emotions were intertwined with orgasms, I felt vulnerable. Eli swept me into his arms and carried me to the little sofa against the far wall.

"I will wait as long as I must, Geneviève." Eli's words were a whisper against my hair as he held me. "There is no other for me."

"But I can't—"

He kissed me, cutting off any careless words that endangered our vow. And when he pulled back, I saw the acceptance in his eyes. I knew that he would accept being banned from his homeland before ending our relationship.

"It's not doubt in you," I whispered. "How do I pass on a chronic disease? What I am . . ."

"I know." Eli smiled, not sadly but in that damned understanding way of his. He made it easy to be vulnerable. He accepted *me*, not the confident façade. Me. All of me.

But I was done being vulnerable tonight. I pulled away, out of his arms.

"Geneviève?" Eli stood, but I put a hand on his chest. He asked, "Did I offend—"

"Hush a minute . . .?" I still sounded vulnerable and raw, but that was where I was today. I reached out and unfastened Eli's trousers, shoved the fabric so they slid to the floor, and then asked, "Rules?"

He smiled. "I have none with you. I never have."

I knelt in front of him. "Still no objections?"

He swallowed hard. "None. . . although I feel like you deserve a more romantic . . ."

His words ended as I took him into my mouth. Anything he said after that was in his own language, which I've yet to learn. To me it all sounds magical, but the taste of Eli, the scent of him, that was magical, too. I loved him, despite knowing I was unable to give him the life he needed.

Today though, I would give him what I could. I would give him my love and my touch.

I felt his hand grip my hair and moaned at the feeling, at the knowledge that I was making him feel as desperate as he'd made me. The vibrations from my moan had him bucking forward, and I thought that right here right now was all I needed. This was romance enough for me. It wasn't fancy meals or any of the rest, but the man was literally trying to make me a queen. He'd fought at my side, stitched my wounds, and met my family. And hearing him beg me in words I couldn't understand, feeling his need for me, was everything.

Afterwards he pulled me back into his arms, and we fell asleep on his office sofa. We both still had our shirts on, but Eli tugged a woven blanket over my bare ass and legs.

. . .

The next thing I knew was that Eli was interrupting a very good dream. He said my name, but not like in the dream. "Geneviève!"

Eli shook my shoulder harder.

"Geneviève . . . love . . . I am trying to follow your rules here." Eli sounded frustrated.

I opened my eyes to realize that I'd been doing more than dreaming. I was astride Eli, and he was holding me away from him like I was a feral cat. It was mortifying.

"Fuck!" I backed away, tangled in the blanket and falling to the floor in a thoroughly graceless heap. I stared at him. "Did we . . .?"

"No." Eli stood and offered me a hand as if I hadn't been trying to mount him in our sleep.

I let him pull me to my feet. "I'm so sorry. Gah. I just . . . you . . ."

"Geneviève." He tilted my head with a finger under my chin, so we made eye contact. "I would only be sorry because it's not what you want."

I hadn't ever been so long celibate, and it's not like we were hands off. It just wasn't enough. I had thoughts, urges, and I felt like I was selfish for mentioning any of them.

"What do you need?" he asked.

"More."

"More?" he repeated.

"Touching. Orgasms. Hell, toys. I feel like I'm constantly on the edge of jumping you," I admitted. "It's worse every day since we started courting."

Eli pulled me into an embrace. After a few moments he said, "Then we'll figure out how to deal with it."

He sounded hesitant, and I was again mortified.

"If you don't want—"

"I do, bonbon. I *want*. Any. All." He cleared his throat before adding, "But I think it's not that simple. I think . . . my mandate to marry is creating a compulsion."

I sighed. "Like a hex on us?"

"Fae magic isn't like that. My people are conduits. The magic is sort of . . . not sentient, really, but it has Will. Our bond is being blessed, and so we are being encouraged—"

"To boink." I shook my head. The will of the fae magic was compelling us to boink like bunnies, as if my own lust wasn't overpowering enough.

CHAPTER SEVENTEEN

I was silent as Eli drove me home. I wasn't angry with Eli, but I was angry. I hated things that controlled me, that overpowered my will. It was part of why I resented my *draugr* side. I wanted to be more than my impulses, hungers, and mood. I wanted to logic my way through trouble or, if that failed, swing a sword at it.

Swords don't do a helluva lot on fae magic.

Okay, maybe they could if the magic was tethered. Swords were steel, and steel was the antithesis of all things fae.

"Could I stab something that was made of faery magic and nullify it because I used steel?" I asked, seemingly out of nowhere.

"Probably." Eli shrugged. "Are you pondering stabbing me, Geneviève?"

"Not you."

"Or you, I hope," he said lightly. "The parts being . . . encouraged by our betrothal are not parts made for stabbing."

I snorted. "I'm not above making stabbing-of-the-naked-sort references right now, and that's weird. You get that, right? I'm not like this."

"Aroused?"

"No, smart ass. Out of control." I scowled.

"Having been on the receiving side of your temper a few times, I beg to differ." Eli sighed. "You are impulsive, impatient, and rather aggressive, bonbon."

"Fine but——"

"You shoved me onto this very car in the parking lot of the morgue, Geneviève."

"*Fine!*" I was more than my libido, more than magic. I pouted briefly. I hated being wrong, but I also hated being out of control unless I chose that.

I glanced at him. "We always have sparked a bit."

"I believe that is a mild but accurate assessment."

I stopped trying to explain. He understood, just as I understood his point. My secret weapon in dealing with our some-times-volatile connection was that I knew when to shut up. Usually. And he did, too.

Eli, luckily, was not bothered by silence. He drove, albeit slower than usual. I was simply at a loss. The choices were impossible. I wanted him before we were engaged, so I couldn't even blame all of my pent-up need on the magic.

We were almost at my door when I blurted out, "I don't want to lose you."

"I know."

"So where does that leave us?" I asked.

He didn't reply until we were at my building. He cut off the engine and turned to face me. "Do not answer now," he started.

Anything that started there wasn't good.

"There are surrogates," Eli said, his voice calm in the way that said he was expecting an explosion.

"You'd have another woman carry . . ." I stopped.

His child? *Our* child? What was the term?

"Not quite." He took my hand. "We have a choice you are not considering."

I paused. I thought I *had* considered everything. Eli *needed* to have a child. That child had to be carried by his wife, or his line of the fae would wither. He—literally—carried his ancestral memory in his blood. A child of the blood was required to pass on the living memory of his family.

I could not imagine passing on the aberration of my genetic soup.

"Your child has to be carried by your wife," I pointed out. For infertile, gay, or lesbian couples, there were Temple Partners to enable the exceptional cases to pass on their genes.

"You would be my wife," he said still carefully. "So . . . the child would be my genetic child, and the ovum would be from a fae surrogate. All you would need to do was *carry* the child and deliver him or her."

I nodded. It was a solution—one that kept his genes forward and mine ended. I'd had no idea that was possible. Unfortunately, it required my body to also carry life.

"I could agree to that," I said quietly. "If my body . . . if I . . ."

He waited.

"I'm not wholly *living*, Eli." I swallowed the embarrassment of the topic. "I don't know if this body . . . if I could carry a live baby."

"I know that, Geneviève." He was out of the car and at my door in the next moments. He opened the door and pulled me to my feet. "Will you make another faery bargain with me, Genevieve Crowe?"

I couldn't help the shiver his words brought. On one hand those bargains were how I ended up engaged, but on the other, I *loved* him. I held his gaze. "What terms?"

"Be my bride *if* I can guarantee an answer that gives me an heir but that you do not have to pass on your condition," Eli asked.

"If I agree to that, how long until we . . .?"

"Marry?"

"No," I said. "Have to have a child."

"Within the next century or when I ascend the throne, whichever comes first," he offered.

"Two centuries," I countered.

"Accepted." Eli knelt in front of me. "Will you be my wife, Geneviève? Not just an engagement, but wife in truth."

I stared at him, trying to stop the swell of emotions that threatened to overpower me. No person had ever understood me as he did. No person had ever accepted me so fully. From making me feel vulnerable to saving my life to accepting my friends and dangerous avocation, Eli had trampled every barrier I'd built. He was everything I could dream of.

"The reason we are so compelled to"—he grinned—"'*boink*' as you put it is because the bond we have is embraced and accepted by the magic of my people. We are, as you already must know, compatible in *every* way."

"Damn it." I heard the emphasis on the word *every*. I heard it and the way his voice darkened with magic that called to mine. "Every way?"

He laughed and took my hand. "Yes. Every way, every position, every—"

"Duck dongles," I muttered.

"Emphatic and thorough yes," he teased. Then he paused, grew serious and said, "I fight at your side as if we are one. You understand me as no one ever has. My heart and yours are as two pieces that had been torn apart and found their way back together. It is not only my loins that—"

"Yes. Damn it. *Yes.* I want to marry you." I felt like something crashed over me. "I want you, and only you, for eternity."

"Good."

As he came to his feet, my hands in his, I braced myself for the panic, the worry, the sheer terror that the hint of commitments evoked. There was none. I opened my eyes. "You deserve better, but if you're fool enough to love me—"

"Geneviève."

I paused and looked at him. "Eli."

"I deserve a person who loves me as I love her." He pulled me closer. "And you deserve a person who loves and accepts you as you love and accept me."

I sighed. "I do love you. Completely. Wholly. To the point of madness."

He kissed me, as gently as if I were the fairy tale princess he should have. And although I wouldn't admit it to anyone other than him, I felt that way. Sweet. Good. Fragile. No one else had ever made me feel like I could lower my weapons, like I could leave my sword at the gate.

"Shall we go catch a murderer?" Eli asked, sounded far too cheerful. "I can be free right this moment . . . or do you still need time to think?"

I gave him a curious look. Admittedly, Eli was always happy to exercise his warrior side. He might feign being a man of leisure, but my beloved was as much warrior as politician, as much shrewd businessman as ruthless fighter.

"What gives?"

The laugh he gave was pure sin, and my entire body responded to the wicked promise in that sound.

"Bonbon, once this case is done, I will inform my uncle of our bargain." He gave me a look filled with promise I wasn't yet understanding.

"So, you are eager to go home?" I asked.

"In a manner of speaking." Eli pushed me toward his car, stalking me in a way that was both new and wholly predatory.

His body protected me from view, despite the fact that we were out in the open. And I thrilled to the thought of his very public attention.

"Eli?" My own voice sounded more breathy than usual. Aggressive Eli was fast becoming one of my many favorite flavors of Eli.

Eli lowered his hand between us, fingers toying with the seam of my jeans. "When there are no rules left . . ."

"Home," I echoed as understanding dawned on me.

I was his home, and he was mine. And once we were able to resolve this one last obstacle there was nothing to stop us from getting "married" in the way of his people. Sex. Intimacy. All of it.

I whispered, "No more rules."

"Exactly, Geneviève." He leaned closer, pressing himself tighter to me.

My eyes fluttered closed as desire made me weak. I was grateful for the car I was leaning against, and I let his magic and mine entwine. I forced my voice to be steady and let my guard down even more than usual. "An eternity making love with you still doesn't seem like enough to fulfill this need."

He chuckled, rubbing against me so that he drew a whimper from me. "We shall try, Geneviève. We shall definitely try, over and over . . ."

I whimpered as he pulled back. Maybe the magic of our bond *was* making us more desperate, but I knew magic—had harnessed it from the moment I first drew breath in this life and so had he. We'd use this magic as we'd used the magic in both of our lives. I was no longer frightened, no longer angry. The force of this thing between us was heightened because we were so damnably compatible. Why not accept it?

"When do we speak to the king?" I asked, shoulders back and ready to move forward. Finally. I was done resisting. Fae bonds only affirmed what I already hoped: we were perfect together. That's why Eli was already so sure of us, why he knew we could work around my fears, his heritage, my genetics.

"Soon. First, we must resolve this case," Eli pronounced. "I cannot spend our wedding looking for threats to your life. Find out who is targeting you. Get married."

I took several moments, shoving my needs back into their box, before I said, "I expect a honeymoon. Days and nights and weeks with no clothes, no work . . ."

"It will be my pleasure . . . and yours," Eli promised.

Words escaped me as thoughts, ones he was projecting as hard as he could, crashed into my mind. Images. Sounds. Tastes.

"Tease," I whispered.

"*Promising*, not teasing. I plan to deliver on every promise," he countered.

And as much as I wanted to drag him inside and continue to enjoy my newfound acceptance of our future, I knew that the rules were still in place until we went before the King of *Elphame* to plead our case. And once I had Eli naked and able to be fully mine as my spouse, I wasn't going to want to interrupt it for beheading *draugr*.

"To Houston then?" Eli prompted.

"To Houston," I agreed.

Madame Hebert, hopefully, had the answers I needed to resolve that dilemma. Then, on to the question of my mysterious grant benefactor—and who was behind the corpse poker party.

Woe to anyone in my path! I had crises to resolve and a rather incredible incentive to do so sooner than later.

CHAPTER EIGHTEEN

ELI CAME INSIDE THE APARTMENT WITH ME, ONLY TO FIND Ally and Iggy sharing a laptop screen. Files were stacked on my breakfast table. I made a mental note to get a desk for Ally's use. I felt securer knowing she was safely ensconced in my home. *Renfield.*

"Boss!" Ally had the proud smile I'd seen when I liked her blood cocktails, but she was waving a file. She hopped up and charged me. "I have Mrs. Hebert's address in Houston. And I have a lead on the grant."

I accepted both her hug and the file. Briefly, I wondered if that hugging was part of why my friends found her so irritating. I allowed Ally liberties that typically took years to acquire.

"I bribed a few people," Ally announced proudly. Then she pointed at Iggy, who stood the moment Ally had bounced out of her seat. "And Ignatius hexed one!"

I hadn't realized until then that Iggy could still hex people. Magic, at least the sort most people practiced, required a pulse. It was why so few *draugr* could hex anyone—although my grandmother was an exception. She was the only one I knew of, and her mastery over it was why she was extra terrifying. My family tree was, apparently, a messed up one even back when Beatrice was breathing.

"I have questions, Iggy."

He smiled. "I exist to teach you, Hexen. Literally, in fact, which means you *ought* to have questions. Perhaps, you ought also to stay here to hear the answers."

"Killers to catch, questions to ask." I shrugged.

"How well I remember," he murmured. Then, he asked, "And how were the mutton shunters?"

"The . . . what?"

"Police," Eli offered quietly at my side. "Master Blackwood is peppering his answers with 1800s phraseology to appear mysterious or perhaps subtly remind you that he is of another era."

Iggy laughed, clearly caught off guard.

"Subtle stuff is not great with the boss," Ally whispered loudly. "She's the most direct person in the world, which makes her engagement to a faery super fun to study."

I stared from one to the other. Then I handed the file to Eli and headed into my fight space to collect a few things. I tossed a few daggers on the bed, a bag of hand-crafted salt rounds, and started to pack an overnight bag.

"Need a place to stay tonight, Ally," I called out. "Fae friendly."

"On it," she sang back. "New delicates in the bureau drawer."

I winced. "Woman!"

"Your underthings were positively *pedestrian*, Boss." Alice sounded horrified, as if boring knickers were a mortal sin. "Prince Eli deserves better things. He's a faery." She said the last word in a whisper as if that were a secret.

I waited for Eli's usual objection to being called Prince Eli, but he was grinning and reading the file, clearly pretending he couldn't hear us.

"New knickers are okay," I allowed. Then deciding to stir things up, I asked, "None of those little see-through nighties, though, right?"

"Three. I didn't include red because it would clash with your hair but—"

"I'll retire to my room," Iggy announced, positively scurrying out of the room.

I wasn't sure if he was scandalized or lamenting his own lack of a woman in need of fancy knickers. I waved at him as he departed and called out, "Thank you for assisting Ally. If you want to consider me educated now—"

"Ha! Nothing so simple as that, Hexen." He looked over his shoulder at us before vanishing into the guest apartment.

"The money is coming from a bank within the city," Eli said after perusing the file. "An account owned by Bayou Protection."

"And they are owned by a company owned by a company whose letters of incorporation are routed to an attorney," Ally finished. "Layers. Don't you think I'm done, Boss. I'll get the owners' names one way or another."

Her hand dropped to her purse where I knew a gun that looked too big for her petite self.

"No shooting lawyers," I said.

Ally stuck her tongue out. "Fine, I'll send Tres to talk to them."

I wasn't sure which was worse. Send a *draugr*? Wave a gun? I suppose it was a toss-up. "We'll discuss it, and Ally?"

"Mmmm?"

"Tres is missing time. Devolved a bit. Knows he was in Houston. Knew he was to attend my meeting with NOPD, but he cannot recall *why* he knows." I watched Ally's expression grow darker.

"I could just kill Lydia! The trouble that woman created for my family—"

"Ally? You did kill Lydia," I interrupted.

"I did, didn't I? I shot Lydia. A lot." Ally grinned. "No one messes with my family." She shot a glance at the door where Iggy had gone. "I think that's why I like Ignatius. He's here to protect you, and you and Prince Eli are my new family."

"Look up what you can on where Tres was," I said, skirting right past her proclamation of family. "Call him. Find out what he knows. Track credit cards, and—"

"Boss! I know how to track people." She rolled her eyes. "I was a society wife. I have connections all over."

I turned back to packing.

I pulled out the frothy bit of lace and gauze from my bureau drawer. Like everything Ally added to my closet—or Eli added to the closet for me at his place—this was likely to have cost more than I ever spent on clothes. I made a point of holding it up so that Eli could see part of it.

"Panties to match," Ally said off-hand.

Maybe I ought to be embarrassed to discuss lingerie with Ally. But neither witch nor fae was particularly repressed when it came to sex. Eli was private, but I figured that if he was uncomfortable with the conversation, he'd have left as Iggy had.

As Ally wandered off to book wherever it was that I'd be sleeping that night, Eli came over to join me as I packed.

"I find myself incredibly motivated to solve these problems," Eli whispered as he stood behind me.

"Agreed." I leaned back as his hands gripped my hips so hard that it reminded me that he was strong enough to toss me wherever he wanted me.

We stood for a moment, and then I grabbed the light blue

lingerie, one of Eli's shirts, and a pair of jeans. "Let me get changed, and we can hit the road."

When I returned, Ally held out another piece of paper. "Boutique Hotel. Caters to high end clientele. I booked a suite since the boss keeps different hours."

Eli took the note. "You are a gem at handling matters."

Alice paused, blinked, and immediately hugged him. "You said something nice to me!"

He peeled her off him without frowning. "I shall not make it a habit of doing so if you accost me, Alice."

She cleared her throat, but she sounded extra cheery as she said, "I texted the info to you, Boss."

I opened my arms for the rest of the hug she wanted to give someone, and she squeezed me hard. "Ooof."

Eli had my weapon bag in hand, leaving me with the overnight bag and a sword to carry. I glanced at Ally.

Feeling a little silly, I asked, "Will you be here or at home?"

"I'll keep an eye on Ignatius." She smiled at me in a way that should be irritating but wasn't only because she was Alice. "And I'll be careful. And I'll watch out for Tres. He's been super weird lately, and this explains why."

"Check his holdings," I told her.

"Already planning to." Ally sighed.

I knew that they had a complex friendship, former class-mates turned stepmother-stepson, but I thought he resented her. She was why he was dead, and yet she was the one who had my attention.

Eli looked at Alice. "Please, avoid being alone with him until we know."

She squirmed, but then she nodded after a moment. "So, I guess I'll stay here . . ."

"Excellent idea, Alice." Eli smiled at her, maybe to take the sting out of the awkwardness.

Outside, Eli gave me ample room as we walked. I popped a button on the shirt, making sure he could see the lace. I met Eli's gaze. "How fast do you suppose you can drive to Houston?"

Eli's smile was the most beautiful thing I'd seen that day. "Navigate for me, bonbon, and I'll be there in record time."

"You say all the right things, fiancé of mine." I waited patiently as he put our things in the trunk. "I was thinking of what we could possibly do after we finish our talk with Madame Hebert . . ."

His laugh was everything I loved. He opened my door and said, "I have a few ideas."

"Excellent. I look to forward to hearing all about them." I leaned up and brushed my lips over his. "You have the most delicious voice, Eli."

As I slid into the car, Eli stared down at me. "I like your increased comfort with our pending marriage, buttercream."

I trailed one hand over his thigh. "Oh honey, you ain't seen nothing yet."

CHAPTER NINETEEN

THE DRIVE TO HOUSTON WAS ON ONE OF THE ROADS THAT was still maintained. Many roads had fallen into disrepair. The commuter lifestyle ended when the *draugr* came out of the ruins, so local roads were nothing more than memories of asphalt in many places in the South. In the desert regions, roads were lost under sand from their monsoon season; in the North, ice and snow left cracked rubble. The exceptions—like the mostly stone and dirt roads from the city into the Outs—were local choices.

Freeways between cities were a different thing, however. They were kept up even better than before-*draugr* via inter-city contracts. Hopes of easy tourism fueled the appearance of funds. To keep tourists safe at roadside gas stops, fences stretched on either side for the entire stretch of freeway, and monthly patrols checked the freeway fences for gaps or tears. Much like airports, these high-speed networks were part of the system of connection that proved that we weren't a failing society.

At the gates of the city, mobile medic teams checked for a pulse. No pulse, no access. It wasn't as severe as the restrictions to move into the city. With pulses, we were granted a forty-hour pass. It was a clever bit of tech that was affixed to the wheel of the car. Attempt to remove it, and it would pierce the tire. Similar wristlets or anklets were attached to the arms of each tourist over the age of twelve.

Eli parked the car in the queue for the tire monitor. "I despise this."

I grinned. "Let me boost my temperature and hope that still works."

A weird part of me enjoyed the idea that I was the thing they wanted to keep out, and they had no idea. So far, I could fool a temperature scan—just not a blood test.

I stepped into the rectangular frame; it was akin to the old body-scanners at airports in the early part of the century. No standing still these days. It simply read whether or not a body was alive. Temperature and pulse.

Eli held out a card that had "FAE ANCESTRY" in a purple highlighted stripe. His temperature wasn't going to read as human.

I was about to step out of the remote scanner, when the alarm went off.

"Miss Crowe?"

Panic filled me. I met Eli's gaze. "Monkey nuts."

Maybe this wasn't as okay as I thought. I had no sword. Weapons inside the machines were a no go. I could *flow* to the car. I could summon magic. I sent a pulse, seeking the dead.

"I'm a witch," I said.

"Witches don't usually set it off." The guard didn't draw a weapon, but two others were approaching.

Eli cleared his throat. "Love? I should've mentioned, but I hadn't realized . . ."

"Eli?"

He gave me a smile and then focused on the officers. "Miss

Crowe is my intended. Her genetic make-up is shifting as our nuptials grow near."

The guards exchanged looks, but I was caught off-guard. Eli was a lot of things, but he was—first and foremost—a faery. The fae did not, could not, lie.

I stood flabbergasted as Eli pulled out a second identification card, this one with his actual ancestry, and his actual name. The diplomatic card was basically a "no questions asked" card. The anxious guards were at a loss as he held up the shiny sliver of silver with the royal badge of his people. "I do like my privacy, gentlemen, but I will not have my beloved looked at as if she is anything other than perfection."

Another guard, some sort of supervisor, headed toward us. He was an older man, no longer suited for guard duty when the thing you were trying to keep out was strong and deadly.

Tourists were leaning out windows to see us, undoubtedly expecting to see a beheading.

"May I present the next of queen of the fae," Eli said, louder still.

More phones and cameras began to pop up in cars, and in the next minute the guards and supervisors were bowing theirs heads to me. To us.

I glared at him. In his defense, I was about to be outed as *draugr* before he stepped in with his explanation.

Fae can't lie, though.

Did our pending nuptials really change me?

Either way, he'd saved me from disaster, and that added a lot to my willingness to play to a camera. I hated cameras. I hated publicity. This right here, this was on my list of reasons I didn't want to be queen. I had no idea whatsoever of how to act.

Jeans, his shirt, and a slinky scrap of lace felt too informal for my outing as the future—

I couldn't even think the words.

The guards straightened, and the supervisor stepped in. "We will still affix the security bracelet, so we can aid you if you are delayed," he started.

"Diplomatic immunity," Eli countered with alacrity. "You will not be placing your metal trinket on the skin of the fae."

"So just the w—"

"My bride is an extension of my being." Eli raised both brows. "We wouldn't want to anger the fae, officer. My people are quick to curse if their royals are impugned."

"Let me make a call." The supervisor walked away, leaving us standing there as snap happy people took our pictures.

"Fuck a duck, Eli."

"Smile, bonbon, or I shall be required to make a scene of devotion for these images." Eli had that tone, the one that reminded me of his uncle, the one that reminded me that the fae are not human despite appearances.

"Purpose?" I prompted. I could do this. I could be the future wife and faery queen.

"To show that we are smitten." Eli gazed at me, façade dropping suddenly, and the look that was typically reserved for private moments was right there. "To let your nation's people know that this is the fairy tale."

"An awful lot of blood for a fairy tale," I muttered.

He laughed. "The oldest ones were bloody, gruesome, and graphic."

I reached out an let my hand caress his cheek. "Rating?"

"All ages, Geneviève." He held my gaze. "For now."

I kissed him softly, briefly, and leaned into his embrace. Then, he offered me an elbow and escorted me back to the car. There was no posturing in it. That was simply how he treated me. Maybe, I didn't need a ball gown to look like his queen, after all.

The supervisor approached us, bowed briefly to me and

then to Eli. "Should you need anything . . ." The man extended a card to Eli. "Enjoy Houston, sir."

No wristlets. No delays.

"Perhaps, we ought to notify the others that we are exposed," Eli said mildly as we drove beyond the checkpoint and into the city.

I texted Jesse, Sera, Christy, Ally, and then called the bar. Once they were all updated, I shut my phone off. I wasn't ready for headlines.

"My uncle will be pleased." Eli glanced at me.

"Oh?"

Eli nodded once. "He's been grumbling that I pretend to be a 'commoner' in this world."

"Since the engagement?"

Eli laughed. "No, bonbon. Since I saw my future bride and decided to stay here. . ."

"Oh."

"Oh, indeed." Eli reached out and took my hand. He lifted it to his lips, brushed a kiss over my knuckles, and said, "I play the long game, Geneviève. All fae do."

Awkwardly, I admitted, "I'm far too blunt for that. You realize that, right?"

"Oh, I do. I count on your impatience. It's a beautiful thing."

And to that, I had no reply. I wasn't sure of much in life lately, but I was sure of Eli's love.

CHAPTER TWENTY

I MARVELED OVER HOW MANY MORE PEOPLE WERE ON THE streets of Houston. We had tourists, of course, but this was a city without *draugr*. It was what life had been like before we learned that there were things out there stronger, faster, and older.

"Geneviève." Eli's voice pulled me out of my reverie.

"Mmm?"

"Are you well?" He had that cautious tone again, the one that said there was a distinct possibility that I might lose my calm or that disaster was near.

"I feel like something happened that I missed." It was an understatement. Something had happened. I just wasn't sure if I wanted to know. Carefully, I said, "The fae do not lie, and I am confused . . . it doesn't make sense."

"Are you asking me to elucidate or would you prefer to remain unaware?"

And that was it, another moment of proof that he understood me. *Was* I asking? *Did* I want this clarity that I wasn't grasping yet? I sighed. "After we deal with Madame Hebert. Right this moment, I can't . . ."

"Of course, bonbon. Let us hunt."

Eli relaxed infinitesimally, and I realized that I understood him as well as he understood me. To most people, that flicker of emotion in his eyes, the slight tension shift in his shoulders and the way his hands gripped the wheel differently would not be apparent.

Whatever I was missing was not insignificant.

"So," I said with exaggerated emphasis. "Do you know where we're headed?"

He gave a single nod, and we wove deeper into the city. The towering building made New Orleans look tiny and older. Here was sleek steel and glass, modern pinnacles jutting into the sky like teeth in a massive maw, and roads that were as layered as the threads in a blanket.

Steel. I paused several minutes later, realizing belatedly that I'd brought a faery to a steel city. "Are you in pain here?"

"I am royal, truffle." Eli steered us through the maze of modern atrocities. "It is bearable."

I was careful in my phrasing. "Will you be uncomfortable entering . . . those?"

As I pointed at the skyscrapers, Eli glanced at me and said, "I would."

"Right. Well, I can go in and—"

"I know." He pulled into a lot. "We live in New Orleans. I pass wrought iron each day. It requires re-energizing, but it can be managed. Your bubbly Renfield has booked us into an establishment that caters to such needs."

A flicker of Eli's mental image of Ally catching flies while giggling filtered into my mind, no doubt projected by him.

"Hush." I tried not to laugh as he came around to my door and opened it.

"Nonetheless, if you do not object, I will leave you to handle this on your own if you are amenable." Eli gave me a tight look, and I worried that he was in far more pain than he'd admitted. "I have other tasks I can manage from here."

"I'll be quick!" I grabbed a sword, a dagger, and headed toward the lobby of the sleek monstrosity before me. I could never understand wanting to be so far from the earth. Maybe the view was worth it, or maybe they thought they'd be safer. Either way it made me queasy as I thought about that glass box that shot up the sides of the building. Elevator, my ass! It was a glass coffin in flight.

"May I . . . Oh *my*, you're *her*!" The man at the desk, who practically screamed cultured young gay, stared at me. "The *princess*!"

He shoved a pad at me. "Would you sign this?"

"Sure." I pasted the calmest expression I could on my face and did as he asked, but my other hand was on the hilt of my sword.

"Selfie?" He gave me those pleading eyes that made me think of Ally. There was a charm gene or school or something, but I couldn't do it. I was more of a, well, sword-in-hand, etiquette-impaired mess most days.

"Sure."

He leaned close, smiling like a model.

I, on the other hand, felt self-conscious as I smiled at his camera.

I was very anti-pictures because of my job. Being hired to behead people was illegal in New Orleans, as was *hiring* people to do it. Murdering the dead wasn't illegal, but those who pulled it off were usually lucky. In places like Houston, they stopped *draugr* at the city gate.

I could never live here. I wasn't embarrassed by it, but it frightened me sometimes how much peace I found when I killed. I knew I wasn't a sociopath—or maybe that was just the story I told myself in the daylight. There was a satisfying jolt inside my body when I fought and didn't die.

And I worried that it was a result of my *draugr* genetics. I enjoyed violence. I enjoyed conquering. I enjoyed not-dying. But I had friends, felt love, so I wasn't a sociopath, right?

"How can *I* help *you*, your royal majesty? Or is it 'highness'? Or—"

"Ms. Crowe works." I smiled more genuinely this time. His confusion did more to ease my mood than his exuberance. "I need to see Madame Hebert."

"That old bat knows a—" he stopped himself. "I mean, of course, it is not my place to—"

"Old bat?" I grinned. "I'm here on business."

"Ooooh, do tell." He leaned on the counter as if we were best buds.

I shrugged and admitted, "I'm not here on business she'll like."

My new bestie smiled like we were old co-conspirators. "You, princess, are why I miss New Orleans."

"How'd you know I was . . ." I trailed off as he held up his phone. Some news channel had pictures of Eli and me already. We did, in fact, look smitten, so that was good.

"'Mysterious woman, apparently human, declared fae royalty,'" the lobby clerk read. "No one has shared your name yet. Or that you're an investigator. Just that the car arrived from the New Orleans highway."

"Bet they're paying for that information," I said, feeling uncommonly clever for thinking of how it could benefit me. I usually only thought such things after Eli pointed them out.

"Four figures so far, that's all I know. Wasn't paying attention. What are the odds of needing to know?" He motioned at me. "Princesses with pretty blue hair don't often stroll in *here*.

Bluebloods? Old ladies? Sure. Not . . ." He gestured at me. "Weaponized women."

I snorted. Weaponized women? Blue-haired princesses? I wasn't sure why this man was working a desk, but I thought he should be doing something where his wit was in play. If we were in New Orleans, I might have to hire him.

I had a thought, suddenly. Obviously, *someone* would share my name. Why not benefit from it? I met the man's eyes. "Call in. Get the reward. 'Geneviève Crowe, special liaison to the New Orleans Police Department.' That's my name."

"Catch?"

"You owe me. I have no eyes in Houston, and Hebert? Part of SAFARI."

"Oh, honey, don't I know that?" He rolled his eyes. "They all join their little hate-clubs up in here. She hosts hate soirees. Well dressed, deep pockets, and misquoting the Bible like it's an art."

I nodded. I knew the type. Unfortunately, not all of them had fled my home city. "Get your reward. Call it a finder's fee for keeping tabs on the SAFARAI activity here. We'll work out details."

He was already dialing, and I hoped to hell I wasn't making a mistake. Planning off the cuff had landed me in trouble enough times in my short life that I ought to know better, but sometimes seeing opportunities was a sort of magic. And the sheer truth was that I always trusted gay men more than I trusted most humans. Goddess knew they'd had enough bias to understand what it was like to be targeted by a hate group like SAFARI. Plus, I'd never had to worry about being shocking around any of the gay men I knew—and New Orleans still had a thriving gay community. I'd yet to earn a second glance when I admitted to being a bisexual witch with a job that included beheading the dead. They took me in stride without a blink.

"I can prove it," he said into the phone. "Uh huh. I have a selfie with her."

Pause. He listened to them and mouthed to me, "Penthouse. Go."

I shook my head. If Ally ever left me, I might try to con this man into being my assistant. Of course, I couldn't imagine her leaving for anything short of a new husband, and she was far too deep in mourning for that.

"Let's talk price before I send it," he said as he motioned me toward the elevator. "Impress me, and I'll send the picture in . . . twenty minutes."

I nodded. I had twenty minutes until he sent the photo and the press started crawling all over here. That, incidentally, suited my plans. Press with cameras meant that I'd have my own private stake-out here, and Madame Hebert and her fae-hating friends would all stay put.

A few moments later, I was sitting in a waiting area in the Hebert matriarch's penthouse. Compared to New Orleans old money homes it was modest. Compared to Ally's house, it was downright boring.

"Do I know you?" Madame Hebert said as she joined me. She had the look of a steel-spined granny. Nothing soft here. She was grey-haired, but if she had extra weight, it was well-hidden. Sensible shoes, well-cut dress, and what Ally called "house jewelry"—single strand of pearls, earrings, rings, and watch. Nothing ostentatious but a subtle reminder that she was wealthy.

"You are the mother of Christophe Hebert?" I prompted.

"I am," she said.

A tightening around her eyes belied her calm tone, and my thin layer of patience was already cracking.

"Look. I don't have a lot of tolerance for SAFARI as it is—"

"So you *like* the dead? They're ruining society." Her calm was gone. "If not for them—"

"Lady, they were here for centuries." I stood. "Your dead son's body is missing. Your house was filled with . . ." I paused. Just because she was hateful didn't mean I had to be. I took a couple moments to calm myself before adding, "Your house in the city was the scene of a crime."

The way she smiled told me more than I wanted to know.

"Vermin were exterminated and left there," she said. "The police notified me. I've hired cleaners."

I blinked. Someday the callousness of people would stop shocking me, but this wasn't that day. Admittedly my job was beheading the troublesome dead, but I'd been forced to confront my own bias of late. Not every dead person was a monster. Beatrice was . . . okay, Beatrice was a bit of a monster, but not without reason.

Maybe everyone's monstrosity had reason. I wasn't a therapist, though. I was a necromancer.

"Did you have anything to do with the events that left those people dead?" I asked. "Did Christophe—"

"Christophe is dead."

"His body is missing," I snapped.

"I had him brought to me. Once my grief was under control, I realized he ought to be with his mother." Madame Hebert spoke of disinterring a corpse as calming as ordering take-out. "He is my only child."

"Are you still affiliated with SAFARI? A number of members were injected, and Christophe—"

"I do not need to answer your questions, but I gave you the courtesy of explaining that you need not look for my son in your city. He was dying of cancer, if you must know. All the wealth in the world, and we cannot fix cancer." For a flicker of a moment, Madame Hebert sounded like any grieving mother.

"I'm sorry for your loss," I said, politeness surging to the surface.

Madame Hebert pointed to the door. "Begone from my home, witch. You have no authority here, and I find myself threatened by how you've come here uninvited brandishing weapons."

"I wasn't—"

"I'm a frail old lady, Miss Crowe." She hunched slightly, hand wobbling. "The Houston police are not in your pocket, as NOPD is."

I gaped at her.

She withdrew her phone from a pocket and held it up like a weapon of her own. No longer hunched or trembling.

Stunned, I watched her dial. "Chief Jackson . . . This is Marie Hebert . . . yes . . . good . . ."

I saw myself out.

It wasn't until I was back in the lobby that I realized I hadn't told her my name. She knew my name. She also referred to her son in present tense—she said he "is" her only son. Was that the normal grieving inability to refer to the dead in past tense? Or was it a statement that Christophe was a *draugr*?

I'd seen the woman, and I still had questions—but she had called the Houston police. And my new friend at the desk was on the phone with reporters. It was past time to get out of Dodge.

At the desk, my new friend held out a business card. "Benjie." He flipped it over. "Private digits on the back."

I took it and handed him mine.

"Thanks, princess."

"Anything odd or SAFARI related, you call."

"On it." He blew me a kiss, and I shook my head.

Then I paused. "Does she have a son?"

"Chris? Mmm. Yes, she does. Dish. Not a hate-beast like

her." Benjie leaned closer. "We went on a few dates. The conversation was okay, and the afterward was delish."

"If you see him . . ." I winced. I hated this part. "He died. Buried. Not in the grave."

"Oh dear." Benjie's eyes went wide. "Not my sort of fun. Thanks for the warning."

Whatever Madame Hebert's story was, she wasn't being honest. I'd have Ally check on the disinterment and now that I was freelancing for NOPD, I'd ask there, too. Innocent old ladies didn't issue threats—or know the name of the necromancing witch of New Orleans.

Did SAFARI have anything to do with beheading *draugr*? Or stashing Hebert's *draugr* son? I honestly had less than no idea, but one thing I knew without doubt was that any mother thinking she was protecting her cubs was scarier than most creatures. If Madame Hebert thought she was saving her son, I had a strong suspicion that she'd do exactly as Ally had done when she injected Tres.

CHAPTER TWENTY-ONE

WHEN I REACHED THE CAR, ELI HAD SUCH A CLOSED DOWN expression that I looked around the lot for threats. No lurking people with weapons—or cameras yet. Worse yet, he didn't ask about Madame Hebert. He was typically with me lately, so the fact that he was neither at my side or asking questions had me worried.

"What's going on?"

"I fear we must make a detour to the park," Eli said, but then he added nothing more as he drove us to a park.

I watched him, worried that our trip to Houston had damaged him. Too much toxic metal? He'd explained earlier that he had to recharge. On some level, I understood. Magic had a price.

I rambled, telling Eli about the odd events with Madame Hebert and my new friend Benjamin. After several minutes, I blurted, "Are you injured? Can I do anything?"

He gave me an enigmatic look. "Be patient with me, Geneviève. That is what I need of you."

"What does *that* mean?"

He shook his head. Once we parked the car, a man rose from a bench and approached us.

Eli came around to me door and extended his hand.

I stepped out of the car, reaching for my sword but Eli shook his head. "No steel, Geneviève. Not here."

"Eli of Stonecroft, I am honored to be addressed by you as Japhael." The man, Japhael, bowed so deeply that his hair brushed the ground.

The park itself appeared completely deserted, only birds and whatever insects buzzed about were there. Not a single person —and that was exceptionally odd. Little patches of nature inside cities were typically one of the busiest places there.

The man, a faery I now realized, bowed almost as deeply to me. "It is my honor to serve."

Eli handed him the car keys.

"Wait! My weapons!" I started toward the car, but Eli caught my hand.

"Will be at home when we return, Geneviève." He looked at me as if he wanted to mentally will understanding upon me. "We must travel other ways than car in this moment."

"*Elphame.*"

Eli nodded once. "It is necessary."

The faery drove away in Eli's car, leaving us stranded. The only options we had were visiting the land of Eli's people or travel by foot. Eli couldn't ride in a regular car or bus.

"Are you sick?" I asked again. I stared at him. He was being uncommonly formal with me suddenly, and I was scared. "Just tell me if you are. Please?"

Eli took my hands. "My health is fine, Geneviève. Please know that I did not mean for this moment to come to pass this way. There are things beyond my control."

I swallowed. "Has the king . . . is he *gone*?"

"No." Eli offered me his arm, and I again lamented the casualness of my attire. His every act was formal, and I looked like I was dressed for a quick run to the grocery . . . well, other than the skimpy negligee underneath my jeans and button-up.

As we walked, a blinding slice appeared as if the air itself had been torn open. It glowed with a light and warmth that made me want to run toward it. I hadn't remembered it being so welcoming last time.

I glanced at Eli.

"I love you, Geneviève. Remember *that* truth if nothing else." He caressed my cheek. "And you love me."

"I do." I leaned into the hand that was too-briefly on my skin. "But you're scaring me right now."

"Traditions," he said, voice cracking. "Please remember that not everything always goes as planned, even for the fae."

A sinking fear stabbed me. Had the king found a way to end our betrothal? Was I about to lose Eli? Terror ripped through my soul, and I practically clung to him.

I pulled Eli to me and kissed him with all my fear, my need, my love.

And that was how the king of *Elphame* found us.

"Welcome home," he said. Fergus of Stonecroft was handsome in the way of feral animals, sharp lines and prominent muscles. If not for knowing who he was, I'd suspect him to be a warrior or guard, but he was the king. The fae didn't age like humans, so I had no real measure of age. Fergus had been king for a lot of years, and he looked no older than Eli. He had been king when the world learned the fae were real, and he'd been king when they all retreated to *Elphame*.

I pulled back from Eli, blinking away tears, but I kept my hand on him as I addressed Fergus. "He's mine. Nothing you say or do will change that. And maybe I'm not who you'd choose for him or this place but—"

"Geneviève." Eli held tightly to my free hand, which was reaching for a sword no longer on my body. "He means you no harm."

The fact that I was ready to draw steel on the king of *Elphame* made me pause, as did the wide smile on the king's face.

"*Indeed*, your highness. He is most definitely yours," Fergus agreed. "Woe to any who think otherwise."

"Don't mock me." I glared at the king. "Maybe I'm not who you want to be the 'highness' at his side, but I *love* Eli."

The king glanced at Eli. "This is the danger with our family's tradition. I presume you have not told her?"

"Told me what?" I scowled and looked at Eli. "I'm sorry if my temper is not like your people, but you knew, and you said you loved me for me—"

"Geneviève." Eli knelt before me and stared up at me. "I *do* love you, and *you* love me. Completely."

When he looked at me so intently, I felt like I was to be grasping something in his words, but I wasn't. "We aren't being forced apart? I didn't say something to ruin—"

"Geneviève? Do you love me?"

"I do, Eli." I felt torn between rage that I had to discuss this now and embarrassment that I'd fucked up somewhere. I was standing at the edge of *Elphame*, in the presence of the king no less. "Are you going to stay here without me then?"

"No! Geneviève . . . look at me, love." He sounded worried. "You feel alarmed right now because you're changing. *Look at me.*"

I did. He was kneeling, staring at me. Realizing the other time he'd knelt that way made me take a step backward. What was happening here?

He had not lied to the guards about my genetics.

The fae did not lie.

But if he wasn't lying, if we weren't separating . . .

I opened my mouth but none of my questions came out. Instead, I made a garbled noise and tried to turn around. I needed time to think.

Eli caught my hand and held fast. "Uncle, may I present my wife. Geneviève of Stonecroft, née Crowe."

I shook my head. "You said . . . we said . . . *how*? We were so careful!"

Who doesn't notice getting married? I should've known. It should've felt different. Right? I stared at them both, feeling awkward and wrong. How could I not notice the moment Eli and I—

"Welcome, your highness." Fergus gave what I thought was a genuine smile. "My nephew has chosen wisely. A warrior. A woman who has ties to many creatures, not merely humans."

I still couldn't speak coherently. I nodded. For goodness sake! I nodded at the king as if he was asking questions.

Eli squeezed my hand. "You asked what I need, Geneviève. Patience. Give me your patience, Geneviève."

"Patience," I echoed. Everything had shifted under my feet. What was there to be patient about? It was here. Now. Changed. I wanted to marry him. Why did I feel so odd? It wasn't regret. It was . . . as if all of my emotions were on fire. That didn't make sense, though.

Eli stayed there, kneeling. "Geneviève.?"

"The adjustment will take at least a few days, Niece. You'll feel peculiar as it is happening." The king gave me a small smile. "But afterward, once you are . . . able . . . you can resume your world."

"What does that even mean?" I glared at both of them. "We were careful. No intercourse. No accidental—"

"Sex is not a singular act." King Fergus sighed. "I thought a witch would be more alert than an average human. Sex is not merely that which results in conception. You held true love in your heart, Geneviève, when you were in the pleasure state with my nephew. In that moment, you both felt pure love. You both accepted this bond. *Chose* it."

"Sex . . . is . . . we . . ." I glanced away.

Then I remembered the moment, the chimes that I swore I heard. We'd been on his desk. We'd agreed that it was . . . I looked at Eli. "It was 'all making love.' That's what you said."

Eli knew exactly what I meant. He nodded. "I was caught up in the moment, not trying to trap you. Geneviève . . ."

"You both felt it, Niece. The laws are clear, and you were warned." Fergus shrugged. "The timeline was not what you chose, but these are the ways of things. You are the wife to Eli, and he the husband to you. Soon, your body will adjust to this change, as will his. We ought to be grateful you learned this before the change began."

"Oh."

Fergus patted my shoulder in what might have been affection—or possibly sympathy— and then kissed both of my cheeks. "Many years ago, my mother swore Death Herself would ascend this throne. I have not walked where I might meet a wife, have not opened my bed to any but concubines, for fear that I would wed Death. . . that I would leave this burden of this crown to my young nephew." He glanced at Eli. "I wanted to protect myself, so this weight would not pass to you before you were ready."

Eli and I both stared at the king. In a rough voice, Eli said, "Your sacrifice was great."

Fergus shook his head. "Prophecy is a tricky thing, is it not? I worried when you went over there . . . thinking that I would have to embrace my death and force you home or find a woman willing to love me, and thereby sentence both of us to death."

And I felt a flash of sympathy for my uncle, who had—

I startled visibly.

Uncle? My uncle? Fergus was Eli's uncle. Not *mine*.

"You are fortunate to be here in *Elphame* while the process happens, Geneviève. It will be easier on our home soil." Fergus hugged me and whispered, "So mote it be."

He hugged Eli next. "Child of my line. Son of my heart."

Then as I stared at him, Fergus made a gesture, and people swarmed into the clearing. "Attend your future king and queen as they *become*."

The swarm of faeries bodily lifted us and carried us to Eli's home here. The whole process felt remarkably *other*—which was saying something. It took a lot to weird out a New Orleanian, a Jewish witch, a half-*draugr*. But this did it.

I was held aloft by fae hands as they carried our bodies over the soil of *Elphame*.

"We cannot touch the earth until we are complete," Eli called, reaching out to me.

I caught his hand, almost tumbling to the ground at the wave of need and intense knowing of his need. It was as if a wire looped between us, and the current grew and grew.

I blacked out and when I opened my eyes, we were in his house on bamboo mats. I looked at Eli. "What's happening?"

"We are bleeding together," he started.

I looked at him. No injuries. No blood.

"Not literally, Geneviève." He crawled toward me and pulled me closer for a kiss. "The more we touch, the tighter the bond. We will meld together, as two lights become one flame, as two fragmented souls become complete."

The words were pretty, and maybe later I could say that. Right now, I simply wanted him closer than close. I was suddenly wrapped around him.

But then his magic surged into me like a fist of daggers, and I jerked away. Crab-crawling backward, I managed to stand, but in the process, I stumbled and would have fallen back to the floor if not for the dozen or so hands that were suddenly on my back, arms, and legs.

"Don't!" In my current state, I hadn't even noticed they were there. I looked around, needing to know who they were, wanting to verify that they were not the dead.

Two dozen faeries stood in the room with us. At least six had steadied me. They watched, almost reverent in their regard.

I tried to walk, stumbled and had they not caught me, I'd have face-planted.

"We are here," one faery said.

I pulled away, and again, I stumbled. "Monkey nuts!"

"What are monkey nuts?"

"She wants the food of primates!"

"Or the bollocks?"

"Is that a human delicacy?"

"She is witch! Do they require other special diets?"

"I can fetch monkeys. Which type? How many?"

I stared at them as if they were all mad, but Eli saved me from replying by saying, "She is expressing her shock. The bollocks will not be needed."

Then, to me, he said, "These fae are not of my familial line. They are here to ease you to stability when the bleeding becomes too much."

"How?" I had a series of thoughts that were too outlandish to speak, but in his way, Eli knew exactly what I'd been wondering.

"Not that way . . . unless it would please you, love." Eli's expression grew heated. "I would be fine with whatever you need to do."

I swallowed against a suddenly parched mouth. Images not of me with these beautiful faeries but of him, naked and in nonstop pleasure. I bit my lip until I tasted blood.

"Or that," Eli said, voice rougher than I could stand suddenly.

My knees buckled, and I forced myself to sound calmer than I felt. "Not the honeymoon I was promised, bonbon."

There was nothing wrong with such fantasies, of course, and I'd enjoyed them with others in the past, but right here, right now, all my body wanted was Eli.

"Don't want them," I bit out. "Or an audience."

"Geneviève." He stepped toward me. "If we . . . the process is brutal."

And suddenly, brutal sounded like exactly the path I needed. At the least, I didn't want strangers here. "Just us."

"Go away." Eli ordered.

The entire room seemed to take a collective breath.

"Out," I declared. A ripple of magic—not just my own— rolled out, toppling faeries like dominoes. I wasn't sure what would happen when my magic slammed into Eli's. I had enough trouble being a witch with a *draugr* side. Seeing them falling like children's toys tossed aside had me worried about what would have happened if this melding had occurred in New Orleans.

I stared at Eli for . . . I had no idea, actually, but when I jerked my gaze from his, there were no people in sight. And the house was in ruins.

"Shockwave." Eli reached for me. "Hold on to me, love. Just hold on."

Somehow, we crept, crawled, fell together, and then my eyes rolled back. Magic lashed out from the building, lighting the sky in streaks.

"Monkey nuts," Eli muttered.

I started laughing at his immediate consternation at the words he'd just uttered. "Oh, buttercream, we are so incredibly fucked," I murmured to him.

And that was the last semi-coherent thing either of us

managed to say. The force of our bleeding, as he called it, was horrible. I felt like I was being hollowed out and filled with nature, like my skin could no longer contain me, and as I blacked out however much later, I was fairly sure my beloved had sprouted fangs.

CHAPTER TWENTY-TWO

AT SOME POINT, I REALIZED THAT ELI WAS AWAKE. WIDE-
awake. Prowling. There was no other word for the way he was
stalking around the ruins of his home.

"Everything is louder," he said.

"Quieter," I said. The world felt less jarring, and I wondered
briefly if this was what most people's hearing was like.

He looked at me, and then was *there* as if he . . .

"You can *flow.*" I stood and did the same, checking that I
still could. Panic. That's what this feeling was. I was panicking.
"Answers, Eli. I need them."

"We're married." He paused. "And sliding a few traits back
and forth, I guess. I'm not usually so . . ."

"Blunt." I grinned. "Maybe I'll develop patience."

Eli looked at me. "Your first move at noticing that I could
flow was to do so yourself. So, maybe not."

I sighed, pretend pouting. "So . . . what do I get out of this
deal?"

"A man who loves you." Eli pulled me into his arms, and it
really did feel like home. It always had, but now whatever the

piece of me was that felt restless suddenly calmed. Maybe that was part of what he'd always offered, but this was *more*.

"Anything else?" I teased.

"Eternity."

"Kinda had both of those already." I kissed his shoulder, mostly because it was all I could reach the way he was holding me. "Not exactly the fairy tale wedding and honeymoon I was promised."

I paused, realizing belatedly that the elaborate wedding and month-long honeymoon were his desires. He wanted the very public ceremony, seeing me walk toward him, barefoot and smiling. And I could picture it as clearly as if I had done it. Because of his desire, I wanted that ceremony, too.

"Where was my giant wedding?"

"We can have a wedding, if you want it." Eli shrugged as if he was okay with me dismissing the idea. He wasn't, and suddenly, I wasn't either.

"We *will*. Big fancy wedding. One here. One there," I suggested. "Just . . . not today."

Outside the wreckage of his home, my world still waited. I guessed this was my world, too, now, but I wasn't ready to deal with that truth—or a lot of other ones. Where would we live? Was the whole no passing my genes on still kosher? Did we boink while we were unconscious? I'd wanted to.

"Did we?" My hand went to my belly. Fae traditions around marriage included some powerful fertility stuff. "I mean . . . are we?"

"No." Eli twined his fingers with mine. "We had a bargain. Your womb will not quicken accidentally."

"Good. That's good." I stared at him, feeling like the morning after the most intense what-did-we-do-last-night of my life. "So, we . . . didn't?"

"Couldn't." He shrugged. "We couldn't even stand at first. I remember that."

"I don't remember much after kicking them out," I admitted. Snippets of trying to reach him. Of blood. I licked my teeth. "Did I attack someone? Monkey nuts! Eli, did I kill someone?"

"No." He let out a long sigh. "No one was killed, Geneviève. My word."

I nodded. I didn't know what the next step was, but I was fairly sure that leaving this place wasn't a thing I wanted. We could stay here in the wreckage, ignore the world. No more death threats. No more *draugr.* A part of me suddenly wanted nothing more than an eternity right here.

"Wife," Eli said, as if he was testing the word on his lips.

I looked at him, curiously.

"*My* wife," he said. "Geneviève Stonecroft."

And it was silly to feel shy, but I did. I'd avoided this, fought it, and only just accepted it. It felt too fast, but it didn't feel *wrong.*

"Which makes you my husband," I said, lightly, as if it wasn't the most momentous thing that had ever happened to me, including my near-death experience. "Because you felt love for me that completely."

"And you for me," he reminded me.

I swallowed sudden nerves. "I want to . . . be *here.* Understand this. Try to settle into this."

Eli rested his forehead against mine.

"But I'm not changing my name, Eli," I muttered. "Still Geneviève Crowe. Still me."

"Geneviève Crowe of Stonecroft," he suggested.

I snorted. "Because *that* rolls from the tongue so easily? No."

"Here . . . here you are Geneviève of Stonecroft. My ancestors reside in *our* blood. Their memories, their strength. We carry them with us." Eli had that cautious tone, which I realized now was fae in its nature. Patience rode in those sounds.

"And I accepted that when I chose this," I reassured him. "But *my* ancestor is in New Orleans. Alive-ish and sending me heads in boxes. My mother is there. My friends. And right now, our king has *Elphame* in hand. Once I know how long we have been here—"

"Four weeks."

"Damn it," I grumbled. "Are you sure?"

He gave a single nod, and I glanced at him.

"You were out a bit longer than I was," he hedged.

"How long?"

"Two weeks." Eli caught me before I walked away. "We didn't realize you needed blood during the process. I should've thought of it sooner. Once I felt your hunger and fed you—"

"Fed me?"

He paused, and then pulled his shirt aside. A pair of angry red slashes on his chest were barely healed. "I chose you, Geneviève, and you . . ."

"What?"

"Fed me, as well." He held my gaze. "I don't recall most of it, but you needed a lot of blood because I savaged you."

I shook my head. Eli was a lot of things, but savage?

He reached down and rested his palm against my inner thigh. "Here. I woke with my face wet with your blood. The vein pumping blood into my mouth." He refused to look away. "I stopped when I came to, but we were both dressed in blood by then."

I hated the way he looked, as if he'd done something awful.

"We melded, Eli. That's *me*. That hunger and restlessness, that's *me*. Until you nothing satisfied me. Not in bed or in life. I could chase it away, but I was never sated."

He watched me, and I realized that we were both rattled by the suddenness and intensity of our marriage.

"I'm sad I missed it, though," I teased. "I do like you between my thighs . . ."

And just like that the shyness and awkwardness between us vanished. We were still us. For a moment, I wanted to remind us of that. Ignore the world. Four weeks here was only a few hours in New Orleans. Maybe we could stay?

"Geneviève? Eli?" Fergus strode into the wreckage, looking like he was late for a court ball. Ermine trimmed cloak. "Ah. You *are* both awake again."

"You have lousy timing, Uncle Fergie."

The king of *Elphame* opened his mouth, and I winced, expecting a dressing down for my impertinence. Then he started laughing, guffawing as if I'd told a raucous joke.

After a moment, he pushed debris off what was possibly the remains of a table or shelf. "You might blame Beatrice then, Geneviève. She's been trying to breach the gates. I'm not sure how or why she'd think such a thing necessary, but I've been amusing myself for days with batting away her spells and hexes."

"You've been . . ." I frowned.

The king gave a shrug that was feigned ease. "It passed the time more interestingly than when I was simply worrying that death had, in fact, come for the throne. If you did not wake, Geneviève, my nephew would weaken and die."

I paused. I hadn't considered that. Admittedly, I'd only just woken, so there wasn't a lot of time to think, and there was a plethora of things to think about already.

"I'm glad you are not dead," King Fergus said solemnly. "Both of you. . . and not only because I'd be forced to spend eternity rebuffing Beatrice's attacks."

It hit me then. Perhaps my great-times-great grandmother

thought that Fergus was trying to do me in. He was her first suspect when the topic of the grant was broached.

"Did you by any chance fund the NOPD so they could hire me?" I asked.

"Why would I do that?" Fergus asked.

"*Did* you?" I asked.

The king of Elphame looked truly flummoxed. "If you have need of funds, the treasury can be opened."

"So that's a no?" I pressed. "You aren't behind it?"

"It is, in fact, a *no*." Fergus looked at me as if I'd just asked him to do the chicken dance.

I paused, made a mental note to require the chicken dance at my wedding reception. The image of the *Draugr* Queen and the Faery King doing the chicken dance had me muffling laughter.

"Have you asked Beatrice?" Fergus prompted.

Eli and I exchanged a look.

"She said the same about you," I told him.

"Impertinent chit." Fergus scowled. "I would not harm my nephew's wife."

"But would you harm a witch with *draugr* blood who wasn't *yet* his wife?" I shook my head. "And for what it's worth, you do realize she's my great-gran, I hope."

"I'd held hope that this was an . . . exaggeration, perhaps a ploy to make you seem more frightening," Fergus admitted.

"Nope." I popped the "p" and grinned. "And since you're basically father of the groom, and she's grandmother of the bride . . ."

Fergus let out a long-suffering sigh. "And you intend to have a wedding?"

"Yep." I popped that "p," too. "Two of them, in fact, and you, Fergie, are invited to both."

I expected him to be surly or object. Instead, he smiled

widely, bowed, and said, "I would be honored, but Beatrice cannot come here."

I'd expected that. Hell, I'd expected a fuss over him attending the wedding over in New Orleans, so I was pleasantly surprised by the king's reaction. I shrugged. "No Grannie Bea, but my mother will be here, and I warn you now: she has Opinions."

The king of *Elphame* gave me a look. "I would expect nothing less from the woman strong-willed enough to raise you, Geneviève Crowe of Stonecroft." Then he motioned toward the world beyond Eli's home. "Now, go deal with the dead woman. She's begun to vex me."

CHAPTER TWENTY-THREE

I FELT LIKE ELI AND I OUGHT TO GATHER POSSESSIONS OR . . . something, but I'd brought no weapons. We had nothing near us but the wrecked remains of his home.

"Open it." Eli motioned to the air in front of me.

I glanced at Eli. I'd been to *Elphame* and back a few times, but only the fae could open a passageway. I'd waited, captive in that only someone else could open this door.

"Think of home. Then part the veil." Eli motioned to the nothingness in front of us.

I thought of my home, not in the Outs, but the city. The sheer determination to overcome any obstacle, the music that seemed to rise up from the very soil and river that made this city, the vibrancy of her people, the assault of the scents of chicory coffee and liquor and the flowers that were trapped in the humid air. I thought of New Orleans, and as I reached forward, my city in my mind and heart, I grasped the air itself and tugged.

The sensation was that of damp silk sheets in my hand, and I almost let go. Instead, I folded the air back as if it was a curtain, and I was opening the fabric to let in the light.

I stepped through, and Eli came with me. We were standing on the street in front of Eli's house. It was near dusk, possibly thirty minutes until sunset.

As I glanced over my shoulder, I could see the fields of *Elphame*. Trees. The brighter air.

"Let go," Eli whispered. His hand was on mine, unfolding my fingers, releasing the veil that I'd parted. The glimmering opening slipped away, like a curtain still; this time it was the curtain closing the play.

"So . . ." Beatrice was there, looking like a warrior goddess. She had on honest-to-Pete leather trousers and a tunic top with metal shin guards and a shirt of chain—one that was hand-fashioned for her body by the look of the fall of the precise interlocking circles—over her clothes. She had a vicious looking sword at her hip, poleax in her hand, and a gun holstered on her other side. The gun was one I would like to study one day. It was antique in the way of museum pieces, but it gleamed like new.

"A *halberd?*" Eli said.

Beatrice smiled. A poleax—or halberd—was a fierce looking thing that combined the reach of a staff with both spear and axe tips. It was heavy, brutal, and intimidating. Of course, my dead grandmother had one at the ready.

"So, you are wed, then?" she asked me.

"We'll have a ceremony here," I answered.

"And one in *Elphame*." Eli motioned for her to walk with us. As we approached the gate, it slid open for us, but rather than lead us to the house, Eli followed a stone path that took us to a grotto to the back of the house.

Oaks and willows surrounded a small pond, offering both shade and privacy despite being in the city. When I'd first seen his home, I was struck both by how unassuming it was, how natural the grounds were, and the sheer size of the lot. The

Garden District had once been the home of wealthy 1800s Americans, then in the later 1900s and early 2000s, more than a few celebrities bought homes here. Actors. Musicians. These days, it was still well-patrolled, gated, and secure.

But now that I knew that my *spouse* was the heir to the throne of *Elphame*, a number of things made more sense. Eli didn't buy things to scream status. He bought land because the fae were of the earth, and he bought the finer things in liquor and food and fabric because the fae had a fondness for decadent tastes.

"Wool gathering?" Beatrice said mildly.

"Sorry. I've changed, and—" I shrugged "—adjusting."

Beatrice propped her halberd against a tree. "I'd seen news. And then you vanished. I had worries. Lauren was most insistent I locate you."

"It's been maybe *four* hours."

Beatrice gave me a look. "Which is a month in the fae lands. That was a long time. And you know Lauren does worry."

"How is my mother?"

"Ordering my household around with the cheer of a retired general," Beatrice said with an odd catch in her voice. "I think Eleanor has decided to switch her loyalty, and Sir George offered Lauren a half-chewed turtle. My daughter is rather hard to refuse."

"Ergo you battering the gates of *Elphame*?"

Beatrice shrugged. "How am I to know what devious things Fergus has done?"

"My uncle *didn't* fund the grant," Eli said, taking a seat of a chair that looked to be woven of wood and vine. "And he does not come here. The king has nothing to do with the threats. Of this truth, I am certain."

Beatrice paced, seeming like a feral creature. Typically, she carried the calm of the grave. Austere and calculating were her default, not restless.

"What news do you have?" I prompted.

"Daphne has vanished. The imbeciles you sent to me identified *her* as their Baba Yaga." Beatrice pressed her lips together. "They asked who I was. *Me?* I am the fucking queen of their kind, despite their denial of what they are."

I blinked. I'd never heard her so talkative. "I thought you—"

"Daphne *claimed to be me!*" Beatrice said, voice harsh and irritated. "I was . . . played. That is the word, yes? I was played. I thought she was lovely but harmless. And all the while, she was murdering *draugr* and assigning the deaths to me by this deceit."

I wanted to hug her. I stepped toward her to do just that, but I was not a hugger and well, she was an angry, armed, fanged *draugr.* I paused.

"Have I grown complacent?" Beatrice met my gaze. "Have I lost my edge in the joy of finding family?"

"Frog freckles," I muttered. Then I *flowed*, and I hugged her.

After a moment she patted me on the back—much like a mother patting a gassy baby. I guess my great-times-great grandmother wasn't a hugger either. For some reason, that made me hug her a second time. Then I stepped back.

"That was . . . pleasant." Beatrice brushed her sleeves as if I'd left them crinkled or something. She seemed to re-center herself. Voice calm and expression implacable. "I dislike this."

"Murder?" Eli asked.

"No, of course not." Beatrice shot a disdainful look at him. "I simply prefer to own the murders I commit. They are strategic decisions to exert control and maintain order."

He met my eyes, as if to say, "do you see what she is?" I didn't think Eli truly objected to my growing closeness with

Beatrice, but sometimes I felt like he had taken on the task of being cautious when I was not.

I nodded at both of them, and then I asked Beatrice, "And the grant?"

"That remains to be seen." Beatrice smiled in a way that would make many a grown man quake; she was far from the knitting grannies of storybooks. My grandmother was a vicious —and proud—creature, and currently, she was livid. "I shall ask her that when we discuss these things. She did, however, leave the avian remains with your name on the package."

Daphne wasn't old enough to provoke a fight with Beatrice. The balance was tragically in Beatrice's favor, so why provoke her? Why be so transparent in leaving crow heads, corpses, and what were the playing cards about? And why pretend to be Beatrice?

"It doesn't track." I rolled what Beatrice had said in my mind. "Hebert likely had her son injected. She says she brought him to Houston, but she spoke of him in present tense."

"Did you feel his presence?"

"Wherever Christophe was, it wasn't at the Hebert place." I paused, pondering what I said next. How much was I trusting Beatrice? At this point, I guess I was as all-in as I got. My mother was at Beatrice's castle, and I was confiding in her. "Hebert knew my name. Knew I was a witch, knew I worked with NOPD. Desk guy at her building says Hebert hosts SAFARI parties."

I shook my head. I had an idea, a suspicion really. I held up my hand to Beatrice and texted my new friend Benjamin: "Have you seen this man?"

I did an internet search on my phone, and then saved and sent a picture of Tres.

"I cannot fathom a SAFARI member like her working with a *draugr*, even one as charming as Daphne," Beatrice continued as soon as I looked up from my phone. "Although . . . mother-hood can muddy the waters of even the dearest beliefs."

"It made my mother scr—"

Beatrice cut me off. "Do not speak ill of Lauren."

"Christophe was dying. Cancer," I said, back on topic.

"And Daphne killed some of the Prague group. The so-called vampires." Beatrice shook her head.

"A rose by any other name . . ." Eli murmured.

My phone chimed with a singular line: "Yummy Suit from NOLA? YES."

I sighed. Tres was connected with more than information. "My guy in Houston saw Tres at the Hebert building."

"We need to speak to him." Beatrice sounded calm, but nothing I knew about her made me think she meant only speak. One didn't rise to control the *draugr* in any way without violence.

"I'll do it," I said.

"No." Eli met my gaze, and I wanted to have the argument somewhere without a witness.

"He's my responsibility."

Beatrice cleared her throat.

"Let us speak of your joyous union. I give you these tokens as a small gift for your nuptials." Beatrice offered the gun to me. Then she motioned to the halberd. "A more suitable gift shall be yours upon the date of the ceremony."

Then she removed a pendant from her neck and walked over to Eli, careful not to let her mail shirt brush against him. Her shirt was steel of some sort, but the pendant was a stone on a long golden chain with an enormous fire opal. Such gems were always costly, but this one had vivid streaks of blue, gold, and orange that marked it as particularly pricy. It truly looked as if a flame burned inside.

"I carried this sunlight, my own reminder of when daylight

welcomed me." She twisted the chain, so the stone was caught and illuminated by the last bit of the day's sunlight that filtered through the trees overhead. "It was the first thing I had when I was free of masters. It was the one thing that was *mine*. I give it to you, Eli of Stonecroft, and I remind you that this that I have worn for *centuries* more than you have lived is nothing compared to the love of my family that burns in my heart. I've moved the seat of my crown to this place because of Lauren and Geneviève. I would cast that away sooner than my daughters."

Eli bowed his head to her, and she dropped the chain around his throat. I flinched, hoping that it was not iron in any way. That he trusted her enough to lower his head to allow this was as much a gift as one of the fae could give any *draugr*.

"With this stone comes my protection," she added, as if it was an aside. That protection, of course, was the real gift. The stone was symbolic. Beatrice added, "Anyone strong enough to be a threat will know that you are under my cloak if they see this."

"You are kind." Eli nodded and then gave her a deeper than usual bow.

Beatrice flashed fangs. "No, grandson. I am not kind at all. I simply know what it means that you are melded to Geneviève. To harm you is to harm her, and I would slaughter the nation for my daughters." She shrugged. "And so, too, with you."

I sighed loudly. "Well, this is festive. Maybe we ought to reconsider ceremonies and just ask for blood gifts."

"You are *draugr*-born. Such gifts are fitting." Beatrice shrugged delicately before she took a seat. She withdrew a carafe-thermos-thing that was decorated with fanged kittens. "Incidentally, I have brought blood. I wasn't sure if you were fed over *there*."

Eli accepted it and sat.

"Kittens?" I said.

Beatrice smiled. "Your Alice sent it to me."

As soon as I sat, too, Eli poured a serving of Beatrice's blood into the lid that functioned like a cheap cup and extended it to me. Something about his expression made me pause.

"Geneviève," he prompted.

That the fae needed to serve the food for one's spouse was going to take time to accept, but in some way, it was already easier because it was Eli. He'd been bringing my drinks to the table at Bill's Tavern for years.

I paused, rolling that detail over. He'd been bringing my drinks *personally* for years.

"You fed me," I accused. "For years now."

"Geneviève?" Eli's expression was unreadable.

"All those times at the bar. You *knew* that I lived on liquor. You *knew* it was my food." I stared at him with growing clarity. "You started doing that *years* ago."

He sounded remarkably calm as he explained, "I was attempting to court you, to indicate my interest in taking you as a bride."

I wanted to be irritated, but mostly I felt charmed. I'd been oblivious to his degree of interest for so long. "Years ago?"

"Years." He smiled. That was it. A smile.

How this amazing person picked me—with my temper, my prickly responses, my general tendency to bleed on his floor and person—would never stop astounding me. I found myself staring at him with a dopey grin.

"Let us speak of murder, though," Beatrice said, her words a big ol' bucket of ice water on my mood.

"Right. Murder. Committing or investigating?" I blinked.

"Yes." Beatrice stayed still, statue-like in the moment. "I have been debating the death of the Chaddock man. He gave them information. Your other servants are loyal, despite being mostly human. That one is not."

"We don't know how involved—"

"He was used as a tool, and we do not know for how long. That is a vulnerability. Vulnerabilities must be eliminated!" Beatrice sounded remarkably upset about it. "He is not mine to slay, though."

"Geneviève, perhaps you could give Tres to your grandmother as a thank you for her kindness," Eli suggested mildly, as if he was uninvested in this. We both knew that Tres Chaddock's attention to me irritated Eli.

It wasn't a bad idea, though. I'd tried to get Beatrice to do just that when I bonded Tres to me. Still, I had a responsibility to him since she'd refused. "I cannot allow his death or torture."

My grandmother scowled. "If I agree not to murder or unduly torture—"

"Define unduly torture."

"Maim. Leave permanent physical scars." Beatrice waved her hand dismissively. "He'd have all appendages when I was done."

"And his businesses?" Eli prompted.

"Would be run well, no loss of business income." She preened a bit. Warrior garb was suitable for her, but so was the "lady of the castle" persona. Beatrice didn't hold the crown simply because she was fierce; she was clever and manipulative —and proud of it. Without false modesty, she added, "I expect I'd increase his profits. I could offer the excess profit over the last three years' average to you as compensation for a twenty-year lease of the man."

"Three years," I countered.

"Fifteen." Beatrice grinned slightly.

"Six."

She smiled outright. "Ten. For ten years he is mine to manage, and the excess profit is your compensation."

"And no maiming, undue torture . . ."

"Yes. Yes. Summon him," Beatrice ordered.

CHAPTER TWENTY-FOUR

WE WERE AT ELI'S HOUSE. MY HOUSE NOW SINCE I WAS married to him. My brain realized that Eli and I needed to have a chat about money at some point. I hadn't married him expecting to have access to his, and I enjoyed the independence of making my own.

"Tres opened an account for me," I told Beatrice. "You can add the residuals to it."

Beatrice gave me that strange smile that was like laughter for her. "Unwilling to give me any information on your accounts."

"Trust issues when it comes to money," I said, not entirely lying but not exactly admitting that my issue was that she—much like Eli, Ally, and Tres—was likely to make random deposits. I didn't mind if I earned it, but I didn't ever want to feel beholden to anyone.

Eli muffled a word that might have been ruder than usual for him.

"Indeed," Beatrice murmured. "I will request that information from him when I am gathering information."

"I don't want to know." I shook my head. "Why don't we

meet at Bill's Tavern. I need to patrol, and then we can have Tres meet us there."

"Patrol," Beatrice echoed.

I stood and grabbed my nifty new halberd. It was overkill, huge and barbaric, but I was there as a result of someone wanting me on the street. Why not go big? It was Carnival.

"Patrol," I repeated. "Official liaison to the NOPD. Here to keep streets safer. The dead deader. And . . . try out my new toy."

Beatrice and Eli exchanged a look.

"How could anyone not love her?" Eli murmured.

Beatrice full-out smiled. "Indeed. Let us patrol then."

I gaped at her.

"Bonding time?" she tried. "That is what it's called today, is it not?" She smoothed her hands over her warrior garb. "I *am* dressed for spilling blood, Daughter of Mine. We can call it a hen party! Technically, it ought to have been before your wedding, but . . ."

Eli cleared his throat. "I'll leave you to your 'hen' party and meet you at the tavern. Midnight?"

I nodded.

"I will be sure Tres will be there, and I will invite the others for after Tres' departure with the Lady Beatrice," Eli said.

I frowned. "Why?"

"To tell them of your matrimony, Geneviève." Eli gave me the same patient look he always did, and I was reminded that while I wasn't a perfect wife by many standards, he still accepted me for me. There was no sanction, no disappointment in his voice or expression. Eli loved me as I was.

I launched myself at him in the sort of kiss that I'd have never offered before, but he was mine.

"Well, I'll see you after work, bonbon," I teased when I pulled back.

"I'll have dinner ready," he said in a similar tone. "Tequila? Or whisky?"

"Surprise me."

I swear Beatrice rolled her eyes, but if so, it was fast enough that I couldn't guarantee it. Did ancient dead grandmothers dressed for battle roll their eyes? I added it to the list of things I didn't know about fifty percent of my heritage.

Together we sauntered into the evening. Halberd in my hand. Sword at her hip. My clothes were shapeless tunic and leggings, tucked into a weathered pair of combat boots, and hers were medieval war garb.

"Just two ladies on the town," I said cheerily.

She snorted. I hear it this time, for sure! I shot her a look.

"St. Charles?" she prompted.

"It ought to be well-guarded. Parade starts soon." I looked at the evening sky, gold and purple streaks in a blue expanse. I'd thought that the sky often looked half-dressed for the coming Mardi Gras, but as we wound through crowds of locals and tourists, I admitted that sometimes it was hard to stand out in our city.

Twelfth Night was a fixed date—one we had passed a couple weeks ago now—but the culmination of Carnival season, Mardi Gras, fluctuated. We were about a third of the way there. Six weeks this year, with two down, meant that things were heating up. Once upon a time the best parades were at the end of the season, and there were fewer parades in the middle. Now, people's desire to celebrate in relative safety meant that by the third week we had three nights per week with impressive parades, and the streets were already a veritable mob.

"Do you feel different?" Beatrice asked as we walked.

"Because I'm married?"

"Because you are melded with a faery." She grinned at a midwestern couple snapping her picture.

I winced when the man said, "Can my wife get a picture with you?"

"Both of you." I suggested, taking their camera and deleting the picture.

Beatrice flashed fangs, licked her lips, and hissed. The couple scurried away, leaving their camera behind in haste.

"Was that necessary?"

She shrugged. "I didn't bite them. Tourists come here, end up dead, and yet the next year . . ." Beatrice gestured to the crowds in the street.

Locals had portable grills, lawn chairs, coolers. They sat and chatted, safety in numbers, staking their spots on the parade route as they had before the *draugr* were public. This was their city. Their entertainment. They celebrated as their ancestors had: as if it were a giant block party. The tourists, though, came here for something else. Drunk, lost, and easy to mug or bite.

"Show us your titties!"

"Yeah!"

Several men, raucous and stumbling, hollered at us. I ignored them. Beer-bellied middle-aged men were low on my priority list. I was strong enough that five men weren't as much of a threat as they would be to most women, but if I fought every drunk man—or sober one—who thought catcalling or posturing was manly, I'd run out of time in my days.

"Centuries pass, and buffoons are still the same." Beatrice's voice was thick was irritation. "I so rarely go into the city unaccompanied. . ."

She sounded disappointed, but not surprised. I made another mental note to ask her about the world she'd known as a human—and the changes she'd seen in her many centuries.

"Come on." I motioned for Beatrice to step in front of me. "Just ignore them."

"Awww! You protecting your girlfr—" The man's sugared

mocking voice was abruptly cut off as my dear old gran grabbed his balls.

"Do not come to my city with your vile"—she squeezed and the man let out a yip of pain—"behavior. If you are here, you are subject to the rule of the city."

"What rule?" one of his drunk friends said.

"*Mine.*"

They laughed. Obviously, they came from a city without *draugr.* Beautiful, fast, angry woman who is not intimidated by a group of large drunk men? Oh, and walks through the city dressed like she's an extra from a Renaissance Faire?

"Beatrice," I started.

"Daughter?" Her tone matched mine.

"Daughter!" one of the echoed. "Man, were you getting busy as a *kid?*"

"Maybe she had a lot of plastic surgery of that Botox stuff," another drunkenly offered.

I sighed. "Or maybe she's *dead.*"

They laughed—except the man whose balls Beatrice held captive. He was trying not to say a word. The rest laughed. Drunks. I drank a lot, but if it made me act like them, I think I'd be a teetotaler.

I gaped at them.

"Give me your words that you'll be courteous to women." Beatrice looked around at them. "That you'll stop behaving like swine."

I heard the intent in that question, the rushing threat, just as I felt a rush of magic.

"Simply say it, and I shall pardon you." Beatrice gave them a chilly smile. "One word."

For a split second I thought it was going to be resolved, but then two of them looked at each other. Both started snorting.

In the next moment, I was staring at five feral pigs. "Sweet mother of frog milk . . . you . . . *seriously?*"

People were staring. Cameras flashing.

Beatrice raised a hand, and I felt a surge of electricity wash over me. "What was that?"

"I believe it's akin to what people call E. M. P." Beatrice enunciated each letter with elongated pauses between them. "I have deleted their camera cards, phones, and the like."

"You did *what?*"

Beatrice's laughter was like the sound of warning bells. "Geneviève, how do think we have avoided photographs? Film? It is . . . like your octopus or squid or eel. We have a buildup of these charges for defense."

She smacked the pigs on the hindquarters with the flat of her sword, sending them running into the crowd. A satisfied look came over her. "This is fun!"

"Wait. . . but so all *draugr* can delete photographic proof of their presence?" I asked, needing clarification as much as wondering if I could do such a thing. Society at large had discussed their existence because of photos and film of them a few decades ago.

"Of course." She crossed her arms, watching the pigs run and get chased.

"So revealing yourself was . . ."

"The act of petulant children? Yes." Beatrice glanced at me. "They were emboldened by years of books and shows and films of vampires. They thought we would be welcomed with open arms and veins. That the world was a tolerant place." She shook her head. "As a woman, witch, and Jew . . . I didn't share such faith."

I nodded. What else was there to say? A simple look at history made clear that there were always those who would hate based on any reason—race, religion, gender, culture, political ideology. Hate was a thread through much of history, and I had my doubts that it would ever vanish. SAFARI was the hate group that was creating trouble here, but there were countless others in history and there would be others yet to come.

"Sadly, we can't turn all the haters into swine."

"It's easier than slaughter," Beatrice said. "It wears off, incidentally. My hope is that they'll reflect on their errors and feel remorse. Remorse will return them to human shape."

"So pigs and gators, hmm?" I thought about Sir George.

"The occasional serpent, a few squirrels . . . oh, and I restored the bison for a while. Created enough of them to help repopulate the Bad Lands." Beatrice continued striding through the crowd. "Iggy has a few usual spells and hexes to share with you, as do I."

"Is that what you intend to do with the SAFARI group?"

She laughed again. "No, dear. I intend to torture them until I know everything and feed them to George."

"Oh." I swallowed hard. I was squeamish, but torture wasn't something I could embrace. Hell, the last person who attempted to kill me was my assistant these days. "And Daphne?"

Beatrice patted my cheek, but she said nothing else.

As we patrolled, redirecting tourists, seeking Daphne, and looking for stray *draugr* noshing on tourists, I decided that some questions were best left unanswered.

CHAPTER TWENTY-FIVE

By the time we arrived at Bill's Tavern, I was no closer to answers than when I'd started the day. We'd killed several *draugr*, which didn't bother Beatrice.

"Obedience leads to longevity under my rule." She wiped blood from her face with a silk handkerchief that she then tucked in a pocket. "Never leave blood behind unless you nullify it. Quite a few unpleasant compulsions can be wrought with enough of a victim's blood."

I pushed away thoughts of all the places I'd bled over the years.

"Geneviève!" Jesse grabbed me as we walked toward the bar, scooping me up in a hug.

"Dead lady," I whispered in warning as I was in his embrace.

When he put me down, he stood so as not to block my ability to draw a weapon.

"I gave her those weapons, child." Beatrice sounded calm, but Jesse didn't recognize that she was being friendly. I could see his pulse pounding faster.

"He's mine, grandmother." I put my hand on Jesse's arm.

"This man, the women with him, they are my family as much as Mama Lauren. I would slaughter the nation for them."

She nodded, understanding the weight of my repeating her words to Eli. "I am only here to collect the Chaddock man. These others are your *loyal* minions, and so safe from me."

"Minion?" Jesse echoed.

I ignored him. "I need a drink."

"Rough day at the office?" came a voice from behind me.

And there was Eli. I all but melted into his embrace, tilting my head to invite a kiss. He brushed his lips over mine, still not excessive on public displays of affection.

"Honey, I'm home," I said as we pulled apart. "Did you miss me?"

"Did I miss a memo?" Jesse asked. "I mean, I know you were together but—"

Eli and I exchanged a look. He shrugged. This was my decision, my friends.

"I need to freshen up," Beatrice said, walking away to give me privacy.

A long moment passed as I tried to figure out exactly what to say. Finally, I settled on simple and direct. "We're married." I took Eli's hand. "It's done."

Jesse's eyes widened. "Whoa! You eloped or—"

I squirmed. How much I wanted to share was another question I hadn't quite sorted out. I was kind of winging it.

"The ceremony will be forthcoming." Eli smoothly redirected the topic. "Two, in fact. One here and one in *Elphame*."

Jesse was silent as we walked to a large table where Christy and Sera were waiting. Beatrice did not follow yet.

"Tell them." Jesse watched as Eli pulled out my chair.

Once I was seated, Eli opened a bottle of wine that was dusty enough that I knew it was older than I wanted to know.

He poured glasses for the five of us and lifted his glass in a toast. "L'chaim."

We echoed the toast, and I swore I might melt into a puddle of goo.

Sera looked from me to him and back. "Say it."

"Say . . ." I hedged, but I was grinning. "That I'm madly in love and married?"

Christy had a slow, Cheshire Cat smile creep over her. "Pay up."

Both Sera and Jesse got out cash.

"You had insider info," Jesse groused, not releasing the wad of cash.

Christy gave him a quelling glance. "You're her brother. That's the definition of insider info." Then she looked at Eli and held out a hand. "Pay up, Boss Man."

"Seriously?"

"I had more faith in your willpower . . . or . . . doubt in my charm." Eli shrugged.

And I realized it was love he feared wasn't real. I grabbed him and planted a kiss that had both of us gasping when we separated. "I love you, husband."

Eli stood and raised his voice, "May I present my bride, Geneviève Crowe." He motioned to the bartender. "Drinks to celebrate!"

Then, he looked around. "Tip your bartender and waitresses. My wife is not one to cross."

Laughter and cheers greeted his words, and I was overwhelmed with the way he looked at me here in public, with friends and witnesses.

"*Enjoy this moment*," Beatrice whispered into my mind. "*I shall stand guard.*"

I realized that she'd been at my side for that reason for hours. She'd worried when I was in *Elphame*. She'd patrolled with me. She was taking on the responsibility of Tres. And she was here tonight to watch over me until we knew exactly who funded the grant, what Hebert had to do with it, and where the lovely dead Daphne fit into the puzzle.

"*I have this.*" Beatrice looked at me from the barstool where she sat, lifted her glass and said, "*L'chaim.*"

In the next moment, I felt the approach of at least a six dead people. They were, as before, pockets of emptiness.

"*Friends.*" Beatrice nodded. "*Guards for the perimeter.*"

She'd brought back-up. For a moment, it was enough that I could almost forget that my dead great-times-great grandmother was there because of the threats against me and the threats against her. So, I settled into my husband's embrace and let the joy of celebration distract me for a few moments. I'd resume my patrols once Tres was sorted out, but the grant didn't stipulate that I had to work ten-hour shifts.

T wo hours later, Tres was a no-show. I called a few times. No Tres. No Ally. No Iggy.

My worries were starting to grow, and any remaining peace I had was shattered when a bullet came whizzing into the bar. I *flowed* as it came toward me, faster than was normal for me. *Draugr* were fast, but not bullet-dodging fast.

A high window broke a millisecond before the bullet thudded into the chair where I'd been seated a moment prior.

Shards of wood splintered, one drove into my thigh and others embedded into my forearm and leg. Apparently, even with extra speed, bullet dodging was still, in fact, impossible.

"Geneviève!" Beatrice was at my side. In a blink we were both *flowing.* Less than a second later, Sera, Christy, and Jesse were tucked behind the bar.

I wasn't fool enough to try to separate Eli from me. He had a sword raised and was ready to fight at my side.

"Geneviève?" was all he said.

"Uninjured." I looked around the room. Drunken revelers were cowering. Several people had guns or knives in hand. The expectation was that someone would come through the door or windows.

A few people hastily snapped those absurd bite collars around their throats. Bite Chokers were useless, but I could see the relief on faces—much like the relief that some had as they held beer bottles or knives that looked untested. There was a market for self-defense items these days. Designed and sold by rich folks in cities where they'd never need to field test those items themselves.

This wasn't *draugr*, though. They had even less need for Bite Chokers. The attackers were alive or I'd feel their presence.

I closed my eyes and . . . let go of my restraints. It was always relief to let my magic free. My magic rolled from Bill's Tavern into the streets of New Orleans. I felt the dead. Fallen and no longer moving.

"Beatrice?" I started, trying not to wince as I yanked the splinter of my chair out of my leg. "They're—"

"I know." She sounded like her civility was barely present. "Gone."

Her trusted *draugr*, the ones she'd summoned, were no more. A half-dozen loyal dead soldiers were now twice-dead. I couldn't fathom the planning of such an attack—or the brass balls it took to try to take them out. Who would be fool enough to incite the wrath of the queen of the monsters?

"They were aiming for you," Beatrice said, flicking her hand in the general direction of my wound. "They targeted my lieutenants and my rumored heir. When the ploy to seduce me failed, they resorted to this."

I blinked at her, not sure whether to ask why I was not spurting blood or about the rumored heir remark or how she knew my thoughts.

Beatrice shook her head. "You're projecting, Daughter of Mine. And I've applied a magical bandage. It should hold for an hour at best."

I nodded before letting my magic roll out again. I felt no active *draugr*. Only Beatrice. No walking dead either. "They're humans."

"Yes." Beatrice bit the word out, and I realized that she'd shoved her emotions into whatever cold, dark place she used to store her rage. This was not a calm woman. She was a about to go hunting—and as much as I disapproved of the way the dead preyed on the living, this was different. She was defending herself.

And I intended to be at her side.

I'd been accustomed to hunting the dead, not the living. A part of me rebelled at the realization that those who attacked were not *draugr*.

"I will handle this," Beatrice half-offered, half-declared.

But these were monsters, too. Beating hearts did not make them innocent. Hate thrived in many a mind.

"Bar the doors," someone yelled.

I glanced at Christy.

"Got it." She had passed out guns to Sera and Jesse. "We'll lock up."

Eli made an "after you" gesture, and there we were. My fae husband, my *draugr* grandmother, and whatever species-soup I was . . .

It wasn't the celebration I'd been having, but it would do.

CHAPTER TWENTY-SIX

ON THE STREET, IT WAS AS IF WE'D IMAGINED THE VIOLENCE. Crowds of people, most in varying states of drunkenness, laughed and meandered. Music poured from bars, and the police were increasingly wary. They weren't aware that a sniper had shot at me and beheaded six *draugr*—or maybe they didn't care.

Would I have cared a few months ago?

I couldn't answer that right now. I thought about the peculiar relationship my home city had with the *draugr*, and I wasn't sure how I felt tonight. On one hand, I swore sometimes we had a higher number of *draugr* bites because our public relations team was too good at their jobs. Somehow the fanged monsters that could envenomate victims—or just tear out throats—were a selling point thanks to a long history of mythologizing the city in fiction. Call them vampires, and suddenly folks forgot what they were. Luckily, whatever rules defined the *draugr*, they had a fail-safe: venom from a creature under a century old was unable to infect the living. Enough venom from any of the older *draugr* and a person woke up after death.

On the other hand, there were politics, a brutal sort of vying for power that recalled long ago barbarian tribes that hadn't yet accepted unification. It seemed vicious up close, but was it any different from more recent wars? Dropped bombs was less personal to the bomber—or drone pilot—but it was still vicious.

Deciding where I fell on the "monsters are bad" scale felt more complicated now that I was the granddaughter of the *draugr* queen. The only thing I still felt for certain was that shooting at me—or those I called family—was not forgivable.

Eli followed me as I tracked the pocket of dead in the city that was marked in my mind as Beatrice. I found her, looking like a raging goddess as she shook a human man. Her fangs were out, and her snake-shaped eyes were glittering in the yellow glow of the streetlights.

"Where did you get the information?" Beatrice demanded, lifting the man to her face as if he weighed nothing. His legs dangled and kicked like a child trying to escape. A rifle was on the ground, dropped there by the man.

People were watching in horror. What they didn't realize was that he was a sniper. He'd shot at us, but without that context, he was the victim.

"Audience," I muttered.

I wasn't sure what Beatrice intended, but she was the oldest, strongest person I'd ever met, and she was pissed off.

She *flowed*, carrying the man with her.

"Fuck," I yelled as Eli and I ran toward the angry *draugr*. I didn't want to *flow*, not with this many witnesses. They might be drunk, but they had cameras in hand.

"Hey! That's the faery prince and . . . shit. That's *them*."

"The royals!"

The cameras were on us then, and I made a note to learn that camera erasing trick of Beatrice's. I hated the idea of our images being splashed all over.

"Bonbon," Eli said as soon as we turned the corner. "*Flow*."

And we both did, following Beatrice into a graveyard. I felt her there, watched as she tore open a mausoleum and shoved the bleeding, human man inside.

"Stay," she ordered—not that he had much choice.

He was whimpering, and I had no idea what had been done to him in such a short time or if her rage was enough to frighten him. He looked at me.

"Help?" he pleaded, reached toward me from where he had crumpled in the dirt.

I looked away, turning my back on the man who had shot at me.

"You are lucky she found you before I did." Eli stared at the shooter. "Do we need him alive?"

"We shall see." Beatrice shrugged. "Corroboration and all that."

Eli scowled. "It is easier to handle such things in *Elphame*. No courts."

"Indeed." Beatrice shoed the stone back in place, trapping the man inside.

I tried not to think at the fact that they were lamenting a court of law—or that there was no court of law when I'd beheaded fangers. If one was caught in the act, I was a sword before word person. Why was this different? Was it?

"You're in shock." Eli wrapped an arm around me.

I nodded. It *had* been a lot. I was awake after a soul-meld, discovered that I was married, and nearly shot in a space of mere hours.

"Daphne is working for one of the government agencies." Beatrice frowned. "Her . . . *handler* offered her my empire in exchange for *cleansing* the city. Of me. Of witches. Of fae. They would start a war with such notions. She would rule my *draugr* in exchange for giving them an army of the dead for their military uses."

Eli tensed.

"An army of the dead," I echoed.

"They think to replace me and thereby give her power to command my *draugr.* To use us as weapons in their war machine." Beatrice's voice was radiating rage.

"My people are in *Elphame*." Eli sounded like earth to Beatrice's fire but I knew him too well to think him unmoved.

"They had not identified any of the fae here, but now"— Beatrice gestured at us—"there is you, Prince of *Elphame* and your betrothed. And though Geneviève is merely your betrothed in their knowledge, she is still a target. As if—"

"Grandmother." I took her hand and realized that she was shaking with rage. "Let us find Daphne."

Beatrice nodded, but then she dipped her head to Eli. "My word that this violence toward your people is not the wish of those who are under my rule, Heir of *Elphame*."

"That truth will be shared with my uncle." Eli bowed his head even deeper.

And for a flicker of a moment, I had to wonder if the larger goal had been war between *draugr* and fae. Was this a political plot to eliminate or greater decrease the number of both? Had some faction of the American government decided that they wanted to create bloodshed, so humans were once more the apex creature?

I wanted, suddenly, to send both Beatrice and Eli to safety, to handle this on my own—but I couldn't swear that I could defeat Daphne.

I thought back to her fear in the cemetery, and I had the thread of a plan. *Army of the dead*. I could give them that, but I doubted they'd appreciate it.

"Grandmother?"

Beatrice glanced at me.

"Can you trust me?" I took her hand. "I would ask to handle this."

"She is *draugr*," Beatrice began.

"And what would happen to the city without you ruling them?" Eli met her gaze.

For a flicker of a moment, I was shocked that he would go along with my idea here. Yes, he trusted me, but I was asking to absorb danger that could kill us both. I looked at him. "You could—"

"If you die, I die." He put a hand to my chest, covering my heart with his palm. "One pulse. One life."

I paused. The gravity of our marriage slammed into me. Every time I fought from tonight forward, I was risking *his* life.

"The fae do not wed without considering that." Eli gave me a look that was fraught with things I couldn't process tonight. "Warriors do not often wed for this reason."

I shoved that terror deep down inside. "I would ask that you let no one out of the cemetery. I will handle those inside, but to do that . . . no one who intends to survive can be in there with me."

"Geneviève?" Eli took my hand. "We can try other—"

"She's right." Beatrice gave me an appraising look. "We shall go there, lead them to the trap, and then. . ."

"You will *flow*. Both of you." I met Beatrice's gaze. "He can. I think. He did once before."

"I can carry him if not," she said with a small shrug.

A part of me thought that the plan I was building was more awful, more monstrous, more horrible than anything they'd done. It was certainly as bloody as a war.

But this was a war. This was a fight to protect my people— and the list of people I now had to defend was larger by the moment. I couldn't think on my grandmother's passing remark to me as her heir. I knew, though, with a horrible clarity that if I died, they would raise me as their queen. Witch-*draugr* was a rare thing. To my knowledge, we were the only two.

But dying would mean losing Eli, losing the throne of *Elphame*. They were, as of this marriage, my people. My responsibility. My subjects.

And any government slaughter of me and mine would not exclude my friends. Best case scenario, they were imprisoned. Worst case, they were "collateral damage."

I'd gone from collecting strays, as Eli said, to full-out mother bear. My cubs. Mine to protect. And after years of patrolling New Orleans, Mama Bear was a status I was fine with embracing. Daphne and her handlers had pissed off the wrong person.

CHAPTER TWENTY-SEVEN

ONCE WE HAD THE LARGER PLAN IN PLACE, BEATRICE HAD
argued that they knew they'd injured me, so believing I was
locked away was not a hard sell.

"Daphne is patriarchal," Beatrice muttered as we returned
to Bill's Tavern. "I can tell her that Eli locked you in his home."

To make that believable, Beatrice had paid a large sum to a
drunken tourist in the bar to switch clothes with me and be
swooped away to safety. The woman, of course, would not be
injured. She was accompanied by my closest friends.

As we waited, Eli and Christy cleared the bar.

"Don't want to be here when NOPD shows up." Christy
shooed the patrons out, recommending other bars as they filed
past her.

More than a few glanced at my grandmother, who was
dressed like a medieval warrior but sprouting fangs that looked
very real, or at me with my halberd, blue-hair, and scowl.

"I believe they might find you scarier, bonbon," Eli
murmured as he came to see me.

I stripped my outer layer of clothes, giving the drunk
woman my coat. Beatrice whispered a hex, turning the woman's

hair bright blue so it matched mine. Honestly hair and coat were enough, but sending my friends had the extra benefit of protecting them. Eli's house was impenetrable.

"Be careful." Christy squeezed me hard and gestured at Jesse, who was anxiously waiting, before she added, "I expect you around when I con this one into marrying me."

"She's *my* best woman," Jesse grumbled, shooting Christy a grateful look. "She thinks you'll stand up for her, but she has Sera. You're my sister."

"Married?" I echoed.

Christy shrugged like it was no big deal, but she grinned before saying, "It's contagious, I hear."

For a moment I thought I could pretend it was okay, that this very obvious distraction could allow us to avoid the reality, but reality was what it was. Ignoring it wouldn't change it. "If this goes sideways—"

"Gen!" Sera hugged me. "Shut up."

"No." I hugged each of them. "If I don't pull this off, tell Mama Lauren and King Fergus and Ally that it was my idea. Not Beatrice's or Eli's."

Jesse nodded. We all knew that if this went sideways, if I died, Eli would be dead, too. And somehow, I thought that if Beatrice survived, no one would believe she was innocent. I wouldn't have her second death on my conscience.

Once my friends—and my decoy—were gone, I handed Beatrice my halberd. "I get this back afterward."

She grasped the smooth wood. "To the fields of death, Daughter of Mine."

"Maybe don't mention that death-fields bit to Mama Lauren," I suggested.

Beatrice flashed a fang-filled smile and went to the door, leaving Eli and I alone. With *draugr* hearing, Beatrice could hear us, but the illusion of privacy was still nice.

"My warrior." Eli stared at me, not speaking or reaching out beyond that.

I took his hand. "I want eternity with you."

He nodded, and then he kissed me—not a goodbye kiss but one that spoke of promises to finish. And in that moment, I considered pulling him away and agreeing that the *draugr* could handle this trouble, but if *draugr* attacked known government employees or if the fae sent warriors, it would be the start of war.

I was one lone witch, and as far as the government knew, I was just a human. Defending myself from Daphne wouldn't start a war.

I hoped.

I watched Eli and Beatrice leave, very obviously and publicly hunting for Daphne. They would lead my prey to me.

I waited in the now-closed bar until I was sure that anyone trailing them would have followed. Then I went to Eli's office, peered through the shutters until I knew the coast was clear, and opened the window.

"*Iggy!*" I thought-yelled. "*I could use help tonight.*"

But no ghostly dead aid appeared. Wherever he, Ally, and Tres were, I hoped it wasn't more trouble. A bad feeling came over me, though, because calling for Iggy ought to bring him to me.

Carefully, I made my way to St. Louis Cemetery #1. They prey would be brought into my trap, as if I were a squat spider.

The cemetery was walled and closed at night, but during the day it was a tourist-filled disaster because it was reputedly the home of the grave of Marie Laveau, voodoo practitioner of much legend, as well as the Delphine LaLaurie, murderess and sadist who tortured captive slaves.

I rarely went there, as new graves weren't typically available so whatever dead rested there was not *draugr.* Tonight, however, it was perfect. Surprise again-walkers weren't a variable I wanted to add into an already risky plan.

I scaled the wall and waited, adjacent to the eye-sore of a tomb that some actor had built a few decades ago. In a lovely, mausoleum and memorial-filled cemetery, the modern ugliness of that pyramid made me surly. Apparently, wealth didn't buy taste, though.

I slid my sword out of the sheath, not yet cutting my arm.

And I waited for victims. I could call it something else, but tonight, that was what I was doing. I was a spider, and I awaited the flies.

Thirty or so minutes passed, and then I heard it: the clang of the chains at the wrought iron entrance gate to St. Louis #1. The gates, the chains, the locks, they all creaked and groaned thanks to the humid air rusting it all bit-by-bit.

I let my energy start to roll out, feeling one dead body at that gate. Then I caught the space of one that was both dead and alive.

"To my aid," I whispered, sliding my arm across the blade of my sword and *flowing* through the narrow passageways between mausoleums.

As I went, blood droplets hit the ground, beckoning the dead. I avoided the resting places that had been marked with voodoo symbols, not wanting to find out if LaLaurie or Laveau were in any of them.

Not content with only a few graves tonight, I lowered myself to the soil, letting my blood pour into the ground.

"An enemy comes," I said, spilling magic across the earth. "At my word, I need you."

Within these walls, I had an army, and I would use it.

Then, as I felt the ripple of the dead waking under the soil, I walked toward the center of the walled cemetery. I wanted it to be harder to get away. There would be no survivors in my enemies' forces.

"*No survivors,*" the dead echoed, rasping voices filling my mind like the shiver of serpents through dry grasses.

"*No prisoners.*"

"*Protect.*"

I hopped onto a mausoleum, wanting my dead army to stay still until I was ready. If they were here, no rational soul would walk toward me. I waited, blood dripping onto stone not soil now.

When Daphne finally came, her soldiers had Tres, Ally, and Iggy in tow. Iggy looked furious, and Ally had a black eye. Tres was stumbling, but he had his eyes down.

"Well, if it isn't Beatrice's little witch," Daphne said. "We were disappointed that you were hiding."

A group of maybe thirty to forty people. They weren't dressed in uniforms, but they were human, taking orders from a *draugr,* and the sniper earlier had a military-issued rifle.

"Did they give you the rejected soldiers?"

"These are highly trained—"

"Your sniper missed." I hopped down, my arms behind me. "Ally? Iggy?"

"Fine." Iggy nodded, and Ally shrugged.

Tres looked up, eyes locking with mine. "I shall atone."

"It wasn't his fault, Boss." Ally jerked away from the man holding her bound hands. "They surrounded the building. Shot Ig and Tres through windows."

"You don't want to do this," I said, flexing my hands, milking the blood from my cut so it dripped steadily on the soil. "What do you hope to gain?"

"Grab her." Daphne gestured. "She'll be a useful bait to lure out Beatrice. Since the grant didn't get her killed . . ."

"You funded the grant?" I shook my arm, letting blood fling to the soil.

"My employer." Daphne shrugged. "Since that buffoon wouldn't kill you, I had to try a bribe."

"Buffoon?"

"Chaddock." She scowled at Tres. "I sullied myself with him, and . . ."

"Hands where I can see them." A man with a rifle came toward me and jabbed me with the muzzle of his rifle.

"No." I *flowed* toward Daphne, not underestimating her this time. I wrapped my body around her, both arms holding her, and said, "I like it here."

"Shoot them both." A man spoke, and a clatter of sound followed rifles raising toward us.

"Protect me," I said, voice low. "They mean me harm."

Daphne began to struggle. "Bitch!"

And the ground began to rumble. I felt them, body after body, corpse after corpse. They were awake and ready. My word made the earth roil.

Bullets did nothing to stop the dead. They were already dead, beyond pain and when they returned to the grave any insult or injury would vanish.

I shoved Daphne away and *flowed* to Ally. I jerked her toward me as Tres turned and savaged his captor.

It should have been horrifying, but Ally was mine to protect.

"Give her to the corpse to get her out, Hexen." Iggy's eyes began to glow. "Draw from the dead."

At first, I didn't understand, but then I remembered leaving him desiccated by drawing his magic. I looked at Tres and ordered, "Get her to Beatrice. Stay with her. *Go!*"

As soon as Tres and Ally were gone, I met Iggy's eyes. "Tell me."

I felt images flood my mind, saw the locations of any witch in the earth. "Above."

I shoved my reach into the mausoleums, and I found them —witches, voodoo practitioners, priests, rabbis. Those who connected to something greater than this mortal plane had a spark inside. That was why some bodies were housed in stone. They were dangerous to rouse.

I understood why I could not force Iggy to the grave.

"Questions later, Hexen." He gestured. "Funnel this through me, and I will guide you."

I nodded, and then I tugged, pulling magic from the graves of those who had gone before me. That magic I siphoned into my will and toward Iggy. He was able to direct it, even if I couldn't.

I stumbled, falling to my knees from the weight of it.

"Stay with me, Geneviève. We are so close."

Iggy sounded stronger, and I glanced at him. He was a conduit, sending my will to the dead.

"Tell them to live," he urged. "Order them to remove this threat. Take it to the soil, and then be free."

I echoed his words, shoving them toward Iggy with the magic I'd drawn.

My army of the dead began to embrace the soldiers—and the remains of Daphne. As the dead sunk back into the soil, they took pieces of those enemies in their hands. Those who had the foreign flesh would not rise at any command again.

But neither would my enemies.

No guns. No cameras. No evidence remained. It was all under the soil, and I was prone on the ground, staring up at Iggy. A very alive and breathing Iggy.

"What . . .?" I trying to push myself up, but I was too drained.

"You said to live, to remove the threats, and be free." Iggy smoothed his suit and smiled at me. "I simply obeyed."

"You're a monster, Ignatius Blackwood."

"Indeed I am." He bowed his head. "And a liar, Hexen, but let there be peace between us for now."

And I saw in a flash that the man calling himself Master Blackwood was both more and less than before. The image of Baron Samedi, loa of the dead, hovered over him briefly, but then was gone.

"I've worn many names. I've lived many lives." He looked around. "But if not for a dutiful servant, I'd have been bound in a box as poor Marie was."

"Laveau?"

He nodded. "Someday you will avoid that as you lured a faery into your clutches. Beatrice avoided it by becoming *draugr.* I had to find another option."

"But if I hadn't raised you . . ."

Iggy crouched down beside me, ignoring my question, and said, "My heart beats again, Geneviève of Crowe, because of you. For this, I am in your debt."

Then Iggy strolled away, leaving me there. I was too drained to stand. Alone on the ground, I looked at the green grass, at the repaired grave markers, and I saw that there had been so much magic channeled through me that good had been wrought. There was no battle, no war, and no enemy to carry tales.

But there was something more ferocious than that, and I had raised him myself.

CHAPTER TWENTY-EIGHT

"Geneviève?" Eli crouched down and scooped me into his arms.

"Everyone okay?" I asked.

"Yes." Eli marched through the graveyard toward the still-open gate, carrying me bridal-style. He was angry. I could feel it.

"Sorry." I wasn't sure what I'd done, but I figured I should apologize.

He paused. "I passed out, presumably when you did. Then, Beatrice reluctantly brought me here."

"I'm missing something." I wasn't sure if it was my exhaustion or what, but Eli's tone was reserved.

"The cemetery was under a dome. Impervious." Eli glanced down. "Beatrice, Lauren, and I tried, but could not fracture it. And Blackwood was nowhere to be found . . . was he reinterred?"

"Iggy is alive and . . ." I gestured toward the city.

"Alive?"

"Very." I rested my head against Eli. "Can we wait until later to deal with the next disaster, Eli?"

He kissed my forehead and strode toward the gate, holding

me aloft. Despite the way I typically felt about such a position, I was fine with it. I had little faith that I could stand, and I knew that my husband wouldn't suddenly think I was weak if I allowed him to carry me after exhausting myself protecting all of us.

"Take me home, Eli."

"Yours or mine?" He carried me through the gate. His car was parked there.

I slid from his arms, so I was standing staring at him, leaning against him. His hands fell on my hips, and I swayed toward him. Tilting my face to look up at him, I admitted, "Home is where you are."

He opened the car door, so I could slide-fall-fold into the passenger seat.

"Your house will need repairs." Eli clicked my seatbelt. "And my house is a refuge for Christy, Jesse, and Sera."

"The Outs? *Elphame*? I just want somewhere to sleep in your arms." I was weary in a way that magic had typically not left me. "Take me somewhere we can rest."

"*Elphame*." Eli closed my door and went to the driver's side. Inside the car, he dialed a number and handed me the phone.

"Eli? Have you—"

"Jesse, it's me." I cut into his question. "Tell everyone I'm fine. *Everyone*. Mama Lauren, too. Have her tell my grandmother. And call Ally."

"Damn it, Gen. We weren't able to get to you, not even Mama Lauren." Jesse sounded angry, relieved, and exhausted all at once.

"I'm fine. Threats handled. Witch sleepy." I looked over at Eli as he drove. "We'll park the car at Eli's house. You guys can stay there tonight. We're going . . . home to *Elphame* for a bit."

"Gen . . ."

"I need somewhere safe to sleep." I reached out to take Eli's hand. "And I'm a newlywed, Jesse. I have a husband who owes me—"

"Nope! Don't want to hear it." Jesse laughed though. "You're my little sister, Geneviève. I don't need to hear about some man debauching you."

"Mmm. Debauching," I teased.

"Do not say a word," Jesse ordered. "But, Gen? I'm glad you're not dead. We all are."

I smiled. "So go do my biding, brother. Make some calls. Then relax. I'll be home by morning."

"Morning?"

"Time moves differently," I reminded him. "Love you, Jess. Tell the others, too."

Once we disconnected, I squeezed Eli's hand and admitted, "I'm far too tired for debauchery, love."

He raised my hand and kissed it. "So, we rest first. I have eternity, Geneviève. I can wait a few moments more."

The following morning, waking in *Elphame*, in our home there, I snuggled closer to Eli. My husband. It wasn't what I'd planned, expected, or anything of the like, but I loved him in a way that really was mind-bending.

I traced the line of his ribs, marveling at the fact that we were here. He was a miracle to me. Beautiful in the way of the sort of art that ought to be protected by cameras and guards, but he was here, touchable and close.

I propped myself up and studied him. Muscles and flesh, lips that were full enough that they always looked freshly kissed.

I traced his mouth with my finger.

"Wife." He opened his eyes and stared at me.

I moved so I was straddling him. I loved foreplay, and I

loved Eli, but today, finally, I wanted one thing only. His hand came to hold my hip, squeezing my skin enough to bruise and drawing a whispered noise from my lips.

"I was going to ask if you felt rejuvenated . . ." Eli stared up at me. "But I think I have my answer."

"And an invitation. Make love to me, husband." I bent, covering his mouth and kissing him as he guided my descent onto him.

"Geneviève."

His hips rose, and we moved together. Slow, steady, and never breaking the locked gaze between us. It was both the most direct and slowest thing we'd ever done, but it was exactly what I needed.

"Mine," I whispered.

"As you are mine."

Later, there would be time for things that were less gentle, but on this, our first act as a married couple, I wanted only the one thing we had been denied. Eli filled me, and together we chased bliss as a newly married couple.

CHAPTER TWENTY-NINE

IN THE MORNING—WELL, THE MORNING MANY DAYS LATER—I slipped out of bed after whispering to my drowsy spouse, "I'll be right back."

Eli opened his eyes. "I need to speak to my uncle."

I nodded, and with a lighter spirit than I usually had, told him, "I'm going to work for a minute."

At that, Eli chuckled. "And after work?"

"Oh, I have plans with my husband." I kissed him, trying to resist the urge to crawl back into his arms. "My gorgeous"—kiss—"naked"—kiss—"husband."

"Lucky man." His hand traced up my thigh, and without thought, I parted my legs to give him more access.

Head thrown back in joy, I said nothing but his name, as he reminded me that everything he did was somehow exactly what I needed. Between tongue and hands, my husband had me quaking in mere moments.

"Miss me," he ordered, as my knees gave out under the wave of pleasure. "Come home to me."

I swallowed and nodded. "Yes."

Somehow countless days locked in, barely leaving the bed,

had only taken the edge off my need. I swore that touching Eli made me want more no matter how often I did so, but I needed to check in at home before we locked ourselves away longer.

So I backed away, and then I *flowed* to the doorway.

"If I don't go now, I don't know if I can," I confessed. "It's morning there."

His smug grin wasn't helping my resolve, nor was the sight of his naked body. "Wouldn't want to distract you . . ."

I stared at him as he stood and took a step toward me. "Tease."

"Tease . . . but with promises to deliver."

I flowed out of the house, his joyous chuckle following me.

When I stepped through the veil into Eli's—into *our*—yard, I saw Ally in her car. She was sitting there, singing as if it was any other day. If not for her blackened eye, I might be able to pretend it was.

"Boss!" She was out of the car and running. Her hug was more tackle than embrace, and I stumbled at the force of it.

"Ally." I squeezed her. "I'm so sorry."

"Not your fault." She pulled back and studied me. "They said you were okay but. . ."

"I needed a nap."

"Makes sense." Ally shrugged and walked over to her car. "Beatrice is waiting."

I didn't ask how she knew that, but Ally had no ability to keep secrets from me. She grinned when I got into the car. "I told her I'd check in with her today. She did some sort of calculations between Eli's world and here."

When we parked, Ally held out dark shades and an umbrella.

"It's not raining." I slipped the dark glasses on. The sun still wasn't my friend, even with Eli's blood mixing with mine. I sighed. "I don't need an umbrella, Allie."

She looked at me with a familiar frustration and patience. "It's a *parasol* for sun."

I took it, noting that what I thought were flowers were little blood droplets with thin legs and feet. Ally had given me a dancing blood parasol, but at glance, it looked almost feminine if you thought the cheery blood drops were flowers. I stared at it.

"Don't forget your beet juice!" she called, shaking another travel mug. This one, fortunately, was black.

And then she was gone, snapping open her own parasol covered in some designer's insignia and walking into a small group of people who were headed to the pre-dawn coffee vendors. Ally wasn't quite *this* much of a morning person, and she wasn't entirely sure of her feelings about Tres or Beatrice today.

I sat at the bench in Jackson Square. This early, the city was either recently to their beds or not yet awake. The dawn light was creeping out of the night, and objectively it was lovely.

My grandmother arrived a few moments later. She was put together in the way of regents of old, a high Elizabethan collar topped a fur-trimmed cloak. Under it was a fitted gown that looked like it required corset and other layers.

"How do you breathe?" I asked as she stood beside the bench.

"Dead." She gave me a small smile. "As you may recall. . ."

I motioned for her to sit. "Can you fight in it?"

She quirked her lips. "In all these centuries no one else has dared ask."

Beatrice reached under her cloak and in a moment, the constricting dress fell to her feet, revealing leggings and a corset top.

I laughed. "What fools anyone must be to underestimate you."

"Indeed." She sat beside me, silent for a moment. "No one of import lost to us, as I understand."

"Iggy. . ."

Beatrice sighed. "That man has ever been trouble."

"He's alive now."

She gave me a look, but she said nothing. So, I filled her in on what she'd missed. When I finished, Beatrice stayed silent. "These soldiers . . ."

"More may come." I hoped I was wrong, but I wasn't sure. "And I don't know how Hebert fits."

"Should I handle her?" Beatrice murmured.

"It would be easier," I allowed.

Beatrice flashed a satisfied look my way. It was as close to a gloat as I'd seen her come—well, with me.

"This doesn't mean I'm suggesting she die," I clarified.

"Nor have I offered to commit that act today." Beatrice smiled at Ally, as she approached. "If Miss Crowe grows bored of you, child, you may call me."

Ally straightened up to diminutive height and met my ancestor's gaze. "I'm loyal to Geneviève."

"Well, of course you are child." Beatrice nodded. "I shall allow Tres to remain human for now."

"*Draugr* . . ." I started.

"Not a pig," Beatrice said mildly, clarifying her point.

"A pig?" Ally echoed. "You can do that?"

"I will send someone to watch Madam Hebert," Beatrice said. The glint in her eyes didn't inspire a lot of confidence in the safety of the elder Hebert, but protecting racists wasn't my priority.

Then she was gone.

And I was alone with Ally watching the sun rise. I still didn't know how Madame Hebert fit in, but I knew that

Daphne and her soldiers were gone. I knew that the grant was now harmless.

And my friends and husband were safe for now.

The king of *Elphame* would undoubtedly have opinions about this mess, and Iggy . . . I had no idea what to think about him. Was he a loa? Or had he simply caught Baron Samedi's attention?

"Are you okay, Boss?" Ally asked.

"I am. Weirdly so." I shook my head. "Maybe I shouldn't be, but . . ."

Ally gave me a sad look. "You married your soulmate. That makes even the lousiest things okay."

I hugged her, wanting to chase the sad away. "And I have good friends. That helps a lot, too."

She grinned. "Truth, Boss. Fucking *truth*."

Later, I could conquer the rest. In this moment I was a woman who had great friends, a weird but loving family, a well-paying job, and an amazing husband. Life was pretty okay. And the rest of the disasters could wait. I was enjoying sunrise with my friends, and then I was going home to *Elphame* to my husband.

The Wicked & The Dead is AVAILABLE NOW!

"I loved *The Wicked and The Dead*! A sassy, ass-kicking heroine, a deliciously mysterious fae hero, and a wonderful mix of action and romance. Add that to Melissa's usual great world-building, and I'm already looking forward to book 2!"
— Jeaniene Frost, *NYT* Bestselling Author

GENEVIÈVE CROWE MAKES HER LIVING BEHEADING THE DEAD. But now, her magic has gone sideways, and the only person strong enough to help her is the one man who could tempt her to think about picket fences: Eli Stonecroft, a faery bar-owner in New Orleans.

When human businessmen start turning up as *draugar*, the queen of the again-walkers and the wealthy son of one of the victims, both hire Geneviève to figure it out. She works to keep her magic in check, the dead from crawling out of their graves, and enough money for a future that might be a lot longer than she'd like. Neither her heart nor her life are safe now that she's juggling a faery, murder, and magic.

EXCERPT OF THE WICKED & THE DEAD

The Wicked & The Dead
AVAILABLE now!

CHAPTER 1

Autumn in the South was still both humid and hot. New Orleans was always a wet city. Wet air. Wet drizzle. Beer soaked streets. *Other* things spilling out from behind trash bins. Sometimes, the heavy air and frequent rain was just this side of too much.

Most nights, there was nowhere else I'd rather be. We were a city risen from the ashes, over and over. Plagues, floods, monsters. New Orleans didn't stop, didn't give up, and I was proud of that. Tonight, though, I watched the fog roll out like a cheap film effect, and a good book in front of a warm fire sounded far better than work. The nonstop rain this month would wash away evidence of the things that happened in New Orleans' darkened corners, but I could prevent bloodshed. It was more or less what I did. Sometimes, I spilled a bit of blood, but if we weighed it all out, I was fairly sure I was one of the good guys.

More curves and sass than actual *guys*, but the point held. White hat. Dingy around the edges. I blame my persistent nagging guilt.

A *thump* on the other side of the wall made me pause.

Could I hurl myself over the wall into Cypress Grove Cemetery? It wasn't the *worst* idea ever—or even this month—which said more about my life than I'd like to admit.

I listened for more sounds. *Nothing.* No scrabbling. No growling.

I needed to be on the other side of the wall where tombs were lined up like miniature houses. The tree branches I'd used last time were gone, probably trimmed by someone who saw their potential. Now, there was no graceful way to hurl myself over the ten-foot wall.

Every cemetery in the nation now had taller walls and plenty of newly-opened space for the dead. Cemeteries had become "stage one" of the verification of death process. Honestly, I guess graves were better than cold storage at the morgue. The lack of heartbeat made it impossible to know if the corpses would walk again, and those of us who advocated for beheading all corpses were deemed callous.

I wasn't sure I was callous for wanting the dead to stay dead. I knew what they were capable of before the world at large did.

At least I was prepared. A moment or so later, I shoved a metal spike into the wall, cutting my palm in the process.

"Shit. Damn. Monkey balls."

A ripple of light flashed around me the moment my blood dripped to the soil. At least the light was magic, not the police or a tourist with a camera. While the laws were ever-changing, B&E was still illegal. And I was breaking into a cemetery where I might need to carry out a contracted beheading. *That* was illegal, too.

It simply wasn't a photo-ready moment—although with my

long dyed-blue hair and nearly translucent skin, I was far too photogenic. I won't say I look like I've been drained of both blood and color, but I will admit that next to a lot of the folks in my city, I look like I've been bleached.

I fumbled with my gloves, trapping my blood inside the thick leather before I resumed shoving climbing cams into gaps in the wall. Normally, cams held the ropes that climbers use. Tonight, they'd be like tiny foot supports. If I were human, this wouldn't work out well.

I'm not.

Mostly, I'd say I am a witch, but that is the polite truth. I am more like witch-with-hard-to-explain-extras. That smidge of blood I'd spilled was enough to send out "wakey, wakey" messages to whatever corpses were listening, but the last time I'd had to bleed for them to rest again, I'd needed to shed more than a cup of blood.

I concentrated on not sending out a second magic flare and continued to insert the cams.

Rest. Stay. I felt silly thinking messages to the dead, but better silly than planning for excess bleeding.

At least this job *should* be an easy one. My task was to find out if Alice Navarro was again-walking or if she was securely in her vault. I hoped for the latter. Most people hired me to ease their dearly departed back in the "departed" category, but the Navarro family was the other sort. They missed her, and sometimes grief makes people do things that are on the wrong side of rational.

My pistol had tranquilizer rounds tonight. If Navarro was awake, I'd need to tranq her. If she wasn't, I could call it a night —unless there were other again-walkers. That's where the beheading came in. Straight-forward. Despite the cold and wet, I still hoped for the best. All things considered, I really was an optimist at heart.

At the top of the wall, I swung my leg over the stylish spikes cemented there and dropped into the wet grass. I was braced for it, but when I landed, it wasn't dew or rain that made me land on my ass.

An older man, judging by the tufts of grey hair on the bloodied body, in a security guard uniform had bled out on the ground. Something--most likely an again-walker--had gnawed on the security guard's face. Who had made the decision to have a living man with no special skills stand inside the walls of a cemetery? Now, he was dead.

I whispered a quick prayer before surveying my surroundings. Once I located the *draugr*, I could call in the location of the dead man. First, though, I had to find the face-gnawer who killed him. Since my magic was erratic, I didn't want to send a voluntary pulse out to find my prey. That would wake the truly dead, and there were plenty of them here to wake.

Several rows into the cemetery, I found Alice Navarro's undisturbed grave. No upheaval. No turned soil. Mrs. Navarro was well and truly dead. My clients had their answer—but now, I had a mystery. Which cemetery resident had killed the security guard?

A sound drew my attention. A thin hooded figure, masked like they were off to an early carnival party, stared back at me. They didn't move like they were dead. Too slow. Too human. And *draugar* weren't big on masks.

"Hey!" My voice seemed too loud. "You. What are you . . ."

The figure ran, and several other voices suddenly rang out. Young voices. Teens inside the cemetery.

"Shit cookies!" I ran after the masked person. Who in the name of all reason would be in among the graves at night? I ran through the rows of graves, looking for evidence of waking as I went.

"Bitch!"

The masked figure was climbing over the wall with a ladder, the chain sort you use in home fire-emergencies. Two teens tried to grab the person. One kid was kneeling, hand gripping his shoulder in obvious pain.

And there, several feet away, was Marie and Edward Chevalier's grave. The soil was disturbed, as if a pack of excited dogs had been digging. The person in the mask was not the dead one in the nearby grave. There *was* a recently dead *draugr*.

And kids.

I glanced back at the teens.

A masked stranger, a dead security guard, a *draugr,* and kids. This was a terrible combination.

The masked person dropped something and pulled a gun. The kids backed away quickly, and the masked person glanced at me before scrambling the rest of the way over the wall—all while awkwardly holding a gun.

"Are you okay?" I asked the kids, even as my gaze was scanning for the *draugr*.

"She stabbed Gerry," the girl said, pointing at the kid on the ground.

The tallest of the teens grabbed the thing the intruder dropped and held it up. A syringe.

"She?" I asked.

"Lady chest," the tall one explained. "When I ran into her, I felt her—"

"Got it." I nodded, glad the intruder with the needle was gone, but a quick glance at the stone by the disturbed grave told me that a fresh body had been planted there two days ago. That was the likely cause of the security guard's missing face. I read the dates on the stone: Edward was not yet dead. Marie was.

I was seeking Marie Chevalier.

"Marie?" I whispered loudly as the kids talked among themselves. The last thing I needed right now was a *draugr* arriving to gnaw on the three dumb kids. "Oh, Miss Marie? Where are you?"

Marie wouldn't answer, even if she had been a polite Southern lady. *Draugr* were like big infants for the first decade and change: they ate, yelled, and stumbled around.

"There's a real one?" the girl asked.

I glanced at the kids. I was calling out a thing that would *eat* them if they had been alone with it, and they seemed excited. Best case was a drooling open-mouthed lurch in my direction. Worst case was they all died.

"Go home," I said.

Instead they trailed behind me as I walked around, looking for Marie. I passed by the front gate—which was now standing wide open.

"Did you do that?" The lock had been removed. The pieces were on the ground. Cut through. Marie was not in the cemetery.

Shaking heads. "No, man. The ladder the bitch used was ours."

Intruder. With a needle. Possibly also the person who left the gate open? Had someone wanted Marie Chevalier released? Or was that a coincidence? Either way, a face-gnawer was loose somewhere in the city, one of the who-knows-how-many *draugar* that hid here or in the nearby suburbs or small towns.

I pushed the gates closed and called it in to the police. "Broken gate at Cypress Grove. Cut in pieces."

"Miss Crowe," the woman on dispatch replied. "Are you injured?"

"No. The *lock* was cut. Bunch of kids here." I shot them a look. "Said it wasn't them."

"I will send a car," she said. A longer than normal pause. "Why are *you* there, Miss Crowe?"

I smothered a sigh. It complicated my life that so many of

the cops recognized me, that dispatch did, that the ER folks at the hospital did. It wasn't like New Orleans was *that* small.

"Do you log my number?" I asked. "Or is it my voice?"

Another sigh. Another pause. She ignored my questions. "Details?"

"I was checking on a grave here. It's intact, but the cemetery gate's busted," I explained.

"I noted that," she said mildly. "Are the kids alive?"

"Yeah. A person in a mask tried to inject one of them, and a guard inside is missing a lot of his face. No *draugr* here now, but the grave of Marie and Edward Chevalier is broken out. I'm guessing it was her that killed the guard."

The calm tone was gone. "There's a car about two blocks away. You and the children—"

"I'm good." I interrupted. "Marie's long gone, I guess. I'll be sure the kids are secure, but—"

"Miss Crowe! You don't know if she's still there or nearby. You need to be relocated to safety, too."

"Honest to Pete, you all need to worry a lot less about me," I said.

She made a noise that reminded me of my mother. Mama Lauren could fit a whole lecture in one of those "uh-huh" noises of hers. The woman on dispatch tonight came near to matching my mother.

"Someone *cut* the lock," I told dispatch. "What we need to know is why. And who. And if there are other opened cemeteries." I paused. "And who tried to inject the kid."

I looked at them. They were in a small huddle. One of them dropped and stomped the needle. I winced. That was going to make investigating a lot harder.

Not my problem, I reminded myself. I was a hired killer, not a cop, not a detective, not a nanny.

"Kid probably ought to get a tox screen and tetanus shot," I muttered.

Dispatch made an agreeing noise, and said, "Please try not to 'find' more trouble tonight, Miss Crowe."

I made no promises.

When I disconnected, I looked at the kids. "Gerry, right?"

The kid in the middle nodded. White boy. Looking almost as pale as me currently. I was guessing he was terrified.

"Let me see your arm."

He pulled his shirt off. It looked like the skin was torn.

"Do not scream," I said. My eyes shifted into larger versions of a snake's eyes. I knew what it looked like, and maybe a part of me was okay with letting them see because nobody would believe them if they did tell. They were kids, and while a lot had changed in the world, people still doubted kids when they talked.

More practically, though, as my eyes changed I could see in a way humans couldn't.

Green. Glowing like a cheap neon light. The syringe had venom. *Draugr* venom. It wasn't inside the skin. The syringe was either jammed or the kid jerked away.

"Water?"

One of the kids pulled a bottle from his bag, and I washed the wound. "Don't touch the fucking syringe." I pointed at it. "Who stomped on it? Hold your boot up."

I rinsed that, too. Venom wasn't the sort of thing anyone wanted on their skin unless they wanted acid-burn.

"Venom," I said. "That was venom in the needle. You could've died. And"—I pointed behind me—"there was a *draugr* here. Guy got his face chewed off."

They were listening, seeming to at least. I wasn't their family, though. I was a blue-haired woman with some weapons and weird eyes. The best I could do was hand them over to the police and hope they weren't stupid enough to end up in danger again tomorrow.

New Orleans had more than Marie hiding in the shadows. *Draugr* were fast, strong, and difficult to kill. If not for their need to feed on the living like mindless beasts the first few decades after resurrection, I might accept them as the next evolutionary step. But I wasn't a fan of anything—mindless or sentient—that stole blood and life.

Marie might have been an angel in life, but right now she was a killer.

In my city.

If I found the person or people who decided to release Marie—or the woman with the syringe--I'd call the police. I tried to avoid killing the living. But if I found Marie, or others like her, I wasn't calling dispatch. When it came to venomous killers, I tended to be more of a behead first, ask later kind of woman.

———

BLOOD MARTINIS & MISTLETOE (FAERY BARGAINS NOVELLA)

May 18, 2021
Faery Bargains Book 2

Blood Martinis & Mistletoe (A Faery Bargains Novella)
Coming April 15, 2021
Pre-Order Now

BLOOD MARTINIS & MISTLETOE

Half-dead witch Geneviève Crowe makes her living beheading the dead--and spends her free time trying not to get too attached to her business partner, Eli Stonecroft, a faery in self-imposed exile in New Orleans. With a killer at her throat and a blood martini in her hand, Gen accepts what seems like a straight-forward faery bargain, but soon realizes that if she can't figure out a way out of this faery bargain, she'll be planning a wedding after the holidays.

Note: Takes place between Books 1 and 2

EXCERPT OF BLOOD MARTINIS & MISTLETOE

GIANT ALUMINUM BALLS HUNG AROUND ME EVEN THOUGH I was standing in the cemetery not long before dawn. I didn't know who hung the balls, but I wasn't too bothered.

Winter in New Orleans was festive. We might have *draugr* and a higher than reasonable crime rate, but damn it, we had festivities for every possible occasion. Gold, silver, red, blue, purple, and green balls hung from the tree. Samhain had passed, and it was time to ramp up for the winter holidays.

November--the month after Samhain--was uncommonly active for necromancy calls. Unfortunately, a certain sort of person thought it was festive to summon the body and spirit of Dear Uncle Phil or Aunt Marie. Sometimes the relatives were maudlin, and sometimes they were thinking about the afterlife.

Now, the dead don't tell tales about the things after death. They can't. I warn folks, but they don't believe me. They pay me a fair amount to summon their dead, so I always stress that the "what happens after we die" questions are forbidden. Few people believe me.

Tonight, I had summoned Alphard Cormier to speak to his widow and assorted relatives or friends who accompanied her. I didn't ask who they were. One proven relation was all I needed. Family wasn't always just the folks who shared your blood.

Case in point, the faery beside me. Eli of Stonecroft was one of the people I trusted most in this world—or in any other. I closed my eyes for a moment, which I could do because he was at my side. I was tired constantly, so much so that only willpower kept me upright.

"Bonbon," Eli whispered. His worried tone made clear that a question or three hid in that absurd pet name.

Was I going to be able to control my magic? Did he need to brace for *draugr* inbound? Were we good on time?

"It's good." I opened my eyes, muffled a yawn, and met his gaze. "I'm still fine."

Eli nodded, but he still scanned the graves. He was increasingly cautious since my near-brush-with-death a couple months ago.

My partner stood at my side as we waited in the cemetery while the widow, her daughter, and two men spoke to their reanimated relative. Mr. Alphard Cormier was wearing a suit that was in fashion sometime in the last thirty years.

Why rouse him now? I didn't know and wasn't asking.

"Twenty minutes," I called out. I could feel the sun coming; I'd always been able to do so—call it an internal sundial, or call it bad genes. Either way, my body was attuned to the rising and falling of the sun.

"When he is entombed, we could--"

"No." I couldn't force myself to glance at him again.

I was bone-tired, which made me more affectionate, and Eli was my weakness. Cut-glass features, bee-stung lips, and enough strength to fight at my side, even against *draugar*, Eli was built for fantasy. His ability to destroy my self-control was remarkable—and no, it wasn't because he was fae.

That part *was* why I wasn't going home with him. Trusting

him, wanting him, caring for him, none of that was enough to overcome the complications of falling into his bed. Sleeping with a faery prince had a list of complications that no amount of lust or affection overcame.

"I won't get married," I reminded him.

"Are you sure that's a good idea?" Mr. Cormier asked, voice carrying over the soft sobbing women.

The man with them handed Cormier something metallic.

I felt as much as saw the dead man look my way, and then his arm raised with a gun in hand. The relatives parted, and there was a dead man with a gun aimed at me.

"Fuck a duck. Move!" I darted to the side.

Eli was already beside me, hand holding his pretty bronze-coated sword that I hadn't even known he owned until the last month. "Geneviève?"

"On it." I jerked the magic away from Mr. Comier.

It was my magic that made him stand, so I wasn't going to let him stand and shoot me.

REST, I ordered the dead man.

"I'm sorry, ma'am. They made me. Threatened my Suzette if I didn't . . ." His words faded as my shove of magic sent him back to his tomb.

I could hear the widow, presumably Suzette, sobbing.

"I do not believe those gentlemen are Mr. Cormier's relations." Eli glared in the direction of the men who had hired me to raise a dead man to kill me. They'd grabbed the two women and ducked behind mausoleums.

"Why?"

"They seem to want you dead, buttercream," Eli said. "If they were his family, that's an odd response."

A bullet hit the stone across from me. Shards of gravestone pelted me. Oddly the adrenaline surge was welcome, even if the bullets weren't. Nothing like a shot of rage to get the sleepiness out.

"Not why *that*." I nodded toward the men who were staying crouched behind graves. "Why go through the hassle? Why not simply shoot me themselves?"

"Dearest, can we ponder that *after* they are not shooting at you?"

I felt my eyes change. As my rage boiled over, my eyes reflected it. They were my father's reptilian eyes, *draugr* eyes. The only useful thing he'd ever done was accidentally augment the magic I inherited from my mother. Unfortunately, the extra juice came with a foul temper—one that was even worse the last few weeks. After I'd been injected by venom, my moods were increasingly intense.

I wanted to rip limbs off.

I wanted to shove my thumbs into their eye sockets and keep going until I felt brain matter.

Before the urges were more than images, I was moving from one spot to the next.

I could *flow* like a *draugr*. I could move quickly enough that to the mortal eye it looked like teleportation. I *flowed* to the side of the shooter and grabbed his wrist.

Eli was not far behind. He didn't *flow*, but he was used to my movements and impulses. He had his sword to the shooter's throat a moment after I jerked the gun away from the man.

"Dearest?" Eli said, his voice tethering me sanity.

I concentrated on his voice, his calm, and I punched the other shooter rather than removing his eyes. Then I let out a scream of frustration and shoved my magic into the soil like a seismic force.

The dead answered.

Dozens of voices answered my call. Hands reknitted. Flesh

was regrown from the magic that flowed from my body into the graves. Mouths reformed, as if I was a sculptor of man.

"You do *not* wake the dead without reason," I growled at the now-unarmed man who dared to try to shoot me.

Here, of all places. He tried to spill my blood into these graves.

I stepped over the man I'd punched and ignored the cringing, sobbing widow and the other woman who was trying to convince her mother to leave.

And I stalked toward the shooter in Eli's grip.

"Bonbon, you have a scratch." Eli nodded toward my throat.

"Shit." I felt my neck where Eli had indicated. Blood slid into my collar.

I stepped closer to the shooter. "What were you thinking, Weasel Nuts?"

"Would you mind *covering* the wound?" Eli asked, forcing me to focus again.

His voice was calm, but we both knew that I could not shed blood in a space where graves were so plentiful. I'd accidentally bound two *draugr* so far, and blood was a binding agent in necromancy. Unless I wanted to bring home a few reanimated servants, my blood couldn't spill here.

I had to focus. And I didn't need an army of undead soldiers.

"Take this." Eli pulled off his shirt with one hand, switching the hilt between hands to keep the sword to Weasel Nuts' throat.

I stared. *Not the time.*

Eli's lips quirked in a half-smile, and then he pressed the blade just a bit. "And, I believe you need to answer my lady."

I shot Eli a look--his *lady*? What year did he think this was?--but I pressed his shirt against my throat. I did not, absolutely did *not*, take a deep breath because the shirt smelled like Eli.

Eli smiled as I took another quick extra breath.

"Thou shalt not suffer a witch to live." Weasel Nuts spat in my direction. "Foul thing."

I opened my mouth to reply, but Eli removed his sword blade and in a blink turned it so he could bash the pommel into the man's mouth.

Weasel Nuts dropped to his knees, and this time when he spat, he spat out his own teeth and blood.

If I were the swooning sort, this would be such a moment. Something about defending me always did good things to my libido.

"Geneviève, would you be so kind as to call the police?" Eli motioned toward the women. "And escort the ladies away from this unpleasant man?"

It sounded chivalrous—or chauvinistic--but it was actually an excuse. I needed to get my ass outside the cemetery before I dripped blood. Eli had provided a way to do so gracefully.

"Ladies?" Eli said, louder now. "Ms. Crowe will walk you toward the street."

The women came over, and the widow flinched when my gaze met hers. My *draugr* eyes unnerved people.

But then she straightened her shoulders and stared right into my reptilian eyes as if they were normal. "I do apologize, Ms. Crowe. They have an accomplice who is holding my grandson as a hostage. We had to cooperate."

My simmering temper spiked, keeping my exhaustion away and my focus sharp.

I stared at the women. With my grave sight, I saw trails of energy, the whispers of deaths, and the auras of anything living. These women were afraid, but not evil. They were worried.

The older woman grabbed the fallen gun and ordered, "Walk."

For a moment, I thought I'd been wrong, but she pointed

the barrel at the man who had shot at me. "You. Get up."

Her daughter smiled. "Would you mind helping us, Ms. Crowe?"

Eli and I exchanged a look. We were in accord, as usual. He bowed his head at them, and then scooped the unconscious man up.

In a strange group, we walked toward the exit.

As we were putting the unconscious attacker in the trunk of the Cadillac the women had arrived in, the sun rose, tinting the sky as if it were a watercolor painting.

I paused, wincing. Sunlight wasn't my friend. I wasn't a *draugr*—luckily, because sunlight trapped young *draugr*—but my genetics meant daylight made my head throb if I was out in too much of it. I slid on the dark sunglasses I carried for emergencies.

"It was nice to see Daddy," the younger woman said quietly to her mother. "I wish it had been closer to Christmas, but still . . . it was nice."

The widow motioned for the other prisoner to get into the trunk. Once he did, Eli slammed the trunk, and the widow squeezed her daughter's hand. "It was."

The daughter handed Eli the keys. She was shaken by the shooting, and I was bleeding from the shattering stone. Neither of us was in great shape to drive. However, it wasn't great for Eli to be trapped in a hulking steel machine. Faeries and steel weren't a good mix.

"I'll drive my car," he said, popping the trunk and grabbing a clean shirt. Working with me meant carrying an assortment of practical goods—clean clothes, duct tape, a sword, zip ties, and first aid supplies.

I tried not to sigh that he was now dressed fully again. Don't get me wrong. I respect him, but that didn't mean I wasn't prone to lustful gazes in his direction. If he minded, I'd stop.

He walked to the passenger door and opened it. "Come on, my peach pie."

The widow drove her Caddy away as I slid into the luxurious little convertible that had been fae-modified for Eli.

"Are you well enough to do this?" Eli asked as he steered us into the morning light.

"One human." I kept my eyes closed behind my sunglasses, grateful for the extra dark tint of his windows. I rarely needed sleep for most of my life, but lately I was always ready for a nap. Not yet, though.

I assured Eli, "I'm fine to deal with this."

So we set out to retrieve the young hostage. We didn't discuss my near constant exhaustion. We didn't talk about the fear that my near-death event had left lingering issues for my health. We would have to, but . . . not now.

We arrived at a townhouse, and I *flowed* to where the captor held a smallish boy. *Flowing* wasn't a thing I typically did around regular folk, but there were exceptions.

The boy was duct taped to a chair by his ankles.

The captor, another man about the age of the two in the trunk, was laughing at something on the television. If not for the gun in his lap and the duct tape on the boy's ankles, the whole thing wouldn't seem peculiar.

When the man saw us, he scrambled for his gun.

So, I punched the captor and broke the wrist of his gun-holding arm.

Eli freed the boy, who ran to his family as soon as they came into the house.

The whole thing took less time than brewing coffee.

"Best not to mention Ms. Crowe's speed," Eli said to the women as we were leaving.

The younger one nodded, but she was mostly caught up in holding her son.

The widow looked at me.

"Not all witches are wicked, dear." She patted my cheek, opened her handbag and pulled out a stack of folded bills. "For your time."

"The raising was already paid," I protested.

"I took it from them," she said proudly. She shook it at me insistently. "Might as well go to you. Here."

Eli accepted a portion of the money on my behalf. He understood when it was an insult not to and when to refuse because the client couldn't afford my fees.

Honestly, I felt guilty getting paid sometimes. Shouldn't I work for my city? Shouldn't I help people? Shouldn't good come of these skills?

But good intentions didn't buy groceries or pay for my medical supplies. That's as much what Eli handled as having my back when bullets or unwelcome dead things started to pop up.

After we walked out and shoved the third prisoner in the trunk of the Cadillac, Mrs. Cormier said, "I'll call the police to retrieve them. Do you mind waiting?"

"I will wait," Eli agreed, not lying by saying we "didn't mind" because *of course* we minded. I was leaning on the car for support, and Eli was worrying over my injury. If he had his way, he'd have me at his home, resting and cared for, but I was lousy at that.

It was on the long list of reasons I couldn't marry him. Some girls dreamed of a faery tale romance, a prince, pretty dresses. I dreamed of kicking ass. I'd be a lousy faery tale queen.

But I still had feelings for a faery prince—and no, I was *not* labeling them.

So rather head than home, I leaned on the side of the Cadillac, partly because it was that or sway in exhaustion. "I'll stay with you."

Once the widow went inside, Eli walked away and grabbed a

first aid kit from his car. I swear he bought them in bulk lately. "Let me see your throat."

"I'm fine." Dried blood made me look a little garish, but I could feel that it wasn't oozing much now.

Eli opened the kit, tore open a pouch of sani-wipes, and stared at me.

"Just tired. Sunlight." I gestured at the bright ball of pain in the sky. Midwinter might be coming, but the sun was still too bright for my comfort.

"Geneviève . . ." He held up a wipe. "May I?"

I sighed and took off my jacket. "It's not necessary."

"I disagree." He used sani-wipes to wipe away my blood as I leaned on the Cadillac, ignoring the looks we were getting from pedestrians. Maybe it was that he was cleaning up my blood, or that he was fae—or maybe it was that there were people yelling from the trunk.

Either way, I wasn't going to look away from Eli. I couldn't.

Obviously, I knew it should not be arousing to have him clean a cut in my neck from grave shards because someone was firing bullets at me, but . . . having his hands on me at all made my heart speed.

"Would you like to take the car and leave?" Eli was closer than he needed to be, hips close enough that it would be easier to pull him closer than push him away.

"And go where?"

He brushed my hair back, checking for more injuries. The result was that I could feel his breath on my neck. "Drive to my home and draw a bath or shower. I'll stay here and . . ."

"Tempting," I admitted with a laugh.

He had both a marble rainfall shower and the largest tub I'd ever seen. It came complete with a small waterfall. I admitted, "I've had fantasies about that waterfall."

"As have I."

I pressed myself against him, kissed his throat, and asked, "Ready to call off the engagement?"

He kissed me, hand tangled in my hair, holding me as if I would run.

I'd sell my own soul for an eternity of Eli's kisses if I believed in such bargains, but I wouldn't destroy him. Being with me wasn't what was best for him.

When he pulled back from our kiss, he stated, "Geneviève . . ."

I kissed him softly. I could say more with my touch than with words. I paused and whispered, "You can have my body *or* this engagement. Not both."

He sighed, but he stepped back. "You are impossible, Geneviève Crowe."

I caught his hand. "It doesn't have to be impossible. We're safely out of *Elphame* now. We could just end the enga--"

"I am fae, love. I don't lie. I don't break my word." He squeezed my hand gently. "I gave you my promise to wed. In front of my king and family. I *cannot* end this engagement."

We stood in silence for several moments. Then he held out his keys, and I took them.

"Meet me at my place. Maybe we can spar," I offered.

Eli pulled me in closer, kissed both of my cheeks, and said, "I will accept any excuse to get sweaty with you."

"Same." I hated that this was where we were, but I wasn't able to change who or what I was. Neither was Eli. He had a future that I wanted no part of, and I felt a duty to my city and friends. We had no future option that would suit both of us. I'd be here, beheading *draugr* and trying not to become more of a monster, and he would return to his homeland. There was no good compromise.

HEX ON THE BEACH is COMING JULY 1, 2021!

GIRLS NIGHT OUT HAS NEVER BEEN SO MUCH FUN--BUT what are they going to do with all these bodies?

New York Times and USA Today Bestselling Authors Kelley Armstrong, Jeaniene Frost, and Melissa Marr deliver a sexy summer read with this novel-length anthology containing three all-new stories from their Cursed Luck, Night Huntress, and Faery Bargains worlds. Kennedy, Cat, and Gen are just trying to enjoy their respective getaways, but when immortals, vampires, and witches come out to play, things are bound to go awry. Let the supernatural hijinks begin!

Note: The Faery Bargains story takes place between Books 2 and 3

COLD IRON HEART

AVAILABLE NOW!

How far would you go to escape fate?

In this prequel to the internationally bestselling WICKED LOVELY series (over a million copies sold), the Faery Courts collide a century before the mortals in *Wicked Lovely* are born.

Thelma Foy, a jeweler with the Second Sight in iron-bedecked 1890s New Orleans, wasn't expecting to be caught in a faery conflict. Tam can see through the glamours faeries wear to hide themselves from mortals, but if her secret were revealed, the fey would steal her eyes, her life, or her freedom. So, Tam doesn't respond when they trail thorn-crusted fingertips through her hair at the French Market or when the Dark King sings along with her in the bayou.

But when the Dark King, Irial, rescues her, Tam must

confront everything she thought she knew about faeries, men, and love.

Too soon, New Orleans is filling with faeries who are looking for her, and Irial is the only one who can keep her safe.

Unbeknownst to Tam, she is the prize in a centuries-old fight between Summer Court and Winter Court. To protect her, Irial must risk a war he can't win--or surrender the first mortal woman he's loved.

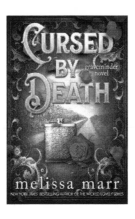

The dead don't always stay dead in Claysville . . . and in the afterlife, Death himself can't be trusted.

Amity Blue has begun to remember strange impossible events, her ex trying to bite her and people vanishing like mist. Everyone in town swears a mountain lion is responsible for the recent deaths, but Amity is sure that there's more to the story.

After a stalker—a dead stalker—appears at the bar where she works, Amity discovers that the dead don't always stay dead in Claysville. Along with the current Graveminder, Rebekkah Barrow, Amity seeks out the enigmatic Mr D, who seems to be Death himself, only to discover that the centuries-old contract to protect Claysville has been broken.

Caught between life in a cursed town and Death himself, Amity and Rebekkah must find a way to put the dead where they belong—because if the Hungry Dead keep rising, everyone in town will be lost.

Return to the world of Graveminder, Goodreads Choice Winner for Best Horror Novel in this stand-alone Graveminder novel (also includes two Grave-minder short stories.).

Available 2022
Pre-Order Now
Dark Sun: A Wicked Lovely Novel

WHEN THE BESTSELLING WICKED LOVELY SERIES ENDED, the Faery Courts were in order. In the years following, peace was still tenuous, but every court seemed devoted to balance.

But now, Urian—son of the former Dark King and the fated Summer Queen, Thelma Foy—has decided to claim his destiny.

Urian knew the secrets that protected his relatives--both the mortal and the faery ones--since childhood. Now, the Dark Summer Prince is ready to claim one—or *both*—of the thrones that should rightfully be his.

When Urian discovers Kyla, unaware of her ancestry, he finally has the ally—or general—he's needed. Far from the world of the fey, Kyla is aware that her bloodlines aren't mortal. When secrets are reveald, she decides to protect her human family by finding her place in the world of the faeries. She can't trust Uri, but she feels drawn to him in a way she never imagined.

Peace is threatened. And neither family ties nor accidental love can keep the balance between the courts now.

Signed Copies:

To order signed copies of my books (with ebook included in some cases), go to MelissaMarrBooks.com

Recent Work:

Cold Iron Heart (2020)

Pretty Broken Things (2020)

Unruly (2020)

Collections:

Tales of Folk & Fey (2019)

Dark Court Faery Tales (2019)

Bullets for the Dead (2019)

This Fond Madness (2017)

All Ages Fantasy Novel:

The Faery Queen's Daughter (2019)

Young Adult Novels with HarperTeen

Wicked Lovely (2007)

Ink Exchange (2008)

Fragile Eternity (2009)

Radiant Shadows (2010)

Darkest Mercy (2011)

Wicked Lovely: Desert Tales (2012)

Carnival of Secrets (2012)

Made For You (2013)

Seven Black Diamonds (2015)

One Blood Ruby (2016)

Faery Tales & Nightmares (short story collection)

Adult Fantasy for HarperCollins/Wm Morrow

Graveminder (2011)

The Arrivals (2012)

Picturebooks for Penguin

Bunny Roo, I Love You (2015)

Baby Dragon, Baby Dragon! (2019)

Bunny Roo and Duckling Too (2021)

All Ages Fantasy for Penguin

The Hidden Knife (2021)

Coauthored with K. L. Armstrong (with Little, Brown)

Loki's Wolves (2012)

Odin's Ravens (2013)

Thor's Serpents (2014)

Co-Edited with Kelley Armstrong (with HarperTeen)

Enthralled

Shards & Ashes

Co-Edited with Tim Pratt (with Little, Brown)

Rags & Bones

ABOUT THE AUTHOR

Melissa Marr is a former university literature instructor who writes fiction for adults, teens, and children. Her books have been translated into twenty-eight languages and have been bestsellers internationally (Germany, France, Sweden, Australia, et. al.) as well as domestically. She is best known for the Wicked Lovely series for teens, *Graveminder* for adults, and her debut picture book *Bunny Roo, I Love You*.

In her free time, she practices medieval swordfighting, kayaks, hikes, and raises kids in the Arizona desert.

facebook.com/MelissaMarrBooks
twitter.com/melissa_marr
goodreads.com/melissa_marr

PRAISE FOR MELISSA MARR'S BOOKS:

PRAISE FOR THE WICKED LOVELY SERIES:

"Marr offers readers a fully imagined faery world that runs alongside an everyday world, which even non-fantasy (or faerie) lovers will want to delve into" --*Publisher's Weekly* (starred review)

"This is a magical novel... the first book in a trilogy that will guarantee to have you itching for the next installment." *Bliss*

"Fans of the fey world will devour this sequel to Wicked Lovely. Marr has created a world both harsh and lush, at once urban and natural." --*School Library Journal*

"Complex and involving." -*New York Times Book Review*

PRAISE FOR GRAVEMINDER:

"If anyone can put the goth in Southern Gothic, it's Melissa Marr. . . . She's also careful to ensure that the book's wider themes —how and if we accept the roles life assigns us, and

what happens to us when we refuse them—matter to us as much as the multiple cases of heebie-jeebies she doles out..."
—NPR.org

"Spooky enough to please but not too disturbing to read in bed."—*Washington Post*

"Dark and dreamy. . . . Rod Serling would have loved *Graveminder*. . . . Marr is not tapping into the latest horde of zombie novels, she's created a new kind of undead creature. . . . A creatively creepy gothic tale for grown-ups."—*USA Today*

"Plan ahead to read this one, because you won't be able to put it down! Haunting, captivating, brilliant!" —*Library Journal* (starred review)

"Marr serves up a quirky dark fantasy fashioned around themes of fate, free will—and zombies. . . . Well-drawn characters and their dramatic interactions keep the tale loose and lively." —*Publishers Weekly*

"The emotional dance between Rebekkah and Byron will captivate female readers. . . . Fantasy-horror fans will demand more." —*Kirkus Reviews*

"No one builds worlds like Melissa Marr." —Charlaine Harris, *New York Times* bestselling author of the Sookie Stackhouse series

"Welcome to the return of the great American gothic." —Del Howison, Bram Stoker Award-winning editor of *Dark Delicacies*